D1231705

MIDNIGHT LACE

Books by MacKINLAY KANTOR

FICTION

Diversey
El Goes South
The Jaybird
Long Remember
The Voice of Bugle Ann
Arouse and Beware
The Romance of Rosy Ridge
The Noise of Their Wings
Valedictory
Cuba Libre
Gentle Annie
Happy Land
Author's Choice
Glory for Me

JUVENILE

Angleworms on Toast

BALLADS

Turkey-in-the-Straw

AUTOBIOGRAPHICAL

But Look, the Morn

a novel by

MacKinlay Kantor

RANDOM HOUSE · NEW YORK

FIRST PRINTING

Copyright, 1947, 1948, by MacKinlay Kantor
Copyright in Canada, 1948, by MacKinlay Kantor
All rights reserved under International and
Pan-American Copyright Conventions
Published in New York by Random House, Inc., and
simultaneously in Toronto, Canada,
by Random House of Canada, Limited, 1948.
Manufactured in the United States of America

813.52
K167m

98312

To

IRENE GIER PAGE SWENSON

PROLOGUE

The girls are in the attic; they are young, giggling girls, still flat-bosomed, still rumply-haired, their noses shining, their voices hoarse; the girls are chattering noisily, they wear the rough woolen socks, the scuffed brown moccasins, the plaid skirts and fuzzy sweaters of their kind; the girls are exploring the attic, carrying their Coke bottles amid garret dust, amid mousy memories; they have opened a closet, they have opened trunks and boxes; the moppet with wild yellow hair—she is lifting a peculiar hat from a shelf, from the paper and silence which have wrapped it; she places the hat jauntily on her head; she is standing with legs wide apart, nose in air and hands on hips, as she cries amid yowls of the others, "Look what Grandma used to wear!"

MIDNIGHT LACE

One

On a September Friday in 1911, a young woman with dandelion hair came down into the lobby of the Saratoga Hotel on Dearborn Street, in Chicago. She was dressed with unusual skill—to catch the eyes of all susceptible men, or to win jealous appraisal from any women who witnessed the taste and drama of her costume.

This girl called herself Dolly Hessian; that was not her real name. She was twenty-six years old, but pretended to be several years younger.

She had with her two substantial suitcases and a small black leather traveling bag of the satchel type, made of pebble-grained leather and lined with rose silk. In this smaller bag Dolly Hessian had packed the toilet articles and the few pieces of clothing as well as her nightdress, wrapper and slippers, which she would need for an overnight journey on the train.

An elderly porter, glad to serve the girl merely because of her beauty (she gave tips seldom at this hotel, and then only dimes), came forward, limping, to take her bags. He asked her if she wanted a taxicab, but Dolly said No; she wished to have the bags checked until evening. It had been necessary for her to give up her room before four P.M. in order to avoid payment of an extra day's charge.

The bags were carried away, and Dolly Hessian paid her

account at the desk. She put her change into a blue purse drawn from her flat reticule, and, with many people watching her, she strolled into the late afternoon confusion of Dearborn Street.

Dolly wore beautiful shoes of black kid. The shoes had sky-blue leather tops, but of course the tops could not be seen beneath the folds of her narrow trimly hung dark skirt and the pleats of blue satin flouncing underneath. The jacket of her traveling suit had wide reveres; stiff-starched lace flowered beneath her chin, and one blue brooch was fastened brightly.

Her hat, more than anything else, contributed to the blazing import of her appearance. The hat was a wide, high, Arabesque turban of a type popular the year before, and still persisting in Western cities and towns of the United States: it was nearly as much a great toque as a turban, and consisted of silk tiers constructed on a capenet foundation. Over the layers of silk a sheathing of thick midnight-blue lace had been arranged, with additional lace in narrow scallops guarding the edge of every tier; and the entire effect was one of richness and flaunting femininity: a manner of challenge and pride which most women might hope to attain at times, but which Dolly Hessian wore—falsely though with effect—each day of her life.

Her face was rather too wide for conventional prettiness; despite plump cheeks, the bones above the jaws were noticeable within the smooth yellowish skin. The eyes made an astonishing humanity out of this face, and were the center and excuse for any beauty attributed to her. They were great gold-gray eyes, rimmed by heavy lashes, and under brows of remarkable thickness and brilliance.

Dolly Hessian's eyes bore an expression of wounded innocence or of mildly quizzical regard or of dreamy, unaware negligence. Strangely, too, they could quiver with infantile laughter. Not once did the eyes themselves reveal the acquisitive desire and the passion for self-exploitation and calculating accomplishment which lurked within. Her eyes were not the windows of Dolly Hessian's soul: they were remarkable paintings hung across the spaces where windows should have been. They had taken men into confusion, into bafflement and perplexity before this; they would do so again.

She walked out of the lobby, toying in serious concentration with the gloves on her skillful square hands as she went. The gloves were already well adjusted; they were on, they fitted perfectly; and yet they were a means of her walking obliviously past the hearty-faced men in derby hats who thronged around the cigar counter. She seemed not too frightened, nor too much the young girl of no experience, nor too much the bold bawd returning gaze for gaze, with a suggestion of invitation or rebuff. There was an appeal in the way the fingers of her right hand closed over the tight little fingers of her left, and pressed and persuaded.

In Dearborn Street, with the glances of men following her as jolly hounds pursue a rabbit, she paused daintily for a moment, then turned toward the north and walked with light vigor up to Madison Street. There she waited with an assemblage of shabby people: a mailman, a solemn Negro minister and his wife, young West Side matrons who had been shopping in the Loop—she waited with these until the next streetcar came rumbling westward, dropping fat crumbs of electric green from its trolley, the bell sounding with a flat pound under the motorman's foot.

Dolly boarded the car—always modesty, always haughty yet

sweetish decorum in her manner; and she rode across one of those hideous bridges with which Chicago had spanned its river. She looked out and down at the substance of oily water, with its burden of soaked paper boxes, orange peelings and other trash. She saw the pewter of the sky reflected there, and knew that she would be glad to leave Chicago.

Not permanently, she thought, not forever. This Chicago which she had attained by bitter degrees—it had too much of the old and worse Chicago remaining in it. Sometimes in her work Dolly had seen girls carelessly stow boxes of cord, ribbons and other trimmings on the high shelves of a room in which the manufacture of their product was made. A girl would reach up in order hastily to drag out a bolt of ribbon or a ball of silver cord from some box; the ends of material would be left hanging out of the box and down. And later, when a lower box in its turn was opened and shut again, beneath its lid might be caught those strands from the box above. Thus the whole series of shelves would soon be in an unbelievable tangle, with bright-colored, twisted lengths trailing from shelf to shelf until no one was sure where the parent hoard might be found.

This metaphor Dolly now applied to her own existence. There were still little cords and ribbons going into the box behind—the one from which she had crawled. She did not wish to return to Chicago until she might come in a package to be possessed by the highest shelf of all, and with no trailing reminders.

She meditated on plans and possibilities. A child came into the car—a child dirty of face, hollow and black of eye—and regarded her solemnly from his hard seat beneath the opposite window; and Dolly Hessian gave the child all the dove-spoken tenderness of her smile and her whisper; but meanwhile she was counting the money in her purse, the little money in her savings account, her salary during the weeks ahead. She was accounting for, and trying to order in advance, each figment of the future which might be intrinsically important to her.

Some ten minutes past Halsted Street, the young woman got down from the street-car and walked rapidly two blocks south and half a block west, turning at last into a narrow space lined with houses of disreputable, unhappy appearance. All the houses were bronzed by soft-coal smoke, and each had a basement built high beneath the first story, with an areaway cut down before the front windows, and tall steps guarded by iron piping leading to the story above. The little street was only one block long—pitted with pavement holes, and ending blankly at its southern extremity against a factory wall where five-foot letters were visible, with a portion of the words FELDSTEIN and PLATING.

Five houses distant from the factory Dolly Hessian halted. She had been consulting a scrap of paper brought out of her reticule. She looked up at the little number fastened above the high stairs; then, tensing herself noticeably and holding her head high and her shoulders straight, she went down into the areaway past a row of flower pots with dead geranium stalks in them. She rapped at the door which waited for her in its thumb-smeared poverty and indignity.

When the door opened there was heard issuing from the interior a kind of moan or wail, which seemed to end in hysterical laughter, and then perhaps in tears. You could not tell. The door closed quickly as Dolly slammed it. She stayed inside at least twenty minutes.

When she came out at last, her face was grimly set, especially about the mouth, and her soft eyes held a blankness.

Dolly hurried up over the few brick steps of the areaway and then, hastening to the north, she cried briefly as she went. She had not been crying before, but now the tears were flowing. They edged into the thinly-powdered channels, the few little lines marked already in the girl's flesh. She took out a blue-edged handkerchief and touched her eyes repeatedly. She sniffled inelegantly—there was no one to hear her—but by the time she turned at the northern terminal corner of the street she had left off crying completely.

The woman was retracing her steps—hurrying toward the Madison Street car line more urgently than she had journeyed away from it. There were few people who saw her go. It was a chilly day: not many children played among dry weeds and bricks of the vacant lots, and this was at an hour when factory workers were not yet released and homing.

But one man—a young one—did see her as she turned east. He had just come out of a saloon west of the intersection at the cross street, and he stood holding a long stare as he tried to decide whether, in fact, this woman was really Dolly. Recognizing her at last, he left the step of the saloon, bruising his shoulder against the green post that held up a corner of the building, and he hurried unsteadily after Dolly Hessian.

He was as unattractive a young man as might be found anywhere in that singularly unappetizing neighborhood. He wore trousers which had once been gay with black and white checks, but were now soiled in weary accumulation—especially greasy around the rims of the pockets. He had on a pair of run-over shoes with great knobs on the toes, and a black raincoat flapped like wings as a gust caught him at the corner.

The young man's name was Rick. Everyone called him that: the diminutive of Richard, which his mother had applied to him when he was a baby. He was now twenty-two years old, and had a short term at Joliet to his discredit. He had a round, weak chin of childish softness, and small eyes the color of white grapes. He wore a plaid cap with a button on top.

Just before Dolly Hessian reached the next corner, Rick caught up with her and called, "Dor!" as she was about to turn the corner.

The girl halted and whirled, almost skating in the disgusted surprise with which she recognized and responded to the name. The young man came directly forward and caught her by the arm. He began to speak in a rapid whisper, glancing occasionally over his shoulder toward the ugly street which they had left; and once he pointed, indicating the direction of the house which Dolly had visited, emphasizing something with a repeated jabbing of his finger.

The girl listened in silence, looking, not at the weak and evil face pressed near to hers, but down at the sidewalk between them.

At last she lifted her right hand and fought to remove his hold on her left arm. Rick tightened his clutch for a moment; but when the girl's voice went higher and she said something about "police," the man released his grasp.

He mumbled, "I ought to murder you!"

"You'll do nothing," said Dolly Hessian. "I've done everything I'm going to do."

"We'll see about that."

"You can see all you want to. I should worry what you do."

She moved away from him, brushed her sleeve as if his clutch had befouled it (which indeed it had, to some visible degree, because the young man was horribly dirty) and then, touching the tips of her gloves to the weighty hat of midnight-blue lace, Dolly sailed north toward Madison Street.

The young man stood watching her, his hands sunk deep in the pockets of his old raincoat. He took a couple of steps, preparing to turn down the westward street from which he had come. Then he spied an empty bottle lying beside a grating in a broken crack of the sidewalk. It was one of those small bottles in which drinks of Welch's Grape Juice were purveyed, and it gave Rick an idea. He snatched the bottle up, stepped back to catch a clear view of the street to the north and the woman walking there; leaning on his right leg, lifting his left leg, he drew back his arm and threw the bottle toward her, as high and as hard as he could throw it.

The bottle smashed to bits on the sidewalk not far behind the girl. She turned and saw Rick . . . she knew that he had thrown that bottle. It might have hurt her badly if the missile had struck her. Catching up her skirts, she began to run awkwardly, as women do, and with the additional awkwardness and impediment of her long corset and the heavy garbing of her costume. She hurried at this speed to the next corner and then looked back again, but Rick was nowhere in sight.

Dolly had to wait some time for a street-car coming east. There was a fire over west on Madison somewhere. Distantly she could hear the clatter of alarm gongs, the outcry of children and rumbling of fire wagons. Then the fire was put out, an engine was dragged away streaming blackest smoke and reddest sparks; and the Madison Street cars, barricaded briefly behind fire-hose, were released and came jingling forward.

The first car had men hanging all over both platforms; but

Dolly managed to get on the second car. Thus she rode, no longer fearing Rick or any assault he might bring against her. She rode to Dearborn Street. The street lamps turned yellow . . . it was growing late.

Dolly Hessian had dinner in a cheap but pleasant coffee shop not far from the Saratoga, and at a convenient hour she picked up her bags and rode in a cream-colored taxicab to the Park Row station at the edge of Grant Park. There she bought a one-way ticket for the town of Lexington, Iowa, where she had never been before.

Two

Benjamin Steele left his livery barn before eleven o'clock on a double errand which he had recollected suddenly as necessitous in two ways. First, he wanted to have a trial spin in Mr. Alfred Pittenger's double-seated buggy before the mended buggy was delivered to its owner; and, second, he was expecting a shipment of six horse-collars—now several days overdue. If those collars were not on the eleven-eighteen train Ben would have to send a telegram to the manufacturers. He hoped that they would be on the train, shipped by express from Waterloo; several of the men who wanted collars would be apt to come by for them during the afternoon. Saturday afternoon and evening comprised the most intense shopping period for the farmers of that region, as was similarly the case in any other Iowa town.

Mr. Pittenger's buggy had been badly damaged, but now it looked like new. A replaced mudguard was tough and shining; smashed boards at the corner of the box had been replaced; a new axle had been installed, and there were two new front wheels. The whole had then been properly painted with the very best weatherproof carriage lacquer in stock.

Ben felt a sensation of pride and affection as he walked around the buggy in a shed behind the carriage works. Ben's father, Madison Steele, would have been pleased to see a repair job like that, performed with promptness and skill. The young man smelled leather and paint as the warm sun came down upon them and seemed thus to liberate the enticing scent of their surfaces.

Ben's father had been dead more than eight months, and the son was living alone in the family house on Third Street, opposite the upper-grades and high-school building. He had Mrs. Fachter (a slow-moving widow who looked like the traditional old maid of cartoon and legend) come in each week day about ten o'clock. She would wash up the few dirty dishes, prepare a midday dinner for Ben, make beds and keep the house clean during the afternoon, and do Ben's mending and the ironing of his clothes; then she would prepare the evening meal—called supper—unless he happened to be eating at a restaurant, or dining out somewhere.

This domestic arrangement was working out very well. When Ben's father was alive, there had been a plump young woman named Anna who "lived in." The Steeles were one of the first families in Lexington to keep a maid; although the maids of that community were usually called "hired girls," and always ate with the family. Anna had not felt that it would be decent for her to live on there, alone with Ben; and released by death from the chaperonage of the father, she moved out two days after the funeral. Later that same week she married a Swedish farmer who had been importuning her for some time. Ben smiled secretly to think how a suggestion of scandal had driven Anna headlong into matrimony.

And yet, even more secretly, he was aware of that hearty young woman alone with him in the house those several nights—aware of her presence, and the female threat and excitement of her mere existence—as he had never been (recognizably at least) before. Probably it was a good thing for Anna to move away and marry. He remembered having stood deliberately in the front hall to wait for Anna coming down the stairs, dust-mop in hand. He had waited to see her firm, rounded legs in their black cotton stockings and low-heeled slippers. She had worn her house dresses quite short . . . it was a good thing she had moved away, probably. Still, it was very odd to know that while his father lived, and before pneumonia smothered him, Ben had paid no attention to the dubious charm of Anna—no attention at all. He supposed vaguely that his father's passing had left an emotional void which needed to be filled by some manner of affection. He said this much to himself, but explored his own attitude no further. He was shy about any investigation of his own emotions or those of others.

Ben Steele was twenty-three years old, and exceptionally tall of build—noticeably taller than his father had been (Mad Steele had stood six feet, two inches in his prime) and nearly as tall as the height attained by his grandfather, Uncle Danny, who was variously reported in exaggerated chronicles to have stood six-feet-four or six-feet-five in his stocking feet.

An Irishman of the Seventh Iowa Cavalry had called Uncle Danny "Long Dan," and the appellation was preserved among the old soldiers. Ben liked to think of his grandfather as being "Long Dan" instead of identifying him with the more affectionate diminutive commonly circulated among townspeople. "Long Dan" had a ring of balladry about it, and Ben liked ballads. For several years now, since he came home from college at Ames, he was expected to recite "Down in the Lehigh Valley" or "The Face on the Bar Room Floor" or a Robert W. Service poem, at the Elks' Club smokers—which were really only moderately dull and disorderly drinking sessions. There was no saloon in Lexington; but always liquor flowed through the domain of the Elks.

The eyes of Ben Steele were small, bright, brown, and set deep in his head under heavy black brows. When he smiled or laughed his eyes seemed to disappear completely. His hair was almost black—very deep brown, with reddish highlights showing when it had been freshly scrubbed. Ben had his hair trimmed each week, and he fussed with it considerably between times, using bay rum and a good clear oil. He was a self-conscious dandy in a rough-and-ready fashion. His attire often seemed unkempt, but this was done deliberately, and in an effort to present a lounging, rakish appearance. This style was completely natural to Ben, and he accentuated it purposely, and thus could not have been accused of being false to himself—even had anyone else known how he pondered at times over certain shirts, shoes and gaudy neckties.

On this Saturday Ben wore an old pair of blue denim pants. They had been washed repeatedly and were a bit tight for even his lean, bony legs, and his flat hips and rear. The trousers were belted around the waist with a Mexican leather strap, ornamented with a silver buckle. Ben had bought this belt in Texas two years before, when he and his father made a hasty trip to the Rio Grande country where they were considering an investment in land. To himself, Ben called it his cowboy belt. He had always wanted to be a cowboy, and certainly he was the Iowa equivalent: he had known reins and saddles since his first memory began.

He wore a shirt of yellowish flannel, and had a blue polka-dotted cotton handkerchief tied loosely around his throat. He was bare-headed as usual . . . he had worn a hat only on

Sundays, or to occasional weddings or funerals, since he left college.

Ben said to Hilton Maxwell, the livery-stable foreman, "Have Uncle Em put a horse into this buggy. I want to see that that axle's all right, before I give her to Pittenger."

"What horse? Want to use Babe? Or Barnum?"

Ben stood for a moment listening to the amiable stamping and thrashing, the occasional whinny which drifted over across the vacant lot amidst good stable smells.

"No. Tell him to harness up Nagger. Nag needs a little exercise."

The traditional domain of the Steeles filled up the entire area at Fourth and Hazel Streets, and extended up the hill of Fourth Street nearly half a block, and along the lower slope of Hazel to an alley that bisected the block between Fourth and Fifth Streets. The harness store and repair shop were next to the alley fronting on Hazel Street, in a building much newer than the other structures. It had been built by Madison Steele when Ben was a little boy, and behind it were sheds and barns, the smithy, the machine shop of the carriage works. A huge hay-barn and a large but creaky stable stood well to the rear of the property, alongside a depression which had been a flower-filled ravine with a stream flowing, in the time when Uncle Danny put up these structures.

But the ravine was mostly filled-in with the trash and debris of two generations. There were still a few wild plum trees, determined to show their blossoms in spring . . . birds and worms claimed most of the fruit, even before the schoolboys could stomach it. Sometimes in the moist, quivering, scenty days of April, folks could find bloodroots and dogtooth violets growing among rusty cans and well-settled bricks . . .

there was one clump of Dutchman's breeches. Ben knew where that was—or where it used to be. He might look again in the next spring.

Beyond the stable, banking up to the sidewalk on Fourth Street, and rubbing also the sidewalk on Hazel Street, were long, low sheds of the livery establishment proper. It was a hollow square, solid and close to the street, open on the interior; and here were kept the rigs which the Steeles rented, and here was space for other rigs which people might choose to leave at Steeles' for repair or for mere storage. The open area hemmed by lines of wide-roofed sheds—a kind of parade ground—was always kept cleaner than was the case in most livery barns. This had not been true in Uncle Danny's time, but it became true when Mad Steele took over; Mad Steele's wife was a regular Tartar. She would never allow her husband or his father to step upon her porch if their footgear showed any traces of their beloved occupation.

A square office was built into the sheds at the exact intersection of those two streets, at the corner of the property, with an open driveway next to it. There were two offices, really: one in the rear of the harness building, where also were kept all books and records pertaining to the wagon-works or carriage-shop—the business was called familiarly by either name—but the livery-barn office was the roosting place of the hangers-on.

Here the workmen were paid; here the fees for rental of horses and buggies were collected; and here also was the unofficial headquarters of the Lexington G.A.R. The Grand Army of the Republic still maintained a hall upstairs above a drygoods store on Sixth Street, the main business district of the town; but there was now talk of giving it up, since the enrollment of the local Post ebbed steadily lower, and rent was getting to be a problem. Uncle Danny in his time was a traditional commander of the Post, and all the men who worked for him in the old days had been veterans. In 1911 there was left of this contingent only Uncle Emory Buckland, who had worked for and with Daniel Steele in the earliest times.

Ben entered the back door of the harness store, in order to find the bill of lading for the horse-collars which had already been sent to him by the firm in Waterloo. Out in the yard, Maxwell cupped his hands around his mouth and began to yell, "Uncle Em!" Soon a small bent figure—still wiry despite the shrinkage of age—appeared in the rear driveway next to the stable. This was Emory Buckland. He had a crooked gray mustache pinched between his nose and upper lip, and he wore a sodden slouched-hat of dark felt, around the crown of which a black-and-gold cord was corroding steadily. Uncle Em responded to the summons with a high-pitched yelp, and Maxwell directed him to harness Nagger to the Pittenger buggy.

A tangle of conflicting circumstance is a wonder to all who regard it: a mystery of strong compulsion—even to the old, who have viewed for long the mix-up of personality, of purpose generous or ill, and the strange and contradictory results which are brought about by the infliction of people upon people. It is a puzzle to those who recognize this perpetual and sometimes disastrous confusion—never of the same pattern, never in most manners identical. . . .

Even men of diabolical imagination can seldom stop and say, "On this moment depends—" or, "This person will bring about—" or, "The creak of this axle, the turning of this wheel, will set in motion a series of events—"

Emory Buckland, standing round-shouldered and long-armed, calling back between the livery sheds, was a symbol of the amusing or fearful events soon to be ordained by all the staggering Fates in this town. He was a symbol of accomplishments comical or ugly by turn, and forever immutable.

The woman who—indirectly, but still selfishly—would bring about his death, was even now being carried toward the outskirts of Lexington; yet none of the people there had ever seen her before. Only two people in the town knew her name, and were aware that she was coming.

Three

Ben Steele walked around the horse and buggy observantly —the understanding turn taken by the good driver who sees to traces, to hub-nuts, all in a flash—somewhat as a modern pilot might look over his airplane when it has been prepared for take-off. In this case, though, Ben took a very long look, as this was the trial run of the Pittenger buggy after its smash-up.

"Looks like new," said Emory Buckland.

"Yes. That's Pete. He got a good do on that lacquer."

"Good man when he's sober," said Uncle Em, but Ben did not reply. He had learned from example of his father never to discuss one employee with another, except, perhaps, for a particular purpose.

He swung up into the buggy, took the reins, and Uncle Em stepped away from the horse's head.

Nagger took the buggy forward swiftly toward the driveway entrance where Ben slowed down again and went out cautiously into Hazel Street. Once, twenty-seven years earlier, a careless driver had run over two little girls at that very entrance, and seldom since then did people forget to drive slowly when crossing the sidewalk.

Maxwell, now busy in the livery-stable office, stepped to the door to call, "You going to the train, Ben?" and Ben yelled back that he was. Two old men seated on the green bench just outside the office door—a bench rubbed smooth and polished by the clothing and bodies of their kind—both chirped and waved their hands, and Ben responded with a swift wriggle of his fingers.

The buggy spun away up the wide ruts of Hazel Street, lifting along the slope to Third Street and the courthouse intersection. The old men watched Ben until he turned west out of their sight, and both were reminded of the young man's grandfather, and in lesser ways of his father, though neither of them spoke about it.

Ben Steele went west on Third, passing between his own house and the tall Gothic bricks of the high school and upper grades where he had received his earlier education. He saw Mrs. Fachter shaking a rug out of one of the upstairs windows at home. He waved to her, but she didn't see him; she was very nearsighted; then he gave himself seriously to seeing how the buggy rode.

There were usually a lot of squeaks in this kind of repair job, and he wanted to have all the squeaks out. Mr. Alfred Pittenger had a musical ear and would be rather particular about squeaks. Ben went west past Maple Street to Willow, and, still keeping Nagger at a slow trot, he turned north toward the tracks. The railroad right-of-way ran some distance beyond Sixth Street and parallel with it. There was no Seventh Street—only a few wheel paths wandering more or less at will among warehouses and coal sheds in the combined railroad yards.

North of the tracks the neighborhood was known as Shoetown, because once there had been a shoe factory there. Over there the streets were named after early settlers; part of the north-and-south streets in the town were named after trees, and some of them had Indian names. There was little rhyme or reason to the nomenclature, and the same was true in most other Iowa county seat towns of, say, four to eight thousand population.

With the C. & N.W. spur curving on its lifted grade across the brown road just ahead, Ben Steele spoke to the horse, and pulled up beneath a row of soft maple trees, in order to make a final inspection of the buggy. Nagger was not too young or spirited; he would stand properly with the reins tied around the whip-stock; Ben had no fear of the horse's becoming frightened and dashing toward the tracks.

He put his hands on each of the front wheels in turn and leaned a share of his weight against them: the axle was rigid, nuts were tightly screwed into the hubs. Ben felt the shafts on either side, and even tapped speculatively against the buggy box. Everything had been substantially repaired.

The man stood for a moment, breathing deeply of the thin September air that warmed as midday approached. In an adjoining block on Sixth Street, several bony young boys trotted along together, making a peculiar happy clatter with the football cleats nailed against their soles. They were bound for one of the early practices of the season, and their tattered gold-and-red jerseys appeared like wads of carnival color against the softer hues of the trees. Ben Steele had been feeling very young a moment before; but now, to Ben at twenty-three, these boys appeared suddenly as messengers, telling him that he was no longer a youth.

His first youth had departed in his father's dying, and in the seriousness of sole business responsibility. "But," he thought, "I am soft inside," and a maple leaf fluttered in front of him, and he grinned. Emory Buckland was, in peculiar moods, a self-conscious philosopher, or at least a mouthy sentimentalist whom some might have called a poet, and some might have regarded as a tiresome old bore. Uncle Em said, "Maples are like folks: the hard ones get all the gold, while the soft are still green." Ben Steele struck lightly at the maple leaf with his fist, missed it, and then Nagger turned his ears forward as the eleven-eighteen passenger whistled for the first grade crossing in Lexington.

Ben sprang into the buggy and set Nagger at an astonished gallop across the C. & N.W. spur, dashing off on a side path beyond. The lane went past outlying shacks of a lumber company, curved widely to avoid some of the railroad coal sheds, and then led across the farther reaches of Maple Street and directly alongside the station.

The engine was shuddering past the platform as Nagger raced close, and Ben turned him skillfully into a narrow vacant space next to the American Express wagon. Tucky Miller—a solemn fleshy man who drove the hotel hack—had planted his vehicle on the opposite side of the express wagon, and he stood back in some alarm as Ben and Nagger and the Pittenger buggy swirled together toward the platform.

There was no smash, no scraping or grating as they halted; nevertheless Tucky shook his head in disapproval and wagged a warning thumb. Ben tied his horse to a platform ring. Ordinarily he would have halted and backed in carefully; but it had been fun to see Tucky jump.

Ben Steele walked down toward the baggage car in the wake of two rumbling hand-trucks which the baggage men were drawing. His horse-collars were almost the first items emerging from the maw of the express car after the mail sacks

98312

were passed out. Ben counted the horse-collars: there were six of them, all wrapped and tied in protective brown paper, and he reached up on the truck to examine a tag.

He hunted the express driver and claimed the collars. "Let me take them now. Save you a trip over to the barn."

"That'll be all right, Mr. Steele." The express man was comparatively new in town; practically any other male would have addressed him as Ben—even little boys. Ben signed for the collars. He dragged three of them off the truck and carried them up to the buggy, piling them against the rear seat. He returned for the other three, and when again he stood beside the buggy he saw, advancing toward him down the platform, Dolly Hessian, who had boarded that train in Chicago the night before.

Ben's first thought was that this woman was either an actress or a traveling prostitute. Instantly he rejected the first theory; no show had been advertised as soon to appear in Lexington. There was always plenty of advance publicity given to the road shows that came at infrequent intervals during colder months and usually once or twice in the summer, under canvas, to play their one- or two-night stands.

The traveling-prostitute theory was more immediately tenable. Yet . . . this girl . . . there had been practices of such kind among the more flagrantly immoral men of Lexington for years. Ben was not sophisticated enough in manners and morals to quite fathom how it was done. All of his boyhood he had heard whispers and guffaws from the middle-aged men lurking about the livery-stable office. He had heard their comments—a tantalizing word or two—but stifled quickly by the warning attitude of Madison Steele whenever the boy came within hearing.

Sometimes the women were in rooms at the Wildwood Hotel, if they could seduce the management into letting them remain, or if the influence of some Lexington patron was mighty enough. More often they dwelt in little "apartments" —dingy rooms with skylights overhead, hidden behind doctors' and dentists' and lawyers' offices upstairs over the hardware or clothing stores.

But just who these creatures were—in what alluring oven they had been hatched, with their provocative swishing of taffeta and their stubborn faces—just how the men found them, and where and how they drifted to town, and how long they stayed and how they left—these things Ben did not know. He had seen a few professionally wicked women when he made business trips with his father to Chicago or Des Moines; and now he was doubly sure that Dolly Hessian was not such a creature.

She excited him in his first glimpse as no woman had ever done before. The hat, with its lavish ornamentation of almost-black lace, was an object from which he could not tear his eyes. The woman blazed against his vision hurtfully. Ben felt a little drunk, and when that feeling passed it was only to yield to an inclination toward recklessness: a desire to impress this girl, to capture her interest by some means or other.

She must have said the same thing before . . . she was repeating it now, and with a degree of annoyance: "I said, will you please drive me to the Wildwood Hotel?"

Ben said, "Yes. Sure."

"Then take my suitcases."

He relieved her of the burdens with which she labored. The smaller suitcase had been clamped against a black traveling bag in her right hand; very heavy, the two of them, for a girl to lug, but still not equal to the weight of the second suitcase which might have drawn her arm straight out of the socket.

While he was stowing the bags above his horse-collars in the rear seat, Ben heard a distant mutter of voices—a shrill snort and giggling. He turned to observe two men standing beside the window of the agent's office which bellied out in front of the station. One fellow was striking the other on his shoulder, and both were nearly doubled up with glee. The station agent himself, passing close, was at that moment hailed by the other two, and, as the men whispered to the agent, all three of them turned to look at the girl and Ben with contorted faces.

Their peculiar actions, compressed quickly into the one mysterious moment of his botherment, told Ben nothing. A second later he heard the sound of Tucky Miller's horse on the other side of the express wagon, and heard Tucky calling Whoa. In a flash Ben realized what had happened. The young woman—this magnificently behatted stranger—must have inquired for the hotel hack. Someone had told her that the vehicle was next to the express wagon, where Tucky always parked it, and since Mr. Pittenger's buggy was on the nearer side, the girl had made the most obvious and understandable mistake. If he were correct in this surmise (it turned out, of course, that he was) Ben had no intention of disillusioning her.

He tucked the traveling case compactly behind one of the other bags, and stepped back up on the platform. He said to the girl, "I guess you'll have to come down here and get in on this side."

She gave him a glance of her yielding eyes; probably she

thought this was indeed a slovenly and inconvenient manner in which to park a hack for the benefit of customers; then she gathered up her skirts. Ben extended a hand and helped her down, and again, when they had passed the horse, up into the buggy. The girl settled herself on the seat with considerable rustling and brushing. She did not prefer to ride on the front seat alongside the hack driver—her manner said as much—and yet she seemed determined to make the best of a bad situation with dignity.

Ben unfastened Nagger's hitch-line from the ring, mounted to the buggy, and backed out from his shelter beside the tall express wagon with its canvas top. While turning—not too short, he didn't want to scrape the buggy box with the wheel—he was aware that Tucky Miller stood beside the empty bus, gazing at Ben and his passenger with astonishment.

The station agent and his two friends were going into rare convulsions at the corner of the platform. Ben heard the youngest of the three cry chokingly, "Hey, Tuck! Come here. Come *here,*" and then he set Nagger into a trot. The corner of the station blocked the men off.

When he had turned south on Hazel Street, Ben stole a glance at his companion. She seemed afraid to permit herself the demonstration of curiosity, and yet desiring mightily to do so.

"I didn't ask you the fare, driver."

Ben said, "It's not very far. Doesn't cost much." He was trying to remember whether the Wildwood Hotel conveyed incoming or outgoing guests free of charge. Their hack was to some degree a public hack. Tucky Miller used it for various taxi chores around town when there were no trains to be met.

"I think the fare is a quarter."

"You think? Don't you know?"

He could smell her perfume, he could devour her with his eyes. There was delight in speculating how, if he slid only a few inches closer on the seat, he might feel her body against his own. Again the brave, blind impulse, the recklessness, possessed him. He found himself turned away from contemplation of the street, and smiling directly at this girl.

"I don't know very much," he said. "I just know that I think that hat is wonderful."

There was a kind of knife-flash of response in her face . . . perhaps he only imagined it, for the gaze she gave him in return was steady, but completely cold and scornful.

She asked if he was in the habit of making such personal remarks to the women who rode with him.

Deliberately Ben restrained the horse, drawing in slightly on the reins. The C. & N.W. tracks were just ahead, and beyond loomed the populous intersection of Sixth and Hazel, with the yellow bricks of the Wildwood Hotel on the southwest corner. "You see," Ben said, "not many people go riding with me—girls, I mean. I've got a much better rig than this—better horse, too. If you're going to be here tomorrow, why couldn't we take a Sunday evening drive?"

The girl smothered almost completely the retort which rose to her lips; she gave only a little gasp or groan of resentment, and turned her face away.

Coming up behind them Ben could hear the familiar loose creaking of the black bus driven by Tucky Miller. He looked around. Tucky was shaking with irrational laughter. He was not one given to small jokes, but he began to wave his hand as Ben turned back again.

They halted a moment at the corner beside the bank; there was a lumber wagon turning ahead of them, and automobiles and teams progressing along Sixth Street. Ben drove across the intersection and pulled up in front of the Wildwood Hotel. He had crossed illegally—working against the new traffic rules of the town—and he turned the buggy toward the left side of Sixth Street so that the woman might descend directly to the sidewalk, instead of having to walk around the carriage. He tightened the reins, wrapped them, got down and dragged out the three bags. He carried the bags around to the sidewalk; the girl was already starting to descend.

"Here, let me help you." He took her hand; she did not resist, neither did she respond. He wondered whether he should tell her of the mistake now, or wait for her to find it out by herself.

Ben said, "I'll carry your suitcases inside," but unfortunately the rubbery little Negro, who had been working at the Wildwood for the past month or two, saw the arrival. He came bursting from the screen door and bounded down the steps.

"Yes, ma'am. Yes, sir, Mr. Steele. Lady coming inside?"

"Yes," said Ben. And then, to the girl, "Sorry. I guess I ought to have explained to you—"

From the veranda the voice of a fellow-Elk called, "Hey, Ben. What you doing—going into the hack business?" Tucky Miller halted his bus before the other entrance on Hazel Street, and there was confusion—and no time for Ben to explain to the girl, because she had her bag open, she was selecting a quarter from her purse.

"Here."

He took the coin—there was no way to avoid taking it; literally she had pressed it into his hand. He had blundered. He should have carried this flirtation, this meeting (he didn't know what to call it)—he should have carried matters off with assurance, with wit and gaiety. He had done nothing of the kind. Already Dolly Hessian (he didn't know her name then, but he would learn it later in the day) was going up the steps of the Wildwood, and Tucky Miller was approaching the corner of the sidewalk next to the porch.

Ben called, "Here, Tucky. Catch," and the quarter-dollar spun brightly through the air. Tucky clapped it between his hands. Ben Steele got back into the buggy and drove rapidly west up Sixth Street without looking back. His self-approval would have been a little livelier at that moment if he had known that Dolly Hessian heard him cry out to the hack driver, and saw Tucky catch the quarter. He would have felt better if he had known that she, too, was enraged at her own stupidity.

Four

The colored boy opened the door of Dolly's room when she first moved in. He used the key, and she had no opportunity to learn the peculiar mechanical properties of the lock of that door when the key was inserted from the hall side.

From within, the lock worked perfectly; but a little later, when Dolly had visited a bathroom near the end of the corridor (there were no private baths in the Wildwood Hotel) she came back to her room—Number 26—and tried, without immediate success, to open the door. The lock was old and stiff and had worn itself into misbehavior. The bolt had gone into the notch with ease when the door was locked; unlocking it was a different matter. The little chunk of steel refused to budge from its position.

Dolly grew angry . . . there she was, without her jacket or hat, clad informally in waist and skirt, struggling with futility to open the door . . . people might come through the hall. Dolly did not intend to be placed at a disadvantage—not at any time, but especially when she was so newly arrived in Lexington.

She thought of going to the head of the staircase some distance up the hall and calling for assistance, trying to attract the attention of the clerk or the bellboy. As quickly she discarded the idea: there had been a number of men standing about the lobby when she came in. She tried lifting on the door-knob as she turned the key; that didn't work. She tried pressing in on the door and then pulling out. No success.

Fumbling more and more desperately, slamming her left hand against the metal plate that held the knob in place, suddenly Dolly felt the bolt glide beneath her pressure. With the door safely open, she tried locking it again, and then reversed the process, with immediate ease. It was very simple when you knew how to do it: you had only to press gently, not on the knob, but on the edge of the brass plate above, and the key would respond.

A little flustered, she now locked her door from the inside and got busy at the washstand—rinsing away the cinders of the train journey, repairing the damage her hair and complexion had suffered.

The device of the reluctant lock was one which she would put to good effect some hours later.

A few minutes after twelve o'clock Dolly Hessian heard a bell ringing downstairs, and, very hungry after the trip, and after the meager breakfast which she had eaten in the dining car early that morning, she went down to the midday dinner. Her attire was the same as when she came from the train, but brushed and freshened; the opulent lace hat rode proudly above her hair. She inclined her head and smiled at a woman who now stood behind the hotel desk.

This was Mrs. Eckersall, wife of the manager: a long-necked creature of fifty, with tiny eyeglasses pressed in front of her eyes, and a gold chain disappearing beneath the round buns above her ears. She was chewing gum avidly, and it struck Dolly that this woman who smiled and gave a shrill Hello in reply to her nod, had the angular face, the impudent gaze and loose mouth of the inveterate gossip. An acquaintanceship with her might prove to be of value.

The bulk of the meal was tasty, well-cooked in farm fashion: tomato soup; excellent fried ham with mashed potatoes and gravy; cabbage salad with a sweetish, tart dressing—good, too, though the cabbage was a little leathery; spiced peaches, inedible sponge cake and hot coffee. Dolly ate hungrily, though successfully concealing her eagerness in a series of table gestures of languid, impeccable deportment.

A spotty waitress had placed Dolly near one of the windows. Many country folks moved in the street beyond, but the girl was more engaged by what went on at a large table across the room, where seven men were gathered. They were most of them middle-aged; two were reasonably handsome, with no uncommon distinction; but one face was compulsive—the face of a slow-spoken man with a calm and unctuous manner.

He sat quartering at the farther side of the table, facing Dolly, and even while he spoke to the other men (sometimes ingratiatingly, but with studied and deliberate choice of speech) she knew that his eyes were studying her, and in one department of his brain, at least, his thoughts may have been far from the subject under discussion at that table. He dominated readily in presence, in unspoken personality and in voice. His words sounded windy; there was a quality of a parlor organ in his tone, a resonance not unpleasant. He had bright blue eyes, and a trick of rolling them toward the upper lids as he hesitated in search of a phrase or an idea. His face was meaty, his hair flat curls of metallic silver. At this distance it seemed constructed of mercuric putty which had been slapped into place by the application of a sculptor's implement.

This man had certain uglinesses which Dolly found unpalatable to her. In the first place he was a generation older than she . . . age did not matter so much, but still there were those brows: not gray like his hair, but jutting out like dark-dyed mustaches above each eye. His nostrils were thick and coarse, and ornamented unfortunately by tufts of hair. But he was the big man of that table—in stature, in weight, and certainly in local importance.

Dolly could hear the voices, most of them kept at a low rumble; very few of the actual words or phrases reached her. She heard the word "caucus" several times; also mention of a man named Ryder, who appeared to be among those not present. Once one of the other men cried with annoyed inflection, "I tell you, if the Democrats in this State ever—" but the rest was lost. Later on, while Dolly was eating her peaches and nibbling the frosting off the gummy cube of cake, she observed that the men must be telling dirty stories. Their heads were drawn closer together across the cloth; there was the unmistakable mutter of a single voice dramatizing a tale, and then, inevitably, the explosive laughter which followed the catch-line.

She took some small articles out of her bag: a pencil and a notebook in which she noted down the recent minor expenses incurred on her trip. She was keeping track of these expenses, not for anyone else, for her own information only. She had at that time one friend in the world upon whose support she could rely—money—her own pocketbook and bank account, and neither was too substantial in cash resource. The clothes she had bought and sewn for this trip had cost much more than she intended.

Musing thus, twitching her nose a little as she worked with

pencil and notebook, she still was keenly aware of the group at the large table. She wanted them to precede her from the dining room; and just as she was about ready to give up hope, the men arose and trailed out singly or in pairs, some of them laughing loudly, some still whispering.

When Dolly left the dining room at a discreet distance behind them, she found that only three of the men remained in the lobby; two of them stood talking to the fellow with the iron-gray curls and the fleshy face. He had put on his hat; he lingered near the front door. He seemed even more imposing than he had appeared when seated at the table. Dolly idled beside the postcard rack. She heard the other men say, "That'll be fine, Abie. We'll all write and tell him so—" and then somebody said something about "inside straights" and there was more laughter.

"I'll see you then, boys," said the big man, "sometime after three." They all murmured together; he laughed again, and then went out into the street.

Dolly Hessian, aware that the woman behind the hotel desk was ready to begin a conversation at the first opportunity, let her glance wander after the big man, and there was only the politest kind of curiosity in the look she gave him. She turned to the postcards. Most of them were done in full color —unreal blues and greens and oranges. They depicted objects of local interest: the Methodist Church; Sixth Street, Looking East; the City Water Works, Lexington, Iowa; A Country Drive Near Lexington; the Public Library—things like that.

"Know who that was?" said the woman behind the counter.

"Who?"

"I mean that big gink that just walked out of here."

"No. I'm a stranger." Dolly smiled appealingly. "I just arrived a while ago."

"You're Miss Hessian, aren't you? In Twenty-six? Frankie told me about you—that's my husband, Mr. Eckersall. He's the manager. I'm Lottie Eckersall."

"How do you do."

"Going to stay with us long, Miss Hessian?"

"I don't actually know," said Dolly, with all honesty. "I really prefer a boarding-house—you know how it is—a lady alone. . . ." As the other woman nodded sympathetically and seemed about to take a new conversational tack, Dolly feared that she must prod her back on the subject.

"Who was it?" she asked quickly. "That man? He must have been somebody important."

"That was our Senator," said Mrs. Eckersall with pride. "Senator Newgate."

"Oh, really? A real— Does he live here in town?"

"Yes. Abie Newgate—he's State Senator, and he just about runs everything, politically speaking. All those other ginks with him—those were the Republican wheel-horses."

"Wheel-horses?" asked Dolly.

"Yes. They were having a kind of meeting today. Later on I guess they'll play poker—they always do. Abie just loves poker."

"Oh," said Dolly. Then, "You said his name was Abie. Is he Jewish?"

"No," screamed Mrs. Eckersall, laughing uproariously at the idea of Abie's being Jewish. "That's on account of his initials: you know, Senator A. B. A. Newgate. No, he ain't Jewish; he comes from a real old family. They say his father was a carpenter here in early days; but Abie he went into law. He's a pretty slick politician."

"And," said Dolly, her tone lowering in the suggestion, "I suppose he's rich, like all slick politicians?"

"Say, he owns five or six farms, and he's got more cash— And he's something or other with the railroad and a stock-buyers' association. Say, did you come here to visit somebody, or something?"

"No," said Dolly, "I'm just going to work here in Lexington for a while this fall."

With Mrs. Eckersall's mouth opening, ready to hurl more questions, the girl added quickly, "I'll take these cards. Let's see: and this and this. How much are they?" She knew already. The sign said: "Postcards, 2 cents each," and she had her dime ready; she was sliding it across the desk top to the manager's wife. For just a little longer she wished to remain a woman of mystery—a woman from another world who had come to Lexington, no one knew why—who brought an aura of select mystery in her garments and in the things she said and in the things she didn't say. Mrs. Eckersall and the rest of Lexington would know soon enough who she was, why she had come, what her work was to be . . . oh, just a little longer—the wonder, the secretiveness, the vague uncertainty that lingered in her eyes and in her walk—uncertainty that gave her a strength which others might feel pressing upon them.

The dime had been exchanged for the postcards, and before Mrs. Eckersall could say more than, "I just wondered what—" Dolly had given her the most lovely smile she could invent, and cried, "'Bye. I've simply got to get these in the mail."

"You can write them in there." Mrs. Eckersall indicated a tiny parlor which opened off the lobby, behind the stairs.

In this ladies' parlor, seated at a fumed-oak desk, Dolly proceeded to indite the five postal cards. The first was addressed to Mrs. McConnell Tavish, 508 Highcliff Lane, Lake Forest, Illinois. On this card Dolly wrote: "Dear Aunt Edna: Arrived here today after a rather weary trip; but the town is really charming. Please don't worry about me: I am really much happier earning my own living. Will write a long letter soon. Your affectionate niece, Dolly."

The second postcard: "Mrs. Richard DeLong, The Beeches, Warrenton, Virginia. Dear Aunt Ellen: You see, my mind was really made up! Here I am in Iowa, quite delighted with myself, pleased with earning my own way. I wish you were here. I would make you something truly delectable! Your affectionate niece, Dolly."

The third card: "Mrs. J. Patterson Van Tuyl, 2401 Broadlawn Drive, Philadelphia, Pennsylvania. Darling Sue: So happy to learn that you and Ralph are going abroad next month. I shall think of you often as I work. Imagine! Spain and Rome and the Mediterranean. I'm absolutely green with envy. Bon voyage, and do write. Affectionately, Dolly."

The fourth card: "Miss Hazel Tavish, 132 Randolph Road, Scarsdale, New York. Dear Hazel: Have been so terribly busy that I was unable to write before, but did want to send you a card. You know how it is with us 'working girls' —or do you??? *Please* be careful when you ride that big black horse; he looks so spirited. Much love, Dolly."

The fifth card: "Mr. Ronald Penwick, Penwick and Carrington, Inc., 109 South LaSalle Street, Chicago, Illinois: Dear Ronnie: That was simply a delectable little dinner: the orchestra, the food, the wine–everything was perfect. How thoughtful of you to take me there. I shall remember it a long time. Dolly."

She drew a stamp-book out of her bag, and carefully licked the five green stamps into place. There was a box on the desk marked "Outgoing Mail" for the convenience of guests. Dolly knew for a certainty that Mrs. Eckersall would read all five of those cards after she, Dolly, was gone from the lobby, and after Mrs. Eckersall had concluded an hilarious conversation in which she was now engaged. She would read the cards; she would tell her friends what was written. . . . Dolly knew small towns; she had worked in many other towns before this. The legend would grow and grow, and she would support it with a few other postcards in strategic season. Eventually the postals would find their way to the dead letter office, or whatever repository waited for missives mailed to people who existed only in Miss Hessian's slyest imagination.

Five

She made an inquiry from a policeman who lounged with other men on the hotel veranda; then, smiling as she picked her way down the steps and past the country women and children who rested there, Dolly turned south on Hazel Street. She was a little disappointed to learn that the address she sought was on this side, or secondary, street. Sixth Street was more crowded; the stores there were larger, many of them had double fronts, and there was a nickel show—perhaps more than one. She had seen the sign when looking out from the window of her room. Still, there were churches and a courthouse not far along Hazel Street, looming among ruddy trees at the top of a slight eminence; of course the residences near these public buildings would be among the best in Lexington, and their people would walk on Hazel Street.

Dolly passed a pool hall, a shoe-repair shop, a restaurant, a furniture and undertaking establishment. She crossed Fifth Street, then passed over to the opposite side and continued south. As she approached the address she sought, she observed to her disgust that it was almost directly opposite a large livery barn. Farm wagons and buggies with their teams were hitched numerously in front of the livery barn; also there was the chugging sound of automobiles in the thoroughfare; the smell of manure was blended with the fumes of gasoline.

The store before which Dolly halted was a one-storied frame building with a false front built squarely across the end of the single gable, and show-windows on either side of the door. High above door and windows was nailed a sign of faded letters sunk flatly into pebbled black: AGATHA COOK, MILLINER. The dusty windows were jammed with hats, and several red-faced farm women hovered outside with their children. The women talked together in German or Swedish; the children shrieked and scuffled. Dolly hoped that these people were not representative of the shop's best clientele.

Dolly appraised Miss Cook's wares in the window display. She saw only two hats of which she approved: a puffy feathered toque was one, and there was another black velvet with a floppy red bow which Dolly appreciated. The rest, she thought, were so much junk. She wondered about the trimmer Miss Cook had employed the previous spring.

Dolly entered the store. It was too dark in there; merchandise displayed at the rear of the room could not be observed to any advantage. There was one counter along the side, filled with a stock of petty gifts: sewing baskets, birthday cards, paper-weights, embroidery scissors, things like that—objects which people gave away for prizes at whist parties.

A portly dame with a swollen bust was trying on a hat in front of the winged mirror, and glowering at herself. Crouched behind her was a frightened old-maid clerk with prominent yellow teeth. A much older woman with high-piled cottony hair was tying up a hat box for another customer.

Here it was—early Saturday afternoon, high tide of the week's shopping—and the other millinery stores on Sixth Street must be getting most of the town's custom.

Dolly lingered among the cases near the front of the store until the white-haired woman had escorted her customer to the door, and then turned toward Dolly. Of course her eyes went first to the lace-trimmed hat: nervous black eyes. This woman had the hopeless smile of a sugar-sprinkled doll, a pathetic little image sold in a confectioner's shop for children who brought their pennies.

"Can I do something for you?"

"Are you Miss Cook?"

"Yes, I . . ."

"I'm Dolly Hessian."

There was only a second of uncertainty before the milliner recognized the name. She came over and squeezed Dolly's hand. "I didn't expect you until Monday."

"I got here this noon. I thought I'd come in and get acquainted, so as not to take up too much of your time—our time—on Monday morning."

Miss Cook patted Dolly's gloved hand. She seemed yielding to the persuasion of heavy annoyance which emanated from the big woman before the mirror.

"And, Miss Hessian, this is Florence Mahanna . . ."

The spinsterish little clerk ducked her head at Dolly, but shrank back immediately to attend the customer.

The customer stood with arms turned aloft—big fingers clamped on the brim and weight of black velvet, band, buckle and glaring metal lace which she had anchored firmly atop her gray biscuits of hair.

"Excuse me," Miss Cook whispered to Dolly, "I've got to get over here with Mrs. Van Dorm."

She edged around the corner of a counter. "Mrs. Van Dorm, is something wrong?"

"Everything's wrong!"

Little Florence Mahanna wailed, "I did fix it, Miss Cook. Just the way she said. That ribbon is just the way she said."

"Too wide," said Mrs. Van Dorm. "The buckle's too big. I didn't think the brim would turn up so high on the side, either."

"You picked out that buckle, Mrs. Van Dorm," cried Miss Cook accusingly, "and it was your own ribbon. You said you got it in Des Moines at Harris-Emery's trimming sale."

"Well, I can't wear this hat." With angry gestures Mrs. Van Dorm began to withdraw the pins.

Dolly Hessian's voice came floating. . . . "Of course Mrs. Van Dorm is quite right."

Dolly saw the three faces swinging toward her: two of them blankly incredulous, the third challenging and resentful. She moved into the group and lifted her hands to accept the hat.

"The ribbon and buckle are much too wide for this brim; but I can understand easily how anyone might make that mistake. It's kind of hard to translate what we see in our minds, isn't it? I mean—make it into flesh and blood?" She laughed brightly. "I mean, into velvet and capanet and darling buckles . . . to make out of cloth the dream we have."

Her words trailed off; they seemed to drift delicately above the nodding plumes and hummocks of velvet all around them.

Mrs. Van Dorm demanded, "Where did you get that hat of yours?"

Dolly's hand moved up to touch the lace above her ear. "Oh, don't you like it? It's just something I fixed up. I was resting one Sunday, and so I thought . . ."

"It's wonderful," growled Mrs. Van Dorm.

Miss Cook cleared her throat. "This is my new trimmer, Mrs. Van Dorm," she said. "Miss Hessian. She'll be with me this season."

Dolly's contemplative gaze was roving over the hideous knobs into which Mrs. Van Dorm had screwed her hair. "Your hair is so lovely," she said. "It has little lights in it, and —I was just thinking of something I saw Mrs. Palmer wearing in Chicago last week."

"What Mrs. Palmer?" demanded the customer.

"Mrs. Potter Palmer," said Dolly. "Her hair is so much like yours. Of course, she was wearing it in a Psyche knot; but I wonder now if . . ." She lifted the hat appealingly, to interrupt Mrs. Van Dorm's stare. "You meant this for in-between seasons, of course? With rather dressy things?"

Mrs. Van Dorm blinked. "My husband wants me to go with him to the Masonic convention in Cedar Rapids. I just got to have a hat—and we're leaving Monday morning."

Dolly said that she would see what she could do. Still as one walking in a blind dream, with her soul tingling as she appraised the comparative and almost identical beauties of Mrs. Potter Palmer of Chicago and Mrs. J. J. Van Dorm of Lexington, she led the way into the workroom at the rear.

This room also was too dark. There were high windows—a south light, and that was bad. The north wall was bare except for shelves filled with boxes of trimmings and buckram shapes; the tables were worse disordered than they needed to be.

Florence Mahanna jerked a light switch, and in the glare of two yellow bulbs, and in the shafts of sunlight from those south windows, Dolly began to search for the proper belting with which to adorn the crown of Mrs. Van Dorm's hat—for satin of which to create rosettes, for scarlet tulle to apply beneath the band and peep bewitchingly from its edging.

Miss Cook went nervously to attend the few customers who drifted in during the next forty-five minutes. The big yellow teeth of Miss Mahanna showed in a perpetual fascinated leer as she supplied tools and materials. Mrs. J. J. Van Dorm sat with docility while Dolly (her own hat and jacket removed, her gloves tucked away, her steely little fingers stitching, twisting and plucking) made minor miracles. Her voice kept up its soothing.

In less than one hour the hat was redecorated—transformed into an original beauty which became immediately an original horror when it was fastened for final inspection on the peak of the customer's head.

The women stood at strategic places, turning from side to side in responsive movement to the customer's preenings, and uttering their delicate clucks of approval.

"Well, Aggie," said Mrs. Van Dorm to Miss Cook, "this isn't bad." She bestowed her final benison on Miss Hessian: "You're a pretty smart young woman if I do say it."

Mrs. Van Dorm's hands went into her bag and drew out a checkbook. Miss Hessian found her voice quite suddenly . . . there was something, in those days, about a checkbook which might invariably bring a positive reaction from Dolly.

"How much," she asked of Mrs. Van Dorm, "was Miss Cook charging you for that hat?"

"She said she could make it for twenty-four dollars."

Dolly shook her head. "But you see, Mrs. Van Dorm, these additional trimmings are terribly expensive; and in the old hat you furnished part of the trimming. You know: the tulle, and those satin rosettes, too—they're very expensive. We"—she used the plural pronoun without conscious effort—"can't possibly afford a hat like that for twenty-four dollars. It should be thirty-five dollars at least. In any Michigan Avenue shop it would be fifty."

There was a dead silence in the dingy room. The smile left Mrs. Van Dorm's face. She turned to challenge Miss Agatha Cook, who was chewing her lip violently and could not speak at all.

"But," said Dolly Hessian, "after all the difficulty, the worry and mental anguish you have gone through . . ." Timidly she made as if to touch the hem of Mrs. Van Dorm's garment. "I know that Miss Cook wants to please you. Why not meet each other half way, and say twenty-nine-fifty?"

The customer turned to look into the short winged mirror on the nearest work table. She bent close, scrutinizing herself once more. It was not Mrs. J. J. Van Dorm, wife of Jan Van Dorm of the Lexington Farm Implement Company, who returned her glare from the mirror. It was Mrs. Potter Palmer, a lioness of Chicago society, bound probably for tea at Mrs. Helen Chatfield-Taylor's.

Mrs. Van Dorm wrote her check and they all accompanied her to the door. They blessed Mrs. Van Dorm out into Hazel Street. They gazed past the hats in the window, watching the customer on her way. Dolly was the first to speak.

"What a first-class old bitch!" she said.

The others, shocked but delighted, went into ecstasies. Florence Mahanna squealed, when she could find her breath, "Oh, how awful to say a word like that!" and collapsed again.

"But she *is*," said Dolly Hessian, and turned her innocence on them.

Six

Dolly arrived back in Room 26 at the hotel well before four o'clock. The Wildwood Hotel, though only three stories high, was pierced in its center by two courts or air-shafts, and on one of these spaces the window of Room 26 opened.

Lights were on, in an opposite room, to give satisfactory illumination to the card game in which several of the Dodge County Republicans participated with their chief and standard-bearer, Senator Amos Bronson Alcott Newgate.

Dolly stood behind her curtains and watched the men, and listened to their talk which reached her ears. She was prudish about smutty stories, and for a very good reason: a horror of smut itself had been beaten into her by certain associations of her childhood. But there was nothing to offend her in the conversation of these men, except for oaths or expletives used for conversational emphasis so frequently that all emphasis was soon lost. They were talking about Mr. Ryder again, though concerned chiefly with the cards before them.

Twice, men left to visit the bathroom located near the main stairway; each time Dolly could hear them tramping past the door of her room. She looked to see whether the door were locked, fearing that someone might blunder in upon her. Then, as she glanced at the old brass knob, a project began to form itself in her mind.

Dolly waited patiently. She felt that sooner or later Senator

Newgate himself would leave the poker table, and she hoped that he would come alone. When at last she did observe him rising in the opposite room, and heard the few broad remarks which attended him in his errand, she was ready. She wore her filmiest shirt-waist; her hair was newly brushed and arranged. She hung against the door, listening, greeting his strong if ponderous tread with satisfaction. When the Senator had been gone for some minutes, Dolly opened her door, and, key in hand, slipped out into the corridor. There she locked the door and stood with her hand on the knob, waiting.

A traveling man came up the stairs—a man whom she had seen in the lobby previously, and whom she had heard talking about overshoes. Dolly turned her face away and worked with the key. The man hesitated behind her; then, to her distress, he offered to help.

"No, thanks," she said, without looking at him, "it's quite all right."

The man went away, and had barely rounded the corner of a bisecting corridor when Senator Newgate emerged from the bathroom and came toward Dolly.

She struggled angrily with the key and the lock. The big man was whistling softly. It was as if he walked in perfect contentment, in all smug satisfaction with himself and the world; and the odor of his rich, well-chewed cigar came ahead of him. He was whistling, "Pony Boy, Pony Boy, won't you be my Pony Boy?" The whistle was terminated abruptly. Senator Newgate halted.

There was nothing wheedling or flirtatious in his manner. "Allow me." His hands came forward to grasp the key and the knob, and his shoulder was close against Dolly's as he bent beside her.

Dolly drifted away from him a little. "Oh, I'm so glad *some-one* came to help me."

"This hotel is very old; most of these locks stick." He rattled the key and pushed with futility. "But this is very stubborn."

"It's a mean old door," said Dolly with spirit. "I'd like to kick it."

Newgate desisted from the task, and gazed down at Dolly's foot, barely visible in the gloom of the hall. He laughed. "Please don't. I'm afraid you might stub that very pretty toe." Then, after another tussle with the lock, Newgate told her, "You know, I happen to be a politician by trade, and I've learned to admit defeat gracefully. Let me go downstairs and bring the boy."

Dolly lied in her even voice: "He just went away on an errand. Here, let's both try it. You work the key and I'll try with the knob."

She allowed the struggle to go on a moment longer, and then her hand slipped away from the knob as if by accident and fell against the brass plate. The bolt slid out of the socket, the door swung open. "Oh, wonderful," breathed Dolly. "We *did it.* How can I ever thank you?"

The man looked down at her with a faint smile. His wet blue eyes seemed aware suddenly of all the subterfuge lurking within her spirit, and the girl felt a momentary panic. But it was only for a moment, and she told herself later that there had been no discernment by the Senator. She had felt merely a dying tweak of that hopelessly browbeaten entity: her conscience.

The Senator's gaze was friendly, fatherly; but still there was a masculine admiration in it which might have shone to the credit of a much younger man. "I am glad to have been of service. May I introduce myself? I am Senator Newgate."

She whispered, "I'm so embarrassed. I'm not accustomed to having Senators open doors for me."

"Have you been long in Lexington, Miss—?"

"I'm so sorry—please forgive me. I was just rattled. My name is Dolly Hessian."

"How do you do, Miss Hessian?" he said gravely.

"How do you do, Senator Newgate?" and they both laughed aloud.

There were a few other words exchanged, but nothing of importance. He said that he had seen her in the dining room; she, too, admitted that she had seen him. He asked her if she were visiting someone. . . . No, she was going to work for Miss Agatha Cook. "I am a trimmer," she said.

Dolly was not certain; he seemed disposed to linger; she could not be sure. It would not do to have him linger—to have him gain the impression that she was a common woman who indulged in flirtations, or even worse, with strange men in strange hotels.

She said, "It was so kind of you, and I do thank you," and she slipped past him into the room.

"Call me when you're locked out again."

"I don't think I shall be. Probably I'll go to live in a boarding-house. Miss Cook told me about one."

"Where?"

"I think the name was Kristensen or something like that."

He rolled his eyes up into his head. "Almost the very best food in Lexington! You'll be fortunate if she has room for you. Good-bye, Miss Hessian. I hope to renew the acquaintance." He saluted her and went away as she shut the door.

Dolly listened for a time, to see whether he discussed her with the other men. He did not, to any degree. The men rallied Abie Newgate about his long absence; but he said quite casually that he had been talking with a very, very charming lady . . . then he demanded two queens to match the two which he asserted he already held.

Dolly drew down the blind of her window. It was not that she suffered from any abnormal addiction to the fondness of men beyond her own age. As a woman she was, for instance, much more interested in the tall lounging fellow who had driven her from the station—and who, she told herself repeatedly, had been provokingly fresh about the whole thing. Still, casual (even though innocent) liaison with the first good-looking youth who came along was a foolish luxury which Dolly Hessian must deny herself. She knew this, and did not dwell long on the illusion of the young man with the small brown eyes and handsome bony face. There were too many things she wanted to do and to have—too many other needs which taunted her so desperately.

Seven

The flattery and consummate artistry with which Dolly Hessian met Mrs. Van Dorm and retained her as a lucrative customer promptly endeared the young trimmer to Miss Cook and to her "maker," Florence Mahanna. Miss Mahanna worked early and late for the milliner, and was paid seven dollars a week. Makers in some shops got only five dollars; sometimes they got nothing at all.

Of course Florence (generally she was called Floss) was not only a maker; she was clerk and general assistant as well. She would never graduate to the haughty role of trimmer. First, she had no great aptitude toward millinery or any other vocation; and, second, she could not plan to leave Lexington because of her invalid mother—at least not until her mother died. That event did not seem imminent, although Mrs. Mahanna prophesied her own demise with persistent regularity.

Floss Mahanna was the product of a middle-aged marriage between a grist-miller and a petulant daughter of one of the town's early grocers. She inherited nothing of her mother's first prettiness; her face resembled her father's. Fortunately for pioneer aesthetics, Caleb Mahanna's blubbery mouth and yellow fangs had been shrouded by a flowing beard. Indeed his daughter Floss had a beard—a very little one: five or six dark, twisting hairs on her chin, and a straggling mustache which was noticeable when she perspired or when light shone at an angle across her face. There was no delectable femininity about her in body, except her hands; they were dainty, nervous hands, sublimely useless to the world.

Her father had been dead for many years. Her mother ruled mercilessly from a padded Boston rocker, out on Hamilton Street. There was a pension, and they owned the house.

The summonses which she sent to Floss were falsely urgent; Floss might never disregard them. For instance, at eleven o'clock in the morning—three hours after she had walked to work—Floss would be called to the telephone. The message would come from a neighbor—one of three or four neighbors who always were made the mouthpieces of doom.

"Is it Mamma?"

"Yes," the voice of Mrs. Cowper would be quacking inside the receiver. "I could hardly hear her on the phone. She said she tried to get you at Miss Cook's but—"

"The line was busy," said Floss. "Yes, I know."

Mrs. Cowper would make a sound of disapproval. "Floss, I think she's really had a spell. I'd go right over there myself, but I've got something on the stove just coming to a boil, and I'm ironing, and—"

Florence used to ask permission of Miss Cook; but long since she had realized that most other people didn't care to be bothered by the evil besetting her life. She would pin on the green-quilled hat which she had made for herself—a dreadful advertisement for Miss Agatha Cook that hat had become—and she would hasten south on Hazel Street, up the hill past the courthouse, the courthouse park; turning west on First Street, south again on Maple, and finally west on Hamilton.

It would take her all of ten minutes to reach the house. Another ten minutes with her mother, and then back again to Hazel Street.

For half an hour at least, her services were lost to her employer, ten or twelve times each month. Miss Cook had not suggested a cut in Florence's salary. Florence used to worry about that; but this had been going on for a long time, and surely the meek, vicious hypochondriac would be sitting in that same rocking-chair, with that same pink comforter around her shoulders, when another ten years had passed.

. . . Floss's hands were on the door knob. In another moment they would be readjusting the wrapping around the fretting woman, and after that they would bring the hot-water bottle, the pills which the lazy little demon had not been able to find, the cup of coffee from a pot which simmered forever on the back of the kitchen stove. Perhaps, Florence agreed, Mrs. Mahanna's heart was not all that it should have been; but nobody's heart is apt to be vigorous when it has been functioning for seventy-odd selfish years.

The coming of Dolly Hessian brought a charm and lightness into Florence Mahanna's life. Nearly certain that she would be turned down, she asked Dolly if she would like to go to church with her on Sunday morning. To her wonder and delight, Dolly accepted with grace.

Floss said that she would "stop by" the Wildwood Hotel for Dolly about ten-twenty in the morning. Actually she was there at seven minutes after ten, so eager was she to leave the mingled smell of camphor and fried bacon in the little house, and to bask in the radiant, provocative presence of the blonde newcomer.

Floss walked down Sixth Street, looking in the store windows, gazing studiously at the motion-picture advertisements propped up in front of the Unique Theatre. There would be on Monday a comedy featuring Flora Finch. Floss Mahanna found no joy or amusement in Flora Finch. She was secretly positive that she herself resembled Flora Finch.

At the appointed time she walked back to the Wildwood and found Dolly Hessian waiting in the lobby, talking with Mrs. Eckersall.

"How nice of you to come for me," said Dolly.

Floss felt a warmth that rose from her middle and turned her face poppy-pink. She showed her teeth. "We won't be late. Not if we hurry."

"I love to be there for the first hymn," said Dolly, as they moved along Hazel Street to the corner, and then turned east on Fifth.

. . . Oh, lovely, lovely . . . that beautiful hat. And she smells so nice . . . I wonder if that's French perfume she has on . . . I think she's the most beautiful girl I ever saw. Oh, if I were *she* . . . perhaps she will let me be her friend . . . perhaps. And everyone will see us together. Everyone. . . .

The Baptist church, where Caleb Mahanna had served as deacon, was at the corner of Fourth and Plum. It was built of yellow bricks, turned pleasantly tan with age and seepage, and the slim spire—freshly painted that season with flat gray paint—went piercing aloft past the drying elm leaves.

They were in truth a little late. Florence had deliberately slowed her pace to prolong the joy she felt in walking with Dolly, and to admire Dolly's clothes. As they were crossing Plum Street and joining the few people who still straggled toward the high wooden steps, they heard a hymn droning out to draw them in.

"Are you a Baptist?" whispered Floss to Dolly. "If you aren't, I hope you won't mind."

Dolly smiled. Her face was so serene: a yellow pansy of a face under her yellow hair, under the leaves of lace on the midnight-blue hat. "No, I'm not a Baptist, but I love to go to church." She had lied so long and so well that she felt no fear, no hint of a threatening blasphemy as she spoke the words. "It starts me right for the week. Always."

"I don't stay to Sunday school any more," said Floss. They went up the steps. "Mamma isn't well—I don't dare leave her alone too long. She gets to fussing. But we have B.Y.P.U. at six-thirty every Sunday night."

"B.Y.P.U.?"

"That's Baptist Young People's Union. I play the piano." The color suffused her thin face again. "I know they're mostly just kids, and I'm older than most of them"—(she was, in fact, eleven years older than the next eldest Baptist young person)—"but every once in a while they have a party." Church parties were the only parties to which Floss Mahanna was ever invited. Floss loved parties.

The minister preached on, "Shall we have only worldliness in the world?" He made it apparent that almost any giddy thing in which people found joy should be indicted by the blanket accusation of "worldly." It was a sermon that in other accents might easily have been preached in Massachusetts Colony two hundred and fifty years before.

The minister, a listless man who had been tortured by a blustering mother through his younger life, had turned rigidly from all sensual pleasures; including in disapprobation his own wife, a worried woman in a made-over brown suit and a tricorn hat on which two moth-eaten parrots had been smashed flat. She sat docilely in a next-to-the-front pew, and represented to the minister all sensual pleasures which he must shun. He mentioned gaming, wine-bibbing and lusts of the flesh. Since abhorrence of such activities constituted a major portion of the Baptist obsession in that community, some of the older and more assertive people nodded or whispered together in approval while the minister spoke.

Children looked through hymn books or played with pledge envelopes filched from wooden pockets on the backs of the pews. There was a surprisingly capable organist who played Bach for the offertory. Dimes, quarters, and occasional half-dollars clinked shrilly in the velvet collection-pouches passed into the rows by ushers. Neither Florence Mahanna nor Dolly Hessian could recognize Bach as such, but Florence found a kind of comfort in the solemnity of the music; and, in all honesty, Dolly Hessian found the same.

The service lasted for one hour and fifteen minutes—it seemed all of three hours—and then once more the two young women stood in a bright leaf-drifting world.

The Rev. E. Kingsley Cobb showed his disapproval of Dolly's sumptuous hat, when his cold fingers touched hers in what he was prone to call, "the right hand of fellowship." But there was a certain counter-signature of moral approval in the fact that this outlander, this perhaps wicked woman from Chicago, had been invited and accompanied to church by anyone as pure as Florence Mahanna—and on her second day in the community, too. Naturally this was the exact reason that Dolly Hessian had been glad to go to church.

The status of the journeyman—or journeywoman—trimmer was peculiar. Sometimes the trimmers were women as virginal and ugly as Floss herself, but with infinitely more imagination in their minds, and with supreme manual skill and native artistry in their natures. Sometimes they were, on the other hand, blowsy creatures—equally competent, but with more than a taint of immorality in the flash of their clothes.

The trimmer came to town twice a year: in the spring to prepare the warm-weather hats, and in the autumn to prepare for winter. She stayed anywhere from six to ten weeks, depending upon the amount of custom involved. She was paid a princely salary: twenty-five or even thirty dollars per week. Before each seasonal small-town session, she served a seasonal apprenticeship on new styles at one or more of the wholesale houses; and between times she sometimes worked actually trimming hats for long-range custom orders at these same wholesale houses.

Traveling about the country as she did, in a time when few women traveled freely, there was essentially a lack of respectability about her, unless sheer ugliness awarded her an ironclad respectability.

Dolly Hessian had labored grimly in certain communities when tarred with the brush of a self-chosen frivolity. Any corruption which she had practiced in other years had brought only complication and distress. She had been a long time learning. . . . Now she had learned: any private and productive wickedness in which she might indulge safely, she would still embrace; but there must be a profit in it.

She had loved several men when driven into their arms through boredom, hope, or a highly concentrated sexual motive. In no such temporary association had she found the gratification she sought. She felt that her first youth was passing away. She must find and satisfy her ambitious desires, or in some way her spirit and body would be destroyed.

Eight

A teen-age girl in a straw sailor turned from a group of her friends and squealed, "Flaw-awss! Oh, Flaw-awss! Come here a minute." Thus Dolly Hessian was left alone at the foot of the church steps, while Miss Mahanna went willingly to join the group. It was not that Floss desired really to leave Dolly's side, even briefly; but seldom was she called by anyone to join in gaiety or gossip, and her appearance at church in the company of this stranger had awakened a new respect and curiosity in the minds of the B.Y.P.U.

Miss Hessian strolled slowly toward the curbstone at the corner, desiring to draw away from the immediate proximity of families who trailed, talkative or silent, away from the church. Dolly gazed in turn in four directions along the streets. . . . East on Fourth: the rusty little shops of this older, less opulent business section that bounded the near-by residences—they had a gloss of sun and autumn haze lingering over them. Simple and unpromising as they were, they wore a beauty. South along Plum Street . . . the bumpy road rising over a hill past other churches and the public library . . . leaves wavered down with straying elegance, and several automobiles chortled impatiently in their beaming brass. West along Fourth, and sloping up another hill, Dolly could see the boards of the livery barn swelling out, warped with age, bowing over the sidewalk; but red barn-paint had been toned by the seasons, and in this shed-wall dwelt the same mystic prettiness.

Northward on Plum the new post office lumped with its massive gray stone, and people who had lock-boxes had stopped for their Sunday mail. A railroad whistle wavered beyond the brick buildings on deserted Sixth Street and the sheds and elevators and water tanks of the railroad yards. The tone of the whistle went sounding off into haze of other trees and other distances.

It was a good town, Dolly Hessian thought; she would like it here. This country was new to white men in the other century of Dolly's childhood; already there lived a rustic antiquity among the roof-tops, the stained metal cornices, the towering maples and the elms . . . Dolly thought of the East. Her acquaintance with the East was limited to a sordid tear-stained week in a Pittsburgh hotel, and yet she had roved the East in imagination, in practiced falsehood. She desired station and respect, and somehow she felt that the Eastern lives of America were shaped more readily to fit these garments than were those in the West or Middle West. She imagined for the moment that she was in New England, or in Virginia . . . the hooves and coach-clanking of colonial days sounded faintly into the blue.

Throughout this dream, which persisted but a moment, she felt the gaze of the newer prairie town. She felt hostility and speculation; she was conscious, too, of the carnal admiration and hunger of certain men walking with their tribes away from the church—sanctified by Sunday, but embracing secretly those elder lusts which the minister had hinted at but never dared describe. Dolly Hessian was aware of the power exuded by her body and her spirit: she loved it, she gloried in it.

She kept her mild, serious face turned toward the leaves and the houses; and she pretended to be thinking about God.

Florence Mahanna was still wrapped tight in the giggling mob of young girls, and Dolly began to grow a little impatient as the crowd around her thinned, drawing away in different directions—the southbound advance checked and confused by a sudden outpouring from the Methodist church on the next corner.

Then Floss came running to her, slipping her hand through Dolly's arm, squeezing the arm tightly, saying amid snickers, "I'm sorry. I'm real sorry; but I can't help laughing. They told me the funniest thing. It's *rich*."

"What about?"

They crossed Plum Street and moved west together.

"That was Edna Appenzeller. You know, her father's in the furniture business. No, I guess you don't know him. Anyway . . ." Floss became again inarticulate with stifled amusement, and Dolly looked at her questioningly. "They were talking about you," said Floss.

"About me?"

"When you came from the depot yesterday. Do you remember the fellow you rode with?"

Dolly remembered well enough. She said, "Why— You mean the young man who drove the hack for the hotel?"

"But he isn't, Miss Hessian. Honest! He isn't. He's—"

"I wish," said Dolly, "that you'd call me Dolly."

"I'd *love* to." Floss squeezed her arm again. "Well, anyway, I guess somebody directed you wrong, or you made a mistake or something. The fellow who drives the bus for the hotel is

Tucky Miller, and that's how it happened. I mean, he must have had the hotel hack setting next to the one Ben Steele had, and you got in the wrong one."

"I did?" asked Dolly, wonderingly. "You mean that man wasn't the regular hotel driver?" She was prettily disconcerted. "Oh, goodness! What do you suppose he thinks of me? I paid him a quarter, too. Who is he?"

"Ben Steele. His father runs the livery barn and– I mean his father's dead–he died last year–and Ben runs it now. Right across from Miss Cook's. That's it, right ahead."

"Gracious," said Dolly. "I don't want to walk past there. Let's stay on this side of the street. Just imagine! A man from the livery stable."

"Gee, he's not just– I mean, not just a man from the livery stable. His grandfather was a pioneer."

Dolly would hear that expression often in Lexington: "His grandfather was a pioneer." In the Old East of her illusions people might have said, "Their ancestors came over on the *Mayflower*," or "Her mother is an F.F.V." in exactly the same tone.

They were approaching the corner of Fourth and Hazel now; they moved more slowly. "Floss," said Dolly, "I'm really so embarrassed. Maybe I ought to apologize to him."

"Heavens' sake, he wouldn't care. Ben's just a swell young fellow."

"How old is he?"

"He's–I don't know," said Floss. And then bravely she managed it: "He's a little younger than I am." He was, by eight years.

Floss was stammering, twisting her loose, hairy lip over her prominent teeth–flustered as she tried to speak her invitation. "Dolly. I wonder . . . you know, on Sunday, eating all alone and everything . . . there's just mother and me, but we'd love to have you come on home to dinner . . ."

Dolly hesitated, affected by the pleading, the starry hope in Florence Mahanna's face. Sternly she subjugated her pity, even as it was known to her. "I'd love to, Floss. Maybe some other time, but I can't today. I've got a lot of family letters to write." She smiled. "Auntie's really so stern and particular. I'll tell you very confidentially: my relatives were quite upset at my becoming a milliner. If Auntie doesn't hear from me real soon she'll think—well, heaven knows what! You see, I got to write those letters and get them in the afternoon mail. You see why?"

Florence nodded dumbly.

From the entrance of the livery barn sounded the nervous *clop-clop* of a horse's hooves; the horse was drawing a buggy over the sidewalk and into the street. Ben Steele rode there; he wore his Sunday suit. It was not a bad suit at all: dark gray stripes, long-waisted, and he had a soft-brimmed, yellowish felt hat crushed down over his dark hair. His tie was purple and also (they could see, as the buggy turned fairly in front of them) his socks were purple. He was driving a tall mare: a light bay. She was a pacer, and now she swung her legs in cadence.

Ben Steele sat erect, driving well, keeping a tight grip on the reins. He glanced at the women, he recognized them both. His gloved hand came up to touch his hat and he grinned, nodding, though his amused stare went past Florence Mahanna and slid deep into Dolly Hessian. Then he turned his face away; the mare went swinging her legs up the hill toward Third Street.

"Speak of the devil," said Floss. She burst into snorts again.

"He drives real well," said Dolly.

"Horses—that's all those Steeles ever think about. They're just crazy about horses. I mean, Ben is. He's the only one left."

Dolly inclined her head kindly toward the unhappy little spirit that quivered in Florence Mahanna's flesh. "Floss, it was wonderful of you to take me to church, and thanks for the invitation to eat Sunday dinner."

"Maybe some other time, real soon—?" Floss began.

"Of course. I'd love to. Now I'll run along. Good-bye, dear. See you tomorrow."

"See you tomorrow," echoed Floss hopefully.

With Dolly gone, Florence turned reluctantly to the fretful hours ahead. She comforted herself all the way home with the thought of the pretty girl's graciousness—the daintiness, the choice femininity, the excitement they gave. These wonders were a harmony around her . . . they sang in every tinted leaf that came down.

Dolly, walking steadily toward the hotel and entering it, had driven Florence Mahanna completely out of her mind, and would not make room for the girl there until she met her again. She thought considerably of Ben Steele on the way—there was a hidden deviltry about him. Just a livery stable man, she thought. No, I couldn't. I couldn't possibly.

Nine

Marguerite Newgate watched her husband pass the still-green lilac bushes of the yard. She watched him pass the big iron dog which stood contemplating a neighbor's chicken shed beyond the shrubbery; she watched him open a wooden gate fastened in the metal fence (boys had carried off the old gate on Hallowe'en some years before, and she had never been able to find it or replace the missing gate with a similar one).

Marguerite saw the Senator lift his hat to some Sunday strollers and then he went out of sight. She wondered whether, on this day, he was going to seek a woman, and if so, what woman. Marguerite went back to her butterflies.

On a card table covered with plain yellow oilcloth and set close into the bay window of her living room, Mrs. Newgate had arrayed her mounting-board, an old cigar box—damp and sodden—and the pins and tiny tools she employed. Butterflies in the cigar box were only three in number; she had caught them weeks before, but had not felt energetic enough to mount the butterflies at that time.

Meticulous as any scientist in the preservation of her specimens—extremely resourceful and imaginative when it came to capturing them—Mrs. Newgate was anything but scientific in the arrangement of her collection. She collected butterflies and moths principally because she loved their delicacy and the pigment on their wings. It did not matter to her that she had one genus confused with another, or that she applied fanciful names of her own construction.

Marguerite brought out the three small paper envelopes remaining in the cigar box. The box itself was half-filled with cotton which originally had been dampened with water, with the addition of a few drops of a chemical to prevent mildew. A plain sheet of muslin protected the envelopes in which the insects had been placed after removal from her killing jar. Their wings stiffened quickly after death, and Marguerite always made sure that the wings were tightly folded—that the antennae and legs were guarded from any crushing. Then, at her leisure, she would insert the envelopes in the cigar box for a day or two. Dampness would creep through paper, relaxing the atrophied wires of the insects' wings and bodies. If removed with dispatch, and prepared properly on the mounting board (impaled by long thin japanned pins) they would, like the rest of her trophies, become frail wafers of bliss.

She kept them set into cork on their rows of pins, in strong gray cardboard boxes. In the corners of each box, camphor balls were fenced tightly with other pins to keep away the tinier bugs with which Marguerite was eternally at war. She had nothing else in the world to cherish except her butterflies and moths.

Mrs. Newgate put in proper appearance—sedate, unfashionably groomed and prim-spoken—at the few political dinners in that state where wives were held to be a necessary social adjunct. Every two or three years, Senator Abie Newgate chose to entertain the members of the Dodge County Bar Association in his own home; then Marguerite was compelled to put aside her insects for the worries of fried chicken, waitresses, demi-tasse cups, card tables and after-dinner mints. These chores she performed without enthusiasm, without much efficiency, but with strained attention.

Usually the members of the bar association and their wives had a very good time at Senator Newgate's. Abie offered good cigars, and wine fetched secretly from Fort Dodge into this W.C.T.U.-ruled community. The women chattered limply, played whist and Five Hundred, and those who had new dresses delighted in showing them off.

Marguerite always stayed in bed at least two days afterward, and the Senator never went near her bedroom. He would say to the hired girl: "My wife coming down to breakfast?"

"No."

"Oh."

If Mrs. Lottie Eckersall had lived longer in the community (she came there only in 1904) and if she had been less scatter-brained, more able to accumulate and retail accurate information, she might have told Dolly Hessian that Senator Newgate had earned very little of the fortune he held. Most of the estate had belonged to his wife, whose father was a miserly German. Barney Feldbraun came to Dodge County across the prairie with his few belongings in a wheelbarrow; his wealth at his death, translated into bundles of banknotes, would easily have filled that same wheelbarrow.

In the early days people used to shake their heads about those poor little Feldbraun children. When it was the season for hauling corn to mill, or later to town for shipment, passers-by would see old Barney driving a corn-filled wagon along the frozen road, and another similar wagon would be standing between the unpainted cubical house and the big barns. Children scrambled in a miserable bucket brigade in and out of the corn-cribs, back and forth, to the wagon, up over the high wheels; they dumped their baskets of corn, working against time. Even the three-year-old clutched a tin bucket in her blue hands.

The children toiled in silence, never laughing, calling only curt orders or injunctions to one another—sometimes in English, sometimes in Low German. If their father returned before they had filled the wagon, the children were led into the barn one by one and beaten methodically. Hired men cost too much money—at least until Barney's holdings grew so extensive that he was compelled to pay for extra help, or else witness his acres of rich black earth go unplanted, untapped, unmonopolized.

The Feldbraun children ran away as soon as each was grown up enough to do so. Marguerite herself (she was next to the youngest) worked as a waitress, as a hired girl, a slavey who never slaved so hard as at home. Eventually she fell in with a kindhearted family who allowed her to work for her room and board, and sent her to school. Later she had a job in a grocery store where she learned bookkeeping. The columns of figures frightened her; her accuracy was due only to application and extreme patience. With this grimly acquired ability at figures, she found herself at last in the law office of a veteran jurist where a young man named Newgate, the blarneying, pampered son of a poor widow, was reading law books.

By this time the elder Feldbraun had become so decrepit that he was compelled to give up farming and move disconsolately to Lexington. There he rented three dark rooms over a dirty restaurant. His wife sat in the gloom, clasping and unclasping her flaky hands, reading Sears-Roebuck catalogues, dreaming of the things she would like to order and never dared beg for. Marguerite called on her parents occasionally, scarcely exchanging a word with her father, conversing in half-remembered German with her mother. She sat on the edge of a stiff rocker, eager to leave the persistent smell of fried potatoes behind her. . . . The eldest boy had run away out West; he had joined the army and was killed during an Indian uprising. Two of the other runaways had died also—one in childbirth. There were three surviving Feldbraun children; of these, Marguerite was the only one to remain in Iowa.

Seated on the concrete steps beside the Big Wonder Café, listening to worthless talk of others who lounged there, but seldom joining in it, Barney Feldbraun began one day to swallow rapidly and then to gargle and make funny motions toward his beard. He toppled onto the sidewalk and skinned the side of his face in falling. His was not a beautiful death, but it was a popular one.

He was believed to have left millions; as a matter of fact his entire estate was something more than three hundred and fifty-eight thousand dollars. Thus Marguerite became an heiress. There were four buggies in Barney's funeral procession, following the black hearse, and a few curious people who walked the sidewalks toward the cemetery, quickening their pace to keep up with the horses.

It was hot in the cemetery; July blazed hard all around; the grass was turning brown and no rain came for weeks. The husk of Barney Feldbraun shriveled in its gray coffin within the heat that saturated the soil: a kind of attenuated cremation appropriate to the circumstance, since most of Dodge County knew that Barney's soul was cooking in other regions. Mrs. Feldbraun joined him above the creek-side nineteen months later, not long before Marguerite was married to the pompous young lawyer who had courted her with quotations from Longfellow.

The man treated his wife with studied, almost mocking politeness until he had the bulk of her estate well under his control; then he ignored her. There was a brief flurry of marital interest at the time Marguerite was brought to bed. It was a still-birth; she was ill for a long time—insofar as the town believed, for the rest of her life. There was some kind of elaborate disarrangement of her internals, which would breed more hideous disaster later on.

At forty-eight it was strange that Marguerite Newgate could seem younger than she was. Her hair had been white for years but her skin wore a kind of translucent purity. Her long, thin nose, her high cheekbones—each delicately rounded surface of her face was marble-clear and marble-cool. Only the region around her eyes was lined, and her large, tragic gaze went out to the world seeking pity, seldom able to recognize it when it was offered, never able to reciprocate.

A decade earlier she had become interested in collecting insects, when one humid summer night a great many moths came to her window light. She slew these first ones with camphor, and thrust them raggedly on common pins. Soon she had a box filled with colored, distorted shapes. A longing came back to her . . . she remembered the summer days when, as a child, she had seen swallowtails and fritillaries drifting comfortably over clover beds, lost and wandering and unguarded; and she, bending her back above turnip rows, had felt a great desire to be winged and free-flown. Now the coming of these insects gave her an almost sensual delight—she, who had scarcely ever tasted a sensual pleasure.

She learned more about them; she went to the public library, she peeped shyly into "nature books"; she wrote away and bought other books; she learned how to identify these gorgeous vagrants. She was not interested in the Latin names. She called them to herself, *Blue Eye* and *Japanese Paint* and *Egg-color Lovely* and *The Wanderer* and names like that. It was as if, in terminating their brief existence and spearing them in profusion within her boxes, she tasted slyly of the hidden flower patches, the mystery of afternoon and throbbing forest where they had flown.

Ten

"Provided, always, and these presents are upon this express condition, that if the said party of the first part, his heirs, executors, administrators or assigns, shall well and truly pay, or cause to be paid, to the said party of the second part, his heirs, executors, administrators or assigns, the aforesaid sum of money, with interest thereon, at the time and in the manner specified in the above-mentioned promissory note, according to the true intent and meaning thereof, then and in that case these presents and everything herein expressed, shall be absolutely null and void."

The mortgage which lay with many other papers on the table opposite Abie Newgate's desk, had been drawn up with care, and did not need his attention this Sunday. It would be read and re-examined Monday morning, signed and delivered on Monday afternoon. The correspondence which waited, claiming his interest and ambition, could not be attended to until his secretary came in, also on Monday.

But a persistent tremble of restlessness had drawn him out of the house. He knew that he had married his wife for one reason only; she knew it too. He knew also that she admired him in many ways, still; he wished that she did not. He wanted admiration from the rest of the world: none from Marguerite. It was false in her to voice the timid approbation which sometimes she offered. Marguerite knew too much about him, and thus, intermingled with his physical contempt of her, he held a certain fear.

In Des Moines he had a mistress, an austere-appearing but intensely passionate spinster who had served as secretary to various officials in the State House. She lived in a little apartment out west on Ingersoll, and often Senator Newgate spent nights with this woman. Years before, he had attempted to bully through a number of extremely obvious affairs at home in Lexington; but resulting notoriety was reflected at the polls and had even been hinted at in the press by two or three bolder editors of that senatorial district. The game was not worth the candle, and Newgate performed a variety of public absolution.

There had been later a few love passages with women safely married, dressed in the respectability and security of their homes and their husbands. Such women had, in their own lives, fully as much to lose through scandal as had Abie Newgate, and hence he did not worry about any revelation, so long as these illicit rites were performed with the utmost secrecy.

But it was more than a sexual craving that drove him wandering to his office on this Sunday afternoon. Abie was becoming old enough to look with alarm toward the future, toward termination of his masculinity, his career, and indeed his life. He felt that arch and provocative misery: the desire for an attainment beyond his gifts. He had been defeated twice in Congressional elections and once in the early stages of a gubernatorial campaign. Unless eventually appointed to a Federal judgeship, or happily to the bench of the State Supreme Court, he was now at the peak of his career.

True, minor triumphs might await him still in the Senate. He had craved the chairmanship of several committees and had attained to a few. But when one has been State Senator and State Senator only for more than a decade, he may readily believe that the public has taken his political measure.

Sometimes perversely he had dreamed of making a great deal of money: several swollen fees all at once—in gigantic railroad cases, for instance. He had treasured the thought of carrying this money physically, in gold, into his own house, dumping it down before the ailing woman who picked away at her butterflies, and screaming at her, "Take a look! I made it myself. I didn't worm it away from you. God damn it, Marguerite, I earned it with my own talent, my own personality and wisdom. Now you can take back every dollar I have had the handling of, the benefit of . . . take it all up there to the cemetery, and open that grave, and stick it—"

Thus far, in all his years of legal practice, his largest fee had been for sixteen hundred dollars. Except in illusion he saw no brighter prospects ahead.

To himself in solitary session, in lone bedroom, in bathroom, in secret walks through darkness, A. B. A. Newgate held many doubts about himself, and not too much respect. His easy pomposity had been studied. And the impression it made, together with the professional ruthlessness he was capable of manifesting when necessary—these were all he needed to maintain his control of that political principality. For a smaller, smugger man this would have been sufficient. But essentially Abie was one of those unfortunates who had somehow, in inheritance and youthful longing, acquired too large a dream.

Therefore he tried to transfer his sought-after illusions

into the simple conquest of women. In such transports, when deviously he had conquered, he cried to himself that he was great.

His meeting with Dolly Hessian occurred in a moment when he was bored by the fumbling, fawning littleness of the men about him. The hope of some vague unacquired success had drifted before him again on that Saturday. Once more, working almost consciously, he identified this formless desire with the new young woman whom he found in the hotel. He had made inquiries about her slyly, without seeming to, as he knew well enough how to do.

So she was Aggie Cook's trimmer; that was deplorable. Homely, elderly trimmers Newgate recognized: competent in themselves, of ugly virtue equal to their own ugliness. Pretty trimmers were believed to be flagrantly immoral—unless, as rarely occurred, events proved otherwise. The Senator dared not be seen with this woman in public, except when enjoying the most occasional workaday encounter. How could he progress to satiation of this fresh impulse, deprived of the opportunity for the normal preliminary processes of acquaintanceship and salesmanship?

Senator Newgate's office was well down the first block on Sixth Street below Hazel, two-thirds of the way to Plum Street. The windows of the front room looked out north, facing an old wooden building with a cut-under front where the Unique Theatre was housed. Next to this, reading east, came a barber shop, Fairchilds' jewelry store, a hardware store, and then the Capital Restaurant.

The Capital was a narrow, smelly dive with a half-defaced sign on the window-glass: *Tables for Ladies,* and it had changed hands five or six times in the past ten years. Now a

Greek had it, and astonished report declared that the Greek was not only more scrupulously neat than his predecessors, but turned out better food. There were only three restaurants, including short-order places, which remained open on Sunday in Lexington, and the Capital was one of them. Of course the hotel served meals to its guests and to some outsiders seven days a week; but you had to be very prompt in answering the bell which rang to announce each meal.

It was a little after two o'clock when Newgate (seated close to the front window of his front office so that he would not need to depend on artificial light) saw Dolly Hessian moving slowly down the block on the opposite side of the street. Like most Sunday strollers, Miss Hessian examined the boards which leaned in front of the movie house. On these boards were tacked posters of current or coming attractions, together with small photographs of various scenes: stiff blurred pictures, spotted from mishandling.

Abie watched Dolly eagerly. She was wearing a pigeon-gray suit with a pink blouse, and a scrap of gray fur dangled from her arm. She wore the same hat which he had seen her wearing in the hotel dining room on Saturday: the magnificent hat of midnight-blue lace. She was more desirable than most of the women he ever saw in Des Moines.

He wondered about that air of innocence; he wondered whether she had deliberately planted herself at the door of her hotel room when he came along the hall. But the lock had really been baffling. He had tried, he thought, every concentration of effort in order to open it. He wondered. . . .

She stood for a time examining the things displayed in Fairchilds' jewelry store. There were two windows . . . the one on the left, beyond which the younger Fairchild sat on weekdays with a board filled with watches hanging before him: there was only a silver steak-platter in that window, displayed in solitary dignity on a mound of dark velvet. The steak-platter was by way of becoming a local institution. It was put into the window two or three times each year. The Fairchilds had had the platter for a long time, but the price was too high for casual customers to consider, and the few people who might afford such opulent plate were already provided with something like that. The right-hand window was filled with nick-nacks: chinaware, purses, powder-boxes, such things. Some object in this window claimed Dolly's speculation for a while. Then she went on, passing more rapidly to the front of the Capital Café where she glanced up at the sign and went inside.

Newgate shoved the letters together in a pile and carried them to his desk. He pulled down the roll-top and reached into his pocket for the key. He stood for a moment, staring at the old desk, seeing only Dolly Hessian's skirt hem and smooth rounded hips and the lacy challenge of her hat. It occurred to him that she might have learned the location of his office—she might have stood deliberately in front of the jewelry window for him to appraise her as she pretended to appraise the articles inside. Perhaps she saw his office sign—no, there was no sign: it had been damaged during a near-tornado two years before. It had been taken down and never replaced. Between Spillman's drygoods and Olson's bakery there was only a dark stair leading aloft—a stair with three concrete steps built up from the sidewalk, and faded black-and-pink cards tacked against the upright portion of every fourth step where the wooden staircase ran up inside: *A. B. A. Newgate Att'n'y.* An itinerant sign-printer had appeared in Lexington long before, with a font of large type and whole cords of cardboard slabs in his wagon. He had thus decorated, for a fee, the stairs that penetrated nearly every business building in town. You ascended to doctors, dentists, lawyers, photographers; all the way up you saw their names before your eyes.

Miss Hessian could not have known the location of his office, most certainly, unless she had inquired at the hotel.

The Senator took his hat, locked the office, and went downstairs and diagonally across the street, strolling deliberately to the east window of Fairchilds' store. There was no telling what thing in that window had attracted Dolly's interest. There were bags and vases and purses of many kinds—no jewelry. That was carefully locked up in Abner Fairchild's safe each night of the week and on Sundays.

Some young men passed, and spoke respectfully, and Newgate was cordial. In spite of the perfection of September, the business blocks ahead were almost deserted. Most of the younger people went to the woods on a day like this—it was still warm enough for picnics; and the elder folks sat on their porches or worked in their yards.

Newgate went into the restaurant, and Dolly was the only customer before him. She sat at a small table next to the wall, across the room from the counter, with a meal spread before her and a magazine open beside her plate. As she glanced up, Newgate turned toward the Greek, pretending capably that he had not seen Dolly at all. He sat down on one of the stools fastened before the counter.

"I'd like a cup of coffee, please," he told the Greek. "Black. Just a little sugar."

Alternately stirring and sipping his coffee, he turned at last and discovered Dolly officially for the first time.

He smiled and let his strength—he let the whole source of his strength flow toward her and envelop her.

"Why, Miss Hessian . . ."

"Hello."

He arose, coffee cup in hand. "Would you mind if I joined you?"

"Not at all."

He sat down opposite her. "You are very late for dinner," he chided. "Don't tell me you've been working on Sunday."

"No. I went to church. Then I had some things to do, and—I was busy up in my room; I forgot what time it was. I didn't hear the bell, and when I came down the dining room was closed."

Newgate made a few uncomplimentary remarks about the Wildwood Hotel. "Eckersall's a good sort," he said, "but I'm afraid he's incapable of conducting the kind of hotel we need in a town like this. Well," he added cryptically, "there may be a change. Who can tell? What are you reading?"

"*Munsey's Scrap Book*. Just a magazine that was in my room when I moved in."

"What about Mrs. Kristensen's?"

"I'm waiting to hear from Miss Cook."

Newgate ordered a second cup of coffee. He was beginning to feel more secure about being seen with Dolly Hessian, in case anyone whom he knew came into the restaurant. She had spoken about church, for one thing.

"Did you enjoy church? What is your religious affiliation?"

"Actually," said Dolly, "I am an Episcopalian." This was a total untruth. She was exposed in early childhood to a mildewed Catholicism, and had been inside other churches only a few times in her life. "But I found there isn't any Episcopal church in Lexington. Florence Mahanna asked me to go with her to the Baptist. I'm glad I went; it was really a splendid sermon."

Newgate nodded judicially and said that the Rev. E. Kingsley Cobb was a very fine minister indeed. In all truth, the Senator abhorred every public utterance he ever heard the Rev. E. Kingsley Cobb make, but he did not wish to quarrel with Dolly about this. He was beginning to believe that it might be quite safe to be seen on the street with Miss Hessian—that is, if they appeared to be merely walking together, with nothing prearranged about it.

He tried to lead her into conversation about the millinery business, but found her noncommittal. He teased her, with some daring, concerning mysterious inquiries he had allegedly made about her, between the time of Saturday's dinner and the hour when he helped her with the door-key. Dolly only looked at him with her clearest gaze. Somehow she made him feel embarrassed and foolish; no woman had made him feel like that in a good many years.

With gallantry he reached for her check when she was finished, and said, "Please allow me." And she said, with no fluster, "No, thank you. I think it would be better if I paid my own." Thus they stood side by side, offering their checks, waiting while the Greek made change.

Senator Newgate had small change—plenty of it—in his lower right-hand vest pocket; but he thought it better to feel in his empty trousers' pocket without success, first; and then to bring out his big alligator-hide wallet. He counted through the thickness of bills therein, until he found a one-dollar bill. This was a palpable vanity in which he had never been reluctant to indulge himself—not, at least, since the year after he was married to Marguerite Feldbraun. When working his way through college (it was partly work, and partly the bounty of an ailing aunt which put him through) he was once found to be carrying a ten-dollar bill and two ones, wrapped around a wad of green paper cut to the proper size. Boys had teased him uproariously about this, and he had never tried it again.

Pleased by Dolly Hessian's ladylike demeanor, excited beyond reckoning by the occasional touch of her sleeve and by the odor of crab-apple perfume that anointed her, Newgate escorted her west along the sidewalk for a few paces. He saluted . . . he was taking off his hat and saying that he must cross the street and return to his office. Sometimes Sunday was just another day for him; he had entirely too much to do.

His eyes went beyond Dolly and saw something interesting in Fairchilds' store window. He said, "Excuse me just a minute. I must see this!"

Dolly accompanied him to the window, where he pointed out an ornate comb and brush which he had barely glimpsed when passing before.

"I am sure they're just like the ones my wife saw in Chicago recently. She wanted to get a comb and brush like that for her niece, but didn't. Then she regretted it after she was home, but"—he chuckled tolerantly—"she couldn't remember which Chicago store she saw them in. I must tell her they have something like this, here in Fairchilds'. They have nice things for a small-town store, don't they?"

"I," said Dolly, "like that bag."

"Which one?"

"There. The tiny mesh-bag. It's so cute for evening. You know—going to a party or something."

Abie bent close to the glass and read the card. "It's not white gold. It says Sterling."

"That doesn't matter. It isn't the intrinsic value." Dolly's gold-gray eyes turned up toward him seriously. "It's just that it's a beautiful thing to have. I shall save my pennies," she said with a little laugh.

"Afraid you'll have to save at least dimes." For a moment he let something of his own urgency burn through the gaze he gave her—but not for long, not too long. He didn't want to frighten her.

"Well, back to the chain-gang for me. Miss Hessian, may I thank you? This was a very pleasant interlude in a tiresome day."

She said that she had enjoyed it; she didn't offer her hand; she only smiled and bowed. He took off his hat, replaced the hat and strode away to cross the street toward his office. He turned only when he was in the dark cavern of the staircase. Secure in the shadows, he could look back before he had ascended to a height where the wall above the door cut off his view. He got one more glimpse of Dolly as she walked westward; then she was out of sight.

He debated later that day and long through the evening, about the mesh purse. He couldn't decide whether she had been hinting when she pointed it out. There seemed something so concretely honest, so innocently simple about this girl. Was it possible that she was as guileless as the impression she gave?

Well, consider it: she would not be carrying the bag when she went to work, or when she was shopping. Few people would see it, and fewer of those who remarked on it might recognize the little mesh purse as the one which had been offered in Fairchilds' window. The Fairchilds, father and son, were prosy English Lutherans who would seldom—or never, in any likelihood—encounter Dolly Hessian socially, and thus recognize merchandise which they had sold to Abie Newgate.

As for the girl herself: the worst that she could do would be to return the gift to him. In order to protect herself, she would have to do that privately. If she saw him privately, it would give him a further opportunity for acquaintance. There seemed nothing to be lost and possibly a great deal to be gained.

About eleven o'clock on Monday morning, while Dolly Hessian was holding Agatha Cook, Florence Mahanna and two women customers spellbound with her artistry, Senator Newgate walked into the jewelry store and bought the tiny metal-meshed purse for $17.50. He told Abner Fairchild to wrap it carefully and to tie the box in tissue paper. It was a gift, he said, for the wife of a judge in Des Moines.

With the treasure secured, back in his office Abie wrote a little note on one of his cards, and slid the card upside down under the white ribbon that bound the box.

> "Dear Miss Hessian:
>
> Please let me do this. I had a little daughter once. She would have been just about your age. With my admiration,
>
> N."

The problem of presentation was complicated. He dared not leave it at the hotel desk for Dolly. Obviously he could not take it to Miss Cook's, and he did not know when next he might encounter Dolly on the street.

This difficulty he solved with characteristic ease, if not with much dignity. He went to the Wildwood Hotel before twelve o'clock—he was there in some capacity or other, nearly every day of his Lexington life—ánd climbing to the second floor, he found himself in the deserted corridor in front of Dolly's door. The transom was open wide; light came from the windows beyond. Senator Newgate closed his eyes briefly and envisioned the room the way he had seen it when the door was opened on Saturday. The bed was—just about there. . . . He reached up and tossed the little package through the open transom, and heard it fall upon the bed with a light thud and clink.

Dolly found the box when she returned to the hotel fifteen minutes later.

Eleven

When Dolly read Senator Newgate's card, she could not imagine what might be inside the package. She had, for the time being, forgotten all about the mesh-bag which she coveted. Her first reaction when she saw the gleaming fabric of silver was, "How perfectly wonderful!" and then promptly she was torn by doubts.

Already she had ascertained from Mrs. Eckersall that Senator Newgate was married, and that the Senator evinced, as Lottie Eckersall said between giggly snorts, "an eye for the girls." If that were his reputation locally, Dolly could not afford to be identified with him in public fancy—not unless very quickly she made something more permanent out of the arrangement by compelling this man to divorce his wife and marry her, Dolly.

He had money and community eminence, and these two essentials she had determined to secure for herself. Dolly was not unimpressed by Newgate; there was a fleshy, stallion-esque power about him; but after all, what would the man be like in another ten years, when she was only in her late thirties? Practically he would be ready for death and burial. It was all too fantastic; there were too many opportunities for a slip, for moderate disaster. The structure she had reared instantaneously to surround herself and Newgate went up jerry-built from the flimsiest foundation.

She sat on the edge of the bed and played with the pretty mesh, and once she lifted the little bag and touched its cool trickling weight against the bare skin of her neck. Perhaps it would be safe to retain this gift in the spirit in which Newgate pretended to have offered it: in a manner of expression of a fatherly token, however secret the transaction might be rendered. She did not know . . . she wanted the bag . . . she wanted a great many other things. She was not at all certain that she wanted Newgate, or could secure him if she did.

It would be necessary to talk to him, to see how he reacted, and take her cue from his attitude. Dolly went down to her noon meal. She thought Newgate might be in the dining room. Of course she could not talk to him there.

The doors of the dining room entrance nearest the staircase were kept closed habitually, but there were glass panels. Dolly dropped her handkerchief, and faced the doors as she bent to retrieve it. Yes, Senator Newgate was in the dining room at a table with two other men, one of whom she had seen on Saturday.

Dolly idled at the desk. She bought a roll of Necco wafers from Mrs. Eckersall.

"I love candy, but I daren't allow myself more than one teentsie package a week. Isn't it frightful the way the littlest bit of sugar turns into *fat*?" She lowered her voice guiltily.

"*You* should worry!" cried Mrs. Eckersall.

"Oh, dear. And usually I don't eat lunch so early. It's funny: every town, every store seems to have a different arrangement about lunch. I know you call it dinner here, but —Floss Mahanna comes first in the morning at Miss Cook's and opens the shop, so she goes home at eleven. Then she comes back at twelve and I go. Then I must be back at one, and Miss Cook goes then. I wish she'd suggest trading her lunch hour with me, but she hasn't yet. And men with offices: I don't see how they manage it—to keep their offices open, I mean."

"Lots of them are alone in their offices," said Mrs. Eckersall. "They just have to close up while they eat dinner. Of course, if a man has a girl or a partner or something, he can work it the way Miss Cook does."

Mrs. Eckersall seemed to be a fine, free-flowing hydrant, gushing forth all sorts of valuable information. Dolly was positive that Senator Newgate had a secretary in his office—a Senator would need one. There was the unhappy possibility that the girl's lunch hour might be early, to match Floss Mahanna's; but Dolly would have to chance that. She decided to be late at Miss Cook's. She hated to do that on the very first Monday; but after all, she had trimmed one hat the previous Saturday on her own time.

She lunched at the little window table, but this time with her back turned toward Abie Newgate and the men who sat with him. Thus he could not observe her or greet her publicly without being obvious. Dolly was correct in her surmise that Newgate would leave the dining room without speaking to her. She outstayed him. He left about ten minutes to one, and she followed him to his office shortly afterward.

He was alone. There was a litter of papers on the secretary's desk, but her typewriter was deserted, her chair empty.

Newgate smiled at Dolly. "Please come inside," and he ushered her through the door of the inner office. Here he had another desk, mainly for show. The room looked unused . . . there was a table with chairs around it, which could serve for political conferences, and there were three large bookcases containing law books and the *Iowa Official Register.*

Newgate closed the door and stood looking down at Dolly. She thought for a moment that he would try to kiss her then; he seemed so inclined.

"I shouldn't have come here."

"I'm glad you came."

Silently she opened her reticule and brought out the mesh-bag which she had re-wrapped in its tissue paper.

"Now, now—"

"But, Senator Newgate, I *can't.* What would you think of me? You wouldn't have any respect for a girl who—"

His blue eyes were blander than she had observed them before. "Did you read the card I wrote?"

"Yes. I—I sympathize deeply." And even more softly she asked, "Do I remind you of her?"

"Yes."

The pitiful little baby, born dead, had been a bluish, repulsive object with a scrolled face like an ape. Abie Newgate didn't like to think of this child, but sometimes the memory rose before him. He would have liked a son. He said that sometimes with telling effect, to men who owned sons of their own, and in whom he wished to instill a kindliness toward himself. He would say simply, "I envy you. You have a son to carry on your name. My boy—died. I shall never have another."

"Yes," he said again to Dolly Hessian, "you do remind me of my little girl." As a matter of fact sometimes he was not at all certain of the sex of the still-born infant, and neither were most other people in Lexington. Marguerite remembered.

Dolly asked, "Would you like to have me keep the bag?"

"It would make me very happy." He put his hand on hers. "Please don't be alarmed; I mean nothing by it except—Well, you are beautiful; the bag is beautiful; I want you to have it. I promise that it will be a secret which we will share—we alone."

His hand tightened slightly on hers, but he did not bend down nor attempt to draw her to him. At last Dolly lifted her gaze and smiled tremulously.

"I will keep it always."

Abruptly she turned, twisted the door-knob, and was out, flying across the office. Distantly down the hall came the sound of a dentist's drill. A dropsical, dispirited old incompetent was still practicing dentistry there on any victim who came his way. By the time Dolly reached the foot of the staircase, she had her handkerchief out and was holding it against her jaw. This act was unnecessary; no one was on the sidewalk near at hand. So far as she ever learned, her visit to Senator Newgate at that time and place went unrecorded in the town's annals.

Back at the shop on Hazel Street, Dolly burst in on Floss Mahanna, her lips streaming apologies. She caught up the little turban which had been ordered that morning by a Mrs. Lester—a friend of Mrs. J. J. Van Dorm (who had already departed for Cedar Rapids, proud in the belief that she was the identical twin of Mrs. Potter Palmer).

Floss said it didn't matter; there hadn't been any new customers in the shop, and Miss Cook had already gone to her dinner unresentfully. She feared only that Dolly might be ill—Dolly worked so hard.

"I was actually a little ill. I had a sore tooth. Oo, how it hurt."

Floss smothered her with sympathy. "But you missed the excitement. There was almost a fire."

"Not here?"

"No. Just at one o'clock, over across the street, in the back end of the harness store. All of a sudden, just when Miss Cook was leaving, we heard a lot of yelling and everything, and we looked out and Ben Steele came running, and another man— Somebody yelled Fire and they almost turned in the alarm. I guess somebody had burned something with a little gasoline lantern they were using there in their work, or something. Anyway, Ben put it right out."

Dolly said, after a moment of silent stitching, "But I thought he was the man from the livery barn. You said—"

"Oh, sure, he is. He owns the livery barn, but he owns the harness store, too, and the carriage works and everything—that whole corner. I wish when my poor father died he had left me as many simoleons as Madison Steele left to Ben."

The cow-bell (which Miss Cook kept tied against the front door when they were working in the back room) jingled. Florence ran to greet two high-school girls who might or might not prove to be customers.

Dolly Hessian, left alone at her work-table, felt a fury and disgust. What a bitchy little fool Florence Mahanna was! Good grief—livery stable man, indeed. Why had no one told her about this before? The whole town: they comprised one grand multitude of idiots . . . livery stable!

A rich young man, obviously popular—obviously a recipient of all respect that such a community could give— And there she sat, with that God damn silver mesh-bag closed up in her reticule. She was committed to the bag; she must keep it "always."

Why had no one told her?

Dolly made a very bad job out of Mrs. Lester's Paris turban for the next hour or two. She had to rip all the preliminary silk off the foundation, and it had already been cut to shape. Perhaps it could be pressed out and not wasted. She got more silk and went to work. At last she regained control of herself, and the turban flowered beautifully . . . and outside a wind came up, the sky turned gray and damp. Wind blew leaves in swirls and drifts across the town. It began to rain about four o'clock.

Twenty minutes later there came a degree of sunshine into Dolly's life, by way of a telephone call to Miss Cook from her landlady, Mrs. Anna Kristensen. The vacancy, which it had been hoped since Saturday might occur at the boarding-house, had now come about. Miss Winifred Handstafel, the new teacher of the second grade, had arranged to move to the home of a school-teacher friend who lived in town with her parents, and was even then in the act of packing up. She had warned the landlady of the possibility before; now it was a fact, and Dolly Hessian could move from the Wildwood Hotel to Mrs. Kristensen's this very evening if she wished. She did wish.

She put two tired arms around Miss Cook when the old milliner broke the glad news to her. "You're such a darling. I'd like to give you a squeeze. I think—I will!" and she squeezed hard, and the women laughed delightedly.

Dolly was very glad to get away from the Wildwood Hotel as soon as possible. She had decided that it would be only a matter of days before Senator Newgate would attempt to manage a tryst with her; or before she, in a weak moment, might instigate such action herself. Dolly often told herself that she was weak, weak, weak inside. She had, in actuality, something of the substance of granite. It had been nearly three years since she performed any act not previously calculated, not previously planned. Religiously she had cut herself away from wicked raptures and from most of the affectionate charities which she typified to herself as weaknesses.

Sometime between four-thirty and five o'clock the cow-bell jingled again, and a boy in an oilcloth slicker tossed a damp copy of the Lexington *Daily Ledger* upon Miss Cook's floor. Bereft for the moment of customers, Miss Cook regaled Floss and Dolly with bits of local news gleaned from the *Ledger's* columns. Dolly listened. Already she was trying to formulate a plan.

"Please read some more social items, Miss Cook. I love to hear what people are doing . . . parties and dinners and things. I suppose they have lots of things going on in a town like Lexington every night of the week."

"Not much on Monday. Of course, there's lodge tonight —two or three lodges. We used to have Eastern Star on Monday, but we changed. The Daughters of Union Veterans have their meeting Monday nights. I belong to that—I used to be an officer, but I don't go much any more. Seems like I get pretty tired the older I get."

"There's the Monday Supper Circle," said Floss.

"Do you belong?" asked Dolly.

Floss grinned. "No. Anyhow, I can't leave Mamma even if I did belong to anything—except for church things. Mamma doesn't fuss so much when it's a church thing I go to."

" 'Commercial League supper,' " read Miss Cook.

"Oh, yes," said Floss, "I guess that's on Mondays, at the Wildwood."

" 'Members of the Lexington Commercial League will hold their semi-monthly supper and business meeting at 6:30 P.M. this evening at the Wildwood Hotel. Members are earnestly requested to be on time.' "

Dolly was trimming a fuzz of green cockade which would adorn the turban. "Commercial League," she asked, "what's that?"

"Oh, you know. All the businessmen and everything. You know—they talk about community plans, and decorating Sixth Street at Christmas time, and how to get new factories in town."

"Trying to get more pavement, too," said Miss Cook. "I don't think they'll put it across with the City Council before next year."

"Do you belong, Miss Cook?"

"Oh, no. There's several of us ladies in business here in town, but I don't know— It would be sort of funny sitting there with all those men."

Floss Mahanna thought that it would be wonderful sitting there with all those men. But she said nothing.

"Ben told me, the other day," said Agatha Cook, "that they were going to start a campaign to get the local businesswomen to join. There's several millinery stores, and Mrs. Garrett's candy shop, and Mrs. Pryor that runs the restaurant, and Dr. Ruth Schraeder, and some more. Ben said he felt that ladies ought to belong too."

"Ben?" inquired Dolly daintily.

"You know, across the street. Ben Steele. Your bus driver to the Wildwood Hotel."

Their laughter shrilled.

Dolly looked modest and embarrassed. "Does he belong to the Commercial League?"

"Oh, sure."

Dolly tacked the cockade lightly into place above the smooth-drawn silk. She lifted the turban and turned it slowly on her hands.

Florence Mahanna gasped with rapture, "It's lovely!"

"It must be awfully tiresome," said Dolly, "for a man to work hard all day, and then have to go to a poky old dinner and sit around for hours listening to all that talk."

"No," said Miss Cook, "it doesn't take very long. They usually get through by eight or eight-fifteen. They just eat, and have some of the talks while they're eating."

"Oh," said Dolly, "then it wouldn't be so bad, if they got out early."

Twelve

On Saturday afternoon, Ben Steele had learned, gratis and without much difficulty, the identity of the pretty girl who invited herself to ride with him in Mr. Pittenger's buggy; he learned her name, her occupation, and the fact that probably she was only a temporary guest at the Wildwood Hotel.

Mrs. Eckersall had regaled Tucky Miller with these items of information as rapidly as she acquired them, and Tucky told one of the men at the carriage works, when he came in to have a loose iron tire set more firmly on one of the hack wheels.

Ben was eager to talk with this pretty stranger again. He knew Agatha Cook well—she had been a friend of Ben's father—but he felt that it would be silly for him to wander deliberately into the millinery shop. Neither could he very well stand in the hotel lobby and try to offer explanations and olive branches to the pretty stranger—there in full view of the staff and guests. He tried to think of someone for whom he might dare buy a hat. . . . That, too, was out of the question. First, he had no woman relative in Lexington; and second, he did not court the teasing which would be sure to ensue among his acquaintances.

From time to time Ben "went with" a girl named Cornelia Ritchie. Bernard Ritchie was a docile lumber dealer of the town, very sedentary, well-to-do according to local standards, without much interest in anything except his wife, his daughter and the Masonic lodge.

Ben Steele was a Blue Lodge Mason; not a very active one. His father had embraced Masonry earnestly, and when still a young man had attained to the Thirty-second Degree, complete with both Scottish Rite and Knights' Templar qualifications. On those rare occasions when Ben put in an appearance at a stated communication of the A.F. & A.M., he was welcomed with almost religious emotion by Bernard Ritchie. It was no secret that the Ritchies hoped for Ben as a son-in-law. . . . The father had a disconcerting habit of calling Ben "son" whenever he addressed him privately, and this very nearly frightened young Mr. Steele into precipitate retreat.

Cornelia herself was tall, thin and ash-blonde, with pale and flaccid gaze. She dwelt in empty harmony with her parents in a big slate-colored horror of a house at the south end of Plum Street. She and Ben had never "gone together" when they were in high-school, though they were in the same class. Cornelia had received instead the blundering attention of a good-natured baseball player whom her relatives tried to discourage mightily, and who died at twenty of blood-poisoning engendered by a raw blister on his heel.

Cornelia had not appeared greatly moved by the athlete's demise; she was seldom moved by anything. She was listless, sweet-tempered, and in some ways seemed almost sexless. She presided behind a high desk at the public library building, and was well-liked by numerous children who trooped to borrow *Black Beauty* and the cartoon books of Harrison Cady. She was the kind of girl whose legs were still straight and calf-less at fifteen. Later, after two years at State Teachers'

College she had tried teaching school, but was compelled to give up this career. Several days each month she was bed-ridden at home, and she suffered plenty of sick headaches in between times.

She was a soprano songstress much admired by her household and a few senseless aunts—listened to doggedly by communicants of the Methodist church and by people who gathered to disport themselves at Knights' Templar banquets and at the monthly dinners of the Monday Supper Circle, of which Cornelia's mother was a charter member.

To Ben Steele it sounded as if her voice were as tall and thin and flat and pearly as the girl herself. She would force her mouth into a rigid rose-shaped purse, and through this aperture the notes would be projected from her long, cold throat: a compressed howling, a tingling lupine quaver. That is, until she got into the higher registers; then she screeched.

Ben was amazed to realize that Cornelia had that much breath and power in her body. Her repertoire was limited to hymns, traditional English ballads, and songs like "Last Night the Nightingale Woke Me," and some of the Irish ditties made popular by Chauncey Olcott and rearranged for voices like Cornelia's.

Sometimes Ben Steele had passed or approached the Ritchie residence when Cornelia was singing scales—"exercising her voice," the Ritchies called it. "Cornelia, dearie, you shouldn't try to exercise your voice today. You're too tired." "Mamma, I'm afraid I'll be a little late at the library; but I've simply got to exercise my voice first." When engaged in these toils, Cornelia contrived sounds which Ben believed not fit for human or animal ears. Once, driving behind an old lame horse whom he still exercised in its dotage because he was convinced that the horse liked it, Ben had traversed within ear-shot of the Ritchie dwelling at a pace twice as slow as normal. Before, during and after his approach, Cornelia was singing inside. He wondered whether she had seen him coming down the street, and was sending out those audible messages of allurement.

During this ordeal he contrived a fancy which haunted him forever after when he heard her yells. He thought that she had a lot of wizened, sickly, anemic notes, kept as entities—naked as white hairless dogs. She had these creatures—these horrid little notes with their bald, round heads—imprisoned in a great chest. The notes would try to get out; Cornelia would be sitting, applying all her weight on the lid of the box. The notes would engage in a slimy struggle, attempting to force their way out of jail. Some of them would manage to slide their rubbery little necks through the small opening as they raised the box lid. But Cornelia would squeeze and squeeze . . . the little notes, caught and strangled by the lid crushed down on their clammy necks, would squeal and squeal.

It had been bad enough to hear Cornelia sing in public before—and she would sing willingly, without too apparent eagerness, whenever an opportunity offered . . . it had been bad enough to hear her wringing out, "Jer-*u*-salem! Jer-*u*-salem!" before he envisioned this ghastly allegory of the imprisoned, cold-nosed little notes. But after that, her clabbered melody made him completely nauseated.

During the months since Mad Steele's death, Ben had found himself more frequently than ever a visitor at the Ritchie home. The family ties of church and fraternal organizations were strong, no matter how many soprano solos affrighted the world. Ben's attendance at Sunday dinner was becoming something like a Ritchie ritual. He was disturbed by this. He was not at all in love with Cornelia, and in most ways found her physically repulsive.

Twice, actuated perhaps by the desperation of loneliness, he had become actively affectionate with her. She had whispered modestly, "Ben, please don't let's us get 'mushy.' " But he had persisted, and finally she permitted herself a kind of dutiful response without much ardor. After the second time, Ben swore to himself grimly that he would never try to kiss Cornelia again. He had not liked the flavor of her lips: there was something milky about the taste of her. He had wanted perfumed warmth . . . the tingling excitement and mystery which one bad girl of his college days had given him, before she ran away with a carnival.

Nevertheless, because he was distressed at persisting through Sunday in the monastic existence he led at home on other days, he had driven to the Ritchies' again on this yesterday. That was where he was bound when Floss Mahanna and Dolly Hessian saw him drive away from the livery barn.

After dinner he had taken Cornelia for a long drive. They went down to Boneyard Valley. It was a swampy, wooded area two miles from the town, jutting away from the river: a favorite picnic ground for Lexingtonians since an old slaughter-house had burned down and the forest was happily freed from taint of the abattoir.

There were still a few cattle skulls and grim white pelves among the woodland leaves, and squirrels rushed in profusion. It was a pleasant region for an innocent buggy ride, for Sunday loverlike strollings, and for more wicked revelry alleged to occur at night hours in the buzzing glades.

While driving with Cornelia, and again tormented by a sense of angry masculinity, Ben had tried to envision himself leading Cornelia among the basswood trees in a preliminary to seduction. He turned from this imagining in disgust . . . but wait: he thought of himself escorting Dolly Hessian on such an errand among those same thickets, and his pulse began to pound. He was embarrassed. He shifted abruptly on the seat, slapped his horse with the reins. He drove rapidly up the long grade from the valley, and Cornelia looked at him in limpid surprise and hung onto her hat.

Monday morning Ben was early at the harness store. He peeked through a screen of dangling fly-nets in the window, hoping to see Dolly when she appeared at Miss Cook's across the street. He was called away against his will by certain demands of the carriage works, and thus he missed seeing the girl.

He looked for her, too, at noon, and then there was the excitement of the minor fire which easily could have become a serious conflagration. Ben blistered his thumb in putting out the blaze, and he forgot all about Dolly Hessian for a while.

That evening he sat, in appearance obligingly attentive, but bored in thought and response by makeshift planning of the Commercial League members—basically uninterested in any arrangements for the annual Dime-and-Dollar Sale Day which would give stimulus to autumn shopping in Lexington. There would be signs hung across the street; there would be advertisements in all county newspapers, and broadsides circulated by hand and by mail. The Lexington band was to tender a noon concert at the corner of Hazel and Sixth. Merchants who purveyed less expensive merchandise would offer loss-leaders in their stores: items to be sold ostensibly at the regular price, with an extra and identical piece of merchandise offered with each sale for an additional ten cents. People who sold more expensive items—furniture and jewelry dealers, for instance—might carry out the same plan with identical offerings on each sale for one additional dollar.

All this planning was tiresome in the extreme to Ben Steele. From his father he had acquired the simple belief of the artisan: that there was supreme satisfaction in making what he made, and that the public would buy his product according to the public's natural need.

Some men would have ground munificent meal from the little stones of industry with which the Steeles milled out their livelihood. In other hands the wagon shops, the harness manufactory and store and the livery stable all together might have afforded vast profit. These holdings were intrinsically valuable, for farmers of the region were still horse-drawn and horse-propelled—and so were a large share of the townspeople. There existed many little leaks which no Steele had ever bothered to identify or stop up; they found a neat profit, after all taxes and upkeep on the establishment had been paid, of perhaps only five or eight thousand dollars per annum. This was vastly more than the Steeles really needed to live as they chose to live. Ben loved Lexington; but he saw no need for boosting the town or his business.

Meanwhile, as he gnawed the curved stem of his bulldog pipe and tried to find some humor in the argument with which to beguile himself, Dolly Hessian was scurrying furiously about Room 26 above stairs.

She had not observed Ben at the dinner. The dining room

was divided into two sections by a series of baize screens on such occasions, to give some privacy to whatever organization chose to have its supper served there. The other diners ate in a melancholy scattering at little tables in the third of the room next to the Sixth Street windows. A flow of broken conversation swept toward the diners across and through the screens. Silently they ate their creamed chicken in patty shell, their peas and potatoes, and tried to hear what was going on at the Commercial League dinner.

Dolly's repast was mildly enlivened by the antics of a bumptious drug salesman who sat at a table facing her, and attempted to "mash" her while she ate. At last, giving him a hurt look, she arose deliberately, walked around the table, moved her plate and silverware, and sat down facing the other way. The creature resorted to audible indignant laughter, but bothered her no more after that.

Dolly hastened to her room. She packed all her clothes for the move to Mrs. Kristensen's, regretting that her other two suits (she owned a black, a blue and a gray) must be crammed once more into a state where they would require additional pressing. It took longer than she had realized to pack her things, and every staccato discussion or noisy chair-scraping that came to her up the air-shaft filled her with alarm. She had thought that she would be downstairs, ready packed, with perhaps time to write cards to Aunt Edna and Aunt Ellen before the Commercial League supper guests dispersed. Now she began to fear that Ben Steele would have left the hotel before she had a chance to fasten her hold on him.

This lugubrious fear came nearly true. She was on the stairway with her bags as men ambled through the lobby.

The colored porter was vanished, perhaps eating a late supper; Mr. Eckersall was nowhere in sight, and Mrs. Eckersall busy on the telephone. Dolly had to lug her own bags to the stairway and labor down with them in two trips.

She did not see Ben in her first descent, for all his height: he must have been behind one of the posts in the lobby. The second trip down, she carried the two smaller bags . . . she spied Ben moving with other people toward the Hazel Street door, and some of the men were putting on their hats. Ben had his back turned toward her; there was only one thing to do, short of plunging at full length from the stairs.

Dolly dropped her little black traveling bag. It made a sharp thudding as it tumbled down the last three steps.

Several men hastened simultaneously to pick up the bag. They smiled; they said things—Dolly was not sure just what they said. It was as if her ears were tuned only to the electric reception of Ben Steele's voice.

He said, "Hello again."

"Oh. Hello."

One other man lingered. . . . Dolly bent down, examining the traveling bag, praying that it hadn't been split in any place. It had not. The leather was scratched on one corner, and later Dolly would discover to her chagrin that she had broken a bottle of toilet water and cracked her cold-cream jar.

Ben said, "I guess I ought to apologize."

She looked up at him. The other man had turned away. "Why?"

"Oh, you know. Saturday—" He smiled at her . . . his eyes were narrowing, the lids drooped very low. "All that business about the buggy and the mistake you made. I ought to have explained to you. Though I don't mean that I didn't enjoy driving you to the hotel."

"Really, you were very kind," said Dolly. "I don't think any apology is in order, Mr.—"

"My name's Ben Steele. And I know your name—I found out about it. You're Miss Hessian and you're Miss Cook's new trimmer. It's kind of like we were already introduced; I've known Miss Cook all my life."

"Then you are very fortunate," said Dolly. "She's one of the very sweetest women I ever met."

They discussed Miss Cook's virtues for another minute or two.

"But I don't like those bags," said Ben. "Don't mean to say you're sick of Lexington already, and going away?"

"No, I'm moving to Mrs. Kristensen's. They tell me I'm a lucky girl."

"I know how I'd be luckier than that."

"How?"

"If you'd forget all about Tucky Miller and the hotel bus, and just sit quietly in the parlor in there, and let me go down to the barn and get a rig. Then I could drive you up to Mrs. Kristensen's."

Soon they were driving west through the darkness of Fourth Street. A chill rain traveled lightly across the unyielding fabric of the buggy top, and a little spray blew in past the curtains. Wheels made a pleasant swishing through the puddles. "I love the sound of rain on a buggy top," said Dolly.

"It's nice driving in good weather, too," said Ben, "with the top down. Care to take a drive tomorrow night?"

Dolly Hessian gambled her entire future. "I'd love to,

Mr. Steele," she said quietly, "but there are so many things I need to do. You know, it's difficult getting settled in a new job—new town, new room and everything."

"How about Wednesday night?" asked Ben. "It's the last band concert of the season."

"Where?"

"Courthouse Park."

"I'd love to."

Arrived at Mrs. Kristensen's, Ben carried Dolly's bags to the front door. He would willingly have carried them all the way to Dolly's room, but the landlady called to the sleepy-eyed husband whom she had supported for twenty-seven years. That was just about all Gus Kristensen ever did around the place—he carried bags up and down.

Out on the porch, with rain drumming in increased force against the roof, Dolly thanked Ben Steele, and he said that he would call for her Wednesday at twenty minutes to eight.

When Dolly had finally parted from Mrs. Kristensen, when she had been shown the bathroom, the closet, the way the window worked, and had been instructed on the necessity for prompt appearance at meals, she stood within her bright little oak-trimmed room.

For the moment, in purest satisfaction, she was physically unable even to sit down; she could not touch the fastening of any of those rain-spotted suitcases. She could not even feel of the bed to see whether it was soft or hard . . . she could only stand there. She was pleased with her career in Lexington up to this minute, and appropriately certain that more extensive triumph would soon be hers. Only one thing in the world disturbed her, and that was thought of the silver mesh-bag she had accepted from Senator A. B. A. Newgate.

Thirteen

By the time they reached the Courthouse Park Wednesday evening all the benches were filled, and people thronged along the intersecting sidewalks which met beneath hackberry trees. In the middle of the park was an ugly fountain into which no water except rain had flowed for at least twelve years. The concrete basin was filled with a reek of sodden leaves, crackerjack boxes and fragments of Fourth of July firecrackers.

Close at hand in the triangular section of ground abutting on First Street, toward the south, stood the bandstand: a circular wooden structure with a roof like a pagoda. Electric wiring had been rigged beneath this roof, and in the glare of bright orange bulbs the Lexington town band strove to tune its instruments and find a proper arrangement on folding chairs.

During summer months the proceedings held more gaiety; but with the rain of Monday night the air of this region had turned chill. Many leaves had been blown down before their proper time; they lay plastered, dull green and faintly tan, a slippery peril on the sidewalks. Along the Hazel and First Street boundaries of the park, rows of buggies and automobiles and a few farm wagons had been drawn up next to the curb; and on porches of houses beyond these streets, people of the neighborhood gathered to sit in rockers or on the steps. The older women had shawls around their shoulders. Children shuttled back and forth, darting dangerously amid the slow-turned traffic which still assembled, searching for vantage points to view and hear the concert.

A program had been printed in the *Daily Ledger*:

MARCH	—	Hail to the Chief
WALTZ	—	Blue Danube
POPULAR	—	Medley of Dixie Airs
OVERTURE	—	Light Cavalry
POPULAR	—	Red Wing
CLASSICAL	—	I Hear You Calling Me (vocal solo by Miss Cornelia Ritchie)
MARCH	—	Wooden Soldiers
NOVELTY	—	The Whistler and His Dog
IDYLL	—	Glow Worm
MARCH	—	The British Grenadiers
FINALE	—	Star-Spangled Banner

The band was composed of some two dozen men, old and young, who fancied themselves as instrumentalists, and who enjoyed blowing on their reeds for the mere joy of blowing. Probably half of them had skill, and of these several (a mailman, a farmer, a barber, and Mr. Alfred Pittenger of the Dodge County Savings Bank) would have been capable of playing competently in almost any brass band, anywhere. Old Mr. Pittenger had learned the clarinet when he was a boy. His small bald head and close-clipped gray mustache had been an integral part of the band's scenery for a long time. The less adroit musicians followed their conductor and their more able leaders trustingly. A decisive and melodious blast would soon rise among the trees and be thrown back by walls of the big red courthouse.

What Dolly Hessian did not know was that the ceremony of her attendance at the band concert held a distinct social import. There could be few appearances in public where a choice of partners might seem emphasized to a more complete and inquisitive cross-section of the town, than this. It suggested the plazas in Central American cities where military bands roar tenderly among the gardenias, and young men stroll in steady groups to view the girls on display and on the market—when a promenade in duet is tantamount to the announcement of a betrothal.

Ben Steele could have taken Dolly to a picture show—he could have taken her for a Sunday-afternoon buggy ride or just a walk—and people would have thought no more than that he was "interested in" Dolly, for reasons to be estimated by the deportment and alleged character of the girl herself.

His fetching her along to the band concert was something quite different. It demonstrated to the gaze of the world that he had put his seal of approval upon her.

Even had Dolly known the importance of the occasion to her, she might not have given more thought to her costume of the night. Either one of two dresses would have been preferable, if the weather had been warmer. As it was, she had not yet worn her blue suit in Lexington; the hat of midnight lace was as complementary to that suit as to the black.

She had hoped that there might be time on Tuesday or Wednesday for her to "dish up" something new and astonishing in the way of millinery; but Miss Cook's stock was at such a pitifully low ebb that Dolly dared not expend creative effort upon herself. She reasoned that it would be wiser in the long run for her to devote every possible moment to the presentation of enviable trimmings in Miss Cook's windows, than to ennoble her own head. It would be better so far as Ben Steele was concerned. Evidence was reliable that Miss Cook considered Ben, or at least his deceased parent, as a friend. One way or another Agatha Cook would inform the young man of the devotion and willing talent which Dolly Hessian had given her.

So Dolly wore again the midnight lace. . . . She had it pinned, she had her hair adjusted, and a dotted veil over her face, long before Ben rang the downstairs bell at Mrs. Kristensen's—and he was five minutes early, at that. During the interim Dolly had sat nervously on the edge of her bed, thumbing a late copy of the *Century Magazine* which was one of the perquisites awarded her when Winifred Handstafel moved away on Monday.

There appeared an article on Christian Missions in Japan, also a short story by Elsie Singmaster. In neither could Dolly take any interest at all. She leafed through the ads; she lingered over a full-page advertisement for Thomas cars; she read that they cost four thousand dollars, and wondered if Ben Steele could afford a Thomas car. If so, why did he insist on driving with a horse and buggy?

There appeared also, in color, an afternoon hat designed by Edwin B. Halsey. Dolly sniffed at that hat . . . who were men to design hats, anyway? She had known several men trimmers in the wholesale houses, and two of them were painfully effeminate. The Halsey hat was attractive enough, but mild and plaintive. If Dolly had been trimming that particular item, she would have used rich purple flowers along with the pale roses. The effect would thus have been more arresting. There was no profit in being a woman unless you drew attention to yourself—having first made certain that the effect that you might create was worthy of attention. Dolly was confident of one thing at least: she knew what men liked, though she had a suspicion that many men did not know what they liked, themselves.

She was a little nervous about this date. It seemed that things had happened too easily—that there was something to be afraid of. She tried to reassure herself by the reiteration that matters had come about in this way only because she worked tooth and nail to make them happen so. Yet this knowledge failed to satisfy her completely.

Ben's horse started away down Fourth Street with a great rush and dancing, and Dolly, who had always been a little afraid of horses because she had no intimate familiarity with them—Dolly found herself sinking her hands against Ben Steele's left arm.

"It was just that cat."

"A cat? I didn't see—"

"*Whoa. Whoa.* There, he's all right now." Ben turned toward her through the dimness. "This is Barnum. He always get his dander up when a cat runs in front of him."

"Oh, I hope we don't meet any more cats!"

"You're a little afraid of horses, aren't you?"

"A little. Just a little bit, I guess. I don't know much about them." She added, after a moment, "My aunt used to ride horseback a great deal when I was little . . . great big black horses."

"Where was that? I mean, where you grew up?"

"Oh, Chicago. I mean—the North Shore, of course."

Since Ben seemed waiting to hear more, she continued her resplendent fiction. "Then she used to take me to visit my other aunt in Virginia. They had a lot of horses—kind of red—great big tall ones."

"Hunters, I bet."

"I guess you call them hunters. They used to jump, too, when they were chasing animals and things over fences; but I was always afraid. I used to run in the house and cry."

Ben laughed and said he couldn't believe it . . . afraid of horses. . . .

"I know it was crazy, but I was just scared. They had an old nurse for me down there—you know, a Negro mammy—and she used to try and find me. But I'd crawl clear back under the four-poster bed and just cry all by myself."

"Still afraid, even now? We'll have to get you over that," said Ben promisingly.

By this time they had reached the courthouse corner at Third and Hazel. Ben wanted to point out his own house to Dolly as they passed, but she had been talking; he couldn't have pointed out the house without interrupting her.

They turned south on Hazel Street, and long before they were opposite the old Parrott gun on the south courthouse lawn, Ben could see that there was no space for him to turn in and tie his horse. They had to turn west on First Street, and only on the far side of the primary school building could he find a place for Barnum and the buggy.

While he was helping Dolly to alight, there resounded the first imposing blast of "Hail to the Chief." Together they crossed the schoolhouse grounds, passing the rear door of the building. The lawn, trodden bare in patches, was uneven; Ben offered his arm to Dolly. She said, "Thank you," and took his arm, but relinquished her grasp when they approached the faint circle of light that came from the bandstand. Ben noticed this, and was pleased.

To tell the truth, although the girl had dwelt in his imagining at frequent intervals since Saturday noon, and though he was excited by physical contact with her, he was a little suspicious about this millinery business. One trimmer, a year or two before (she worked not for Miss Cook, but for Mrs. Oliphant on Sixth Street) was briefly notorious in Lexington legend. People said, "What do you expect from a trimmer?"—although all the time they forgot about poor Miss Mersy, who had come twice a year to trim for Mrs. J. T. Dana almost since Ben could remember; and they forgot about old Mrs. Molesworth who trimmed for Miss Cook until her weak little heart flagged out—who was as churchly, as virginal and unappetizing as Florence Mahanna herself.

Dolly Hessian was very pretty; but, like most pretty women who came from far away and had a glint of other civilizations in their dust-ruffles, she could easily be avaricious and immoral underneath. Ben was calmly aware that he was no small fry to be snagged by the first hook dangled in front of him. Local mammas—not only Mrs. Ritchie—had been dangling their fleshly bait in front of him for a good while, and with no success whatsoever. He wondered what his father would have thought of Dolly Hessian. Probably Mad Steele would not have approved—even though Dolly had put in a prim attendance at the Baptist church on the very first Sunday she was in town. She was, again, too pretty—and beauty bred the wickedest suspicion in Madison Steele's soul. He had married a beauty himself, and was rewarded by twelve years of vituperative discomfort. His pink-haired wife had been the terror of salesmen, errand boys, church committees, and Methodist ministers' wives—not to forget the cold comfort she gave her own husband and son.

Ben remembered how he had felt after his mother died. Neighbor ladies, solid and long-time friends of the Steeles, wept affectionately over him . . . he could hear them whispering in dark passages now, hiding around the dusty corridors of his memory, gasping together: "Poor little fellow. He don't know what he's lost. He don't realize what life will be like, without a mother."

Young Ben did realize correctly. It meant that life would be free of threats, scoldings, wranglings, backbitings, sundry slappings. Once in a while he recognized sharply that he was glad his mother had died . . . then he would cry, alone in his bed. But the tears were a mere bemoaning of confusion; they welled from no tarn of personal bereavement.

Perhaps it was the band music which evoked these considerations within him. He was uncomfortable about it . . . he hated to explore himself, his emotions, his ideals and ideas. He was more comfortable just living along, performing a task, deciding the price that should be set on a new product of the wagon works, deciding about fly-nets, and whether he should require a cash deposit from the two gay drummers who wanted to rent the surrey, and whether it would be well to pay the stud fee demanded by some farmer for the service of his big dappled horse.

He knew, in this third meeting with her, that Dolly Hessian had already built a complication into his settled existence —no matter what desolation he knew—and he resented her a little because of it.

They strolled down the northeast sidewalk, far from the

"How do you do," said Dolly.

"How do you do," said Elizabeth Butterfield, and their mutual detestation was intense.

Bet Butterfield was the autumnal daughter of an old doctor who had wedded a "practical nurse." Bet was huge of bone, thick of ankle, heavy of voice. She had worked for years in the County Recorder's office, and there was a time-worn jest around the courthouse: "Mister" Elizabeth Butterfield.

For several years Elizabeth had been friendly with a little kindergarten teacher who came to Lexington from Mason City; then they had a quarrel: the kindergarten teacher did not come back to Lexington the next fall. For two years Bet tramped the streets in stolid routine, walking always alone, felt hat-brim drawn low in front of her sullen eyes, eyes studying the sidewalk ahead, big feet thudding, loneliness sharp within her.

Of late she had centered some attention upon Miss Mahanna, who was a neighbor of hers and whom she had ignored since childhood. The trusting Floss was flattered. She was delighted to have a "chum."

Not yet had any act or suggestion on Bet Butterfield's part made the woman repugnant to Floss. . . . It was nice to have someone to go to band concerts with, to invite to her house for a messy supper—though her mother was always whining and having coughing fits in the background. Just let Floss and Bet Butterfield settle themselves before the sewing table on which the Flinch deck was arranged, or let them sit down with a cribbage board between them, and Mrs. Mahanna was certain to mourn: "Floss, I feel very, very weak. Please come and help Mamma go to bed."

Twice lately Bet had suggested to Miss Mahanna that some

time during the coming winter they should take the train and go to Des Moines to see a show. There was a resident stock company in Des Moines—two good ones, in fact, said Bet—to say nothing of the plays and musical comedies which trouped into the capital city with fair regularity. An expedition like this was fascinating in the mere contemplation. It was expensive, too, but Bet had generously offered to stand treat. They could get a room at the Kirkwood Hotel, she said, for Saturday night, and not come back to Lexington until Sunday evening. Floss had been turning the idea over in her mind; she did not know just who she might get to stay with her mother during her absence, and she was more than a little certain that her mother would have a "spell" if a pleasure journey of such nature were even suggested.

Naturally enough Bet Butterfield regarded Dolly Hessian as a most ferocious threat to any intention she might have for monopolizing Miss Mahanna's affections. Also, Bet was completely jealous every time Ben Steele crossed her range of vision. He was male, and easy-going and tan and bony. There was about him the delicious aroma of tobacco, leather and horse-sweat; furthermore he was the proprietor of that establishment where men snorted and chuckled when Bet Butterfield shambled past.

She stood sulkily, not speaking another word until Ben Steele came back. Generously he offered popcorn to Florence and Bet—he offered one of the two sacks he had just bought, and suggested that he would go and buy more, but the women said No.

Ben and Dolly wandered south along the Hazel Street side of the park. Many young men, strangers to Miss Hessian until this hour, came up to speak to Ben. They halted on the sidewalk or hailed him from benches where they sat, and were duly presented to Dolly. She met, face-to-face, and often in semi-darkness, the scrutiny and speculation of wives and girl friends. If, by the end of the evening, an inquisitive and gossipy little elf in Dolly's pay could have made the rounds and brought back a conscientious report to Miss Hessian, the sum of his detection would have pleased her supremely.

The youths found a physical thrill in merely appraising her, and imagining what her love might be like. Elder people approved her dignity, her pleasant smile, her pretense of polite humility. They said that she was "ladylike" or "womanly." The younger women envied her the hat of midnight-blue lace.

She could not remember all the names . . . there was a slim, lively Jew who fancied himself in the role of a comedian; and most of the townspeople seemed also to accept him contentedly in that role. His name was Sylvester Cohen. He had come to Lexington only a couple of years before; he had bought one of the local drygoods stores, and his business was now flourishing. Sylvester was an Elk, much in demand as an entertainer at home-talent shows. His twittering little wife, Naomi—noticeably pregnant—beamed perpetually upon her husband.

There were Harley Paisley and his wife, Myrtle. Myrtle's father was Mr. Alfred Pittenger—now blasting away in the band—and Harley had of late been advanced to the post of assistant cashier in his father-in-law's bank. There were Wayne T. Croy and his wife, Ella. Croy had smoldering dark eyes and an affected drawl, and until he was snared by Ella Ransom he was the town's leading ladies' man. People weren't so certain that he didn't shine best in that capacity still.

A Universalist minister named Spaatz; a doctor named Conger; youngsters named Masterson, Duckett and Lester. All these people seemed jolly and admiring friends of Ben Steele's; intimates by virtue of childhood association or present day-by-day proximity. They "ran with" the young married crowd of Lexington.

Few of them were accounted rich; none was very poor; most of them attended church regularly, but also liked to play cards; a few of them drank; only two of the women had ever smoked a cigarette—and that was on a dare; they went on bob-rides in winter, singing lustily while snuggled within their straw; the men belonged to lodges, and were beginning to appear pompous and officious when called upon to participate in civic meetings; in the summer they had Sunday picnics in Boneyard Valley, where the men went fishing or played baseball in their shirt-sleeves, and the women hunted for wild-flowers or sat gabbling in hammocks they had hung between the trees, and gabbling sometimes vindictively about any of their friends who were not present; one couple lived in a dark apartment upstairs over Fairchilds' jewelry store, their bosom friends rented a small green house on Hazel Street, and *their* other bosom friends lived with their parents in the oldest brick mansion in town; they were beginning to have babies now; two or three of the men were whispered about whenever they went in concert to Fort Dodge or Des Moines: it was believed that they were "off on a bender"; only one of the wives had a hired girl, and she was not really able to afford it; the more opulent of the young matrons did their own work because they had been well taught how to perform it, and had married with a full expectation of cooking, cleaning and sewing; the ones who had houses and yards had also vegetable gardens in the spring and summer—gardens of which they were proud—and later came rows of zinnias along the garden boundaries; most of them longed for wealth; few of them read very much, though they believed that a college education was indispensable in gaining success; nearly all of them kept dogs or cats as pets; the women put up bread-and-butter pickles, chili sauce and currant jelly from recipes handed down by their grandmothers; they represented in themselves the normal quota of cowardice, bravery, cruelty, generosity and affection; they had dreams sometimes, but were seldom articulate concerning them; they were eternally at strife with economic enemies; eternally they contended against typhoid fever, pneumonia and grippe; simultaneously they loved the town in which they dwelt, and resented it, and dreamed of another place in which to dwell more happily—they did not know where; eternally they were at war with weather, with poison ivy, with the elements of fire and water; they could be extinguished by the tornados which spun in springtime above the Iowa prairie; they could be run-away-with when riding behind horses; they could be upset in motorcars or struck by careless drivers; their children could be infected with lockjaw from the puncture of a nail; the people themselves could succumb in time to valvular heart disease, tuberculosis or cancer of the uterus; when late summer sat upon them in its heat, and the epidemic clenched a dead, dry hand among the white houses, they looked at their sleeping children and felt the apprehensive agony of parenthood, which is like no other fear alive; they thought of little Genevieve lying dead, of little Clifford hauling himself through existence on polio-distorted legs, and a cold sweat broke out on their souls; they talked in trivialities most of the time, and yet they were fighting for survival; in churches they sang a line about "the battle of life" and were only dimly conscious that that was the identical struggle in which they were engaged; few of the women had found the happiness in intercourse which they desired, and most of them lay after their husbands were sleeping, wondering about all this in perplexity and confusion; and thus in time they allowed themselves to be pressed between the limbs of other men, and yet seldom found the joy they had felt they were entitled to; all nature, all economy of society, seemed organized to controvert them; the greater, more malignantly-armed enemy waited forever within their doors—the enemy called Themselves.

Fourteen

The car was a Winton Six. The motor cranked itself (sometimes); the car had metal rods running from the widespread top to the front fenders; the operating levers were inside the car body instead of outside, and forty-eight explosive horses lurked beneath the hood, ready to drive the vehicle on its high-pressure tires with demountable rims.

Mr. Ritchie had paid three thousand dollars for the car, and now he sat in it with his wife; and their pride was turned to amazement and then to a sickening sense of loss and curtailment, as they saw Ben Steele walking with Dolly Hessian beside him.

"No, that's not him, Papa—"

"Yes, it is—"

"It can't be. Who's that woman? Who—?"

"Yes. It is too him," and Mr. Ritchie squeezed the bulb of the automobile horn. He could do that: the band had but lately finished the number which was to precede Cornelia Ritchie's solo; the band wasn't playing at this moment.

Ben turned, and when Mr. Ritchie said quietly, in a voice muffled by dread, "Good evening, son," Ben was carelessly bold. He hesitated only a moment before he conducted Dolly across the parking to the side of the car.

"Good evening."

"Good evening."

"Mrs. Ritchie—uh—Mr. and Mrs. Ritchie, I'd like you to meet Miss Hessian."

"Pleased to meet you."

"How do you do?"

"Nice evening for the band concert—"

"I'm afraid Cornelia will catch cold." Mrs. Ritchie spoke pointedly, as if suggesting that Ben himself should have hovered by with a quilted cloak to lay about Cornelia's shoulders.

"If it cleared up, I shouldn't wonder but what it would frost."

"Yes. I guess it won't be long now. Well—"

"Good evening."

"Good evening."

Dolly and Ben went away, and with them walked a fond father's hope for a delectable little grandchild named Bernard Ritchie Steele: an illusion without substance, a dream with no excuse other than the pathetic desire of its maker.

Fifteen

They met and talked with Senator A. B. A. Newgate. For a few horrid seconds—as Dolly gazed luminously up at Newgate bulking before them in the gloom near the empty fountain, on the edge of which the Senator had presided in tobacco smoke over the trifling political opinions of other gentlemen—in this hasty moment, Dolly entertained a marvelous terror.

She thought, addressing Newgate in grim spiritual secrecy: "Well, you could do it to me now. You could wreck everything, everything. You could cut my throat, strike me in the face, drag me down, kick me beyond revocation into the gutter. You could say, 'I hope you enjoy the little gift I gave you, Miss Hessian.' "

Newgate said nothing of the kind. He joked with Dolly about moving away from the Wildwood; he implied that the dining room had lost its charm when the diners could no longer see her there. He called Ben Steele "Four-spot Steele," and the men behind him laughed.

When they had strolled beyond the fountain into further darkness Dolly asked, "What did the Senator mean—Four-spot Steele?"

"Oh, I used to play poker once in a while with that gang—down at the Elks, usually. You know anything about poker?"

"Of course not," fibbed Dolly.

"Well, anyway, I drew to an inside straight and got a four: that's a hand in poker. I mean— Well, my straight was six high, but Newgate came up with one that was ten high."

"Does that mean he beat you?"

"That's right. Then, just about the next hand, I had a full house—fours over kings. And by golly if Abie Newgate didn't draw three cards to a pair, and end up with a full house—nines over jacks!"

"That means he won?"

"That's right. He's quite a kidder. He's called me 'Four-spot Steele' ever since." He looked down at Dolly through the darkness. "How did you and the Senator get acquainted?" he asked abruptly.

"He helped me open my door. It was stuck, and the key wouldn't work." Dolly prattled on, reciting the incident with more minutiæ than were really necessary.

She said that she thought Senator Newgate seemed like a very fatherly man.

"I'll bet my bottom dollar he wouldn't have stopped to help you with that door if you'd been some kind of a homely old crow."

"Then you think I'm not a homely old crow?"

"What do you think?"

"I—I don't know."

The band spoke volubly; its brazen voice was preparing to inform the world that it, the band, heard Miss Cornelia Ritchie calling *it*. And Miss Ritchie, her last summer's flannel jacket now shed from rose-green-changeable-satin shoulders, was standing like a stick of celery under the electric-light bulbs, preparing to tell the band that she, Cornelia, heard the band calling *her*.

"Let's get out of here!"

"Why? Where could we go?"

"Anywhere! I don't want to hear Cornelia sing. I tell you, I just can't stand to hear her sing—"

"Cornelia?"

"That girl up on the bandstand. How about taking a little ride in the buggy?"

"Do you promise not to stop in any dark lanes?"

He led her once more through the schoolyard. "Why? Don't you like to take buggy rides down dark lanes?"

"No," said Dolly in a small voice.

"All right, I promise."

"But I must be home by ten. I'm not accustomed to staying out late. I have a great deal to do in the morning," and Dolly sighed.

For the better part of the next hour, they drove somewhat disconsolately up one street and down the next, approaching even the Milton Mill Road which led across railroad tracks and on in the direction of Boneyard Valley.

Dolly had said, after they were settled in the buggy seat, with the lap robe laying its familiarity across them, "Now please tell me things about horses. I must learn."

Ben, led by the lure of his favorite passion, required little prodding. Thus Dolly received reliable information concerning surcingles, colts, crib-biting, roans, sorrels, thrush, sulkies, and swelling of the hocks. She heard, in generous and complex measure, the pedigrees, personalities and performances of horses with a fantastic variety of names. She could not well assimilate this information, but she pretended to.

Every now and then she asked Ben what time it was. Sometime during the course of the evening he had mentioned something about an Eastern Star supper which would be held a few evenings later, and she was hoping he would return to the same topic more pointedly. He did not, until reluctantly he had obeyed her injunction to deliver her on the steps of Mrs. Kristensen's.

Ben stood on the sidewalk, Dolly on the steps facing him; thus their faces were opposite. He leaned forward slightly and she drew back just as slightly.

"By the way, there's going to be an Eastern Star supper Saturday night. I wondered if, maybe– Maybe–" In fact, he was thinking, not of the Eastern Star supper, but of his desire to embrace Miss Hessian and press his mouth warmly on hers.

Aware of this intended caress–desiring it mightily, and determined that nothing of that sort should occur on their first date–Miss Hessian extended her hand. "Do you mean you want me to go to the Eastern Star supper with you, Mr. Steele?"

"For goodness' sake call me Ben. Can't I call you Dolly?"

"All right," she laughed, "you call me Dolly. Ben, I'd love to go with you Saturday night. Will it be very much of a dress-up affair? I mean, evening gowns and–"

"Gosh, no. You know–just dress-up–glad rags–the way folks do around here. The only people I ever saw in evening clothes were in Chicago or down at college a few times. One thing, though–"

"What?"

"I wish you'd wear that same hat," he mumbled. "I think it's wonderful."

Dolly whispered, "I will wear it, if you like it."

"I think it's wonderful. I think you're–"

She was wise enough not to let him finish the statement

he had begun. She knew that he would have been annoyed with himself the next morning. She said that it had been a delightful evening, and Goodnight.

She went upstairs, confident of the future, wholly delighted with herself.

She lay awake for a long time, though in honesty she was very tired. She surveyed the unhampered life she would enjoy when once she had become Mrs. Benjamin Steele.

Sixteen

She was determined to implant herself in the consciousness of Lexington as deeply as possible—to brand herself against the town's imagination in the character of an astute, brilliant artisan—before she put on the negligee of domesticity (which, all sense told her, was being tailored rapidly to her measurement).

Agatha Cook was a perfect dub as a milliner. You had only to be around Miss Cook's for an hour to recognize that. Had it not been for The Farm, poor Miss Cook might have starved to death. The Farm had belonged to her parents: a meager survival of the timberland claim laboriously cleared and farmed in pioneer days. Now Agatha rented it out and received a modest income therefrom. In the millinery shop she was barely able to make both ends meet.

Dolly found it difficult at first to wet and warm the seed of ambition in Miss Cook's heart, but she toiled on. It did not matter at all to her that if she were to leave Miss Cook's employ after the trade of a single season had padded the little milliner's pocketbook and stimulated her enterprise, the business would collapse in dusty ruin. Dolly wanted to show everyone what she could do.

Those were the days when one might (by simply summoning a carpenter and talking to the lumberyard on the telephone) have minor remodeling done in the twinkling of an eye.

Soon two high, wide windows were built along the north side of the shop building, and there was even a portion of skylight bent into the ceiling above the workroom. Dolly herself picked out new carpeting; she and Florence Mahanna worked at tacking it down, in order to save money for Miss Cook. Dolly struck her finger with the hammer. It was swollen black-and-blue next day; she taped the injury; her fingers darted furiously among filigree and feathers, contriving ever more delicious gauds to excite favor in the eyes of Lexington's women.

Wicked rumors began to be circulated about Dolly Hessian. The stories might conceivably have been instigated by either of the two rival milliners on Sixth Street. They had never regarded Aggie Cook as a threat to their prosperity before; now they were losing many old customers.

But Mrs. J. J. Van Dorm (recently returned from Cedar Rapids, where her hat had been a sensation among wives of the Iowa Grand Lodge) was fulsome in her praise. Like a bellwether she led the D.A.R. and the Six O'clock Club through those once-rusty portals of Miss Cook's. The little cow-bell rattled testily against the upper rim of the door; it dented the paint; it swung on its wire fastening until the wire snapped short off, and the bell came tinkling to the floor. It was not put up again: there was no need. There were always plenty of people in the front room nowadays.

Agatha was compelled to hire an extra clerk, and she retained a new maker as well—an unpaid apprentice—and then another. These handmaidens fetched the boxes, curled the feathers, steamed the velvet; they ran errands; they sawed at buckram with their scissors. . . .

Surrounded by colorful debris, Dolly Hessian reigned from eight in the morning until long after the normal hour of closing. Her hands began to swell . . . she had had them do that before, when she worked too hard and too long.

But she knew what she was doing. The rumors about her reputation were stoutly disavowed by the elderly women who had become Dolly's delighted patrons and fervent champions. She was so mild, so gracious, so unceasingly polite and understanding– They wished their nieces were like that. Dolly reminded them of someone; they didn't know who. . . .

Younger matrons, and the few jealous unmarried girls who had long paraded their charms unsuccessfully before Ben Steele and die-hard bachelors of his generation–some of these women regarded Dolly as a threat to be put down at any price. Many came to be decked brilliantly by her. They teased their husbands or fathers for extra money (Dolly persuaded Agatha Cook to screw her prices ever upward) but their tongues were ready to waggle the moment they were outside the shop.

No one knew exactly what was so wicked about Miss Hessian. Certainly there was never the slightest departure from the rigid gentlewoman's attitude she had carpentered for herself. But people of Lexington needed only the motive and the desire for gossip: they did not need the fact.

There were misunderstood sentences, half-hinted-at allusions. One woman said, for instance, that Dolly reminded her of an actress she had once seen performing in Des Moines. Within twenty-four hours this story had been remodeled as follows: Dolly Hessian was a burlesque queen, even now sought by the police of Des Moines and heaven knew how many other towns.

This story was tossed from phone to phone, from yard to yard, with the bounding resiliency of a hard-batted tennis ball.

Florence Mahanna became possessed of the disparaging intelligence, and trailed to work, white and silent. She burst into tears at eleven o'clock in the morning, and rushed to the toilet room, where Dolly had to go and comfort her. . . . Floss wailed her tale of scandal; she messed Dolly's shirtwaist with her tears, until Dolly transferred Miss Mahanna's wet-nosed countenance to the safer haven of her sateen apron.

"But, Floss, I can't help what people say about me."

"They're just jealous, that's what they are," Miss Mahanna blubbered. "They just hate you because you're pretty and lovely and everything. They just say that because you're a mmmmmmilliner from Chicago."

When Floss observed her again, Dolly was blinking, and her mouth shaped itself in a tremulous smile. "I only try to be as good as I can."

"I hate Bet Butterfield! I used to like her—she was my ffffffriend—and now I'll never speak to her again. How could she say such a thing about you? I'll never speak to her again!"

Dolly said, with the faintest quaver in her voice, "Please do, Floss darling. *Please* speak to her again. I want you to have friends. I—I want to be friendly with everyone."

Calumnies boiled insistently through the town. It was the last week of September when the final shavings were swept away from the new carpet, and Miss Cook's establishment gleamed and beckoned. Two weeks later, Agatha had acquired at least sixty-five percent of the current custom in that community; and, by Saturday the twenty-first of October, they were a fortnight behind with their orders.

Still the rumors about Dolly were darting like waterbugs. On that same Saturday evening, Ben Steele strolled into the Wildwood Hotel to attend a committee meeting of the Commercial League, and was arrested by the conversation of three men who giggled together near a window. Ben looked beyond the men, and he saw Dolly Hessian braving the wind, her skirt blowing tight against her. She was hastening back to Miss Cook's after snatching a quick supper.

". . . Absolutely: I got it on good authority. The best thing that ever came to town. But expensive, brother—expensive . . ."

Ben Steele pulled the group aside; faces turned goggle-eyed; Ben knocked a young man named Longwell all the way through the overcoat rack. There was blood for the frightened Negro porter to mop up, and Mr. Longwell was aided by friends to an adjacent doctor's office, and the doctor was summoned away from his country sausage and apple sauce at the Greek's.

Ben had a date with Miss Hessian for that very evening: it was to be a brief date, because Dolly was so tired these days. But noisy echoes of what had occurred at the Wildwood preceded him to Mrs. Kristensen's. Dolly thanked him wistfully. "I never had anyone to fight my battles before," she whispered, and Ben's ears turned to the color of beet pickles.

Seventeen

On the second Tuesday night following, a Hallowe'en masquerade was held at the Elks' club. As with similar revels attempted on a wide scale in such towns, the mardi-gras effect was not too successful. Everyone was supposed to come in costume, but many of the members considered such festivities childish, and refused to "put on any funny-does" at all. Some had wives or lady friends who wanted to dress up; and thus was presented the peculiar spectacle of fairies, ballerinas and harem inmates escorted by optometrists and chick-hatchery proprietors in sober business attire.

There were the inveterate exhibitionists—people like Sylvester Cohen and young Doctor Conger—who scampered giddily about, one attired as a red devil, the other as a clown. Young Mrs. Cohen was an affable Geisha girl on the sidelines, and young Mrs. Conger a very shy and speechless ghost indeed.

Ben Steele had longed to appear at the party as a cowboy, complete with tooled leather boots and a six-gun. These articles he owned and loved, and would have worn daily about his business if custom permitted. When he discussed the party with Dolly, he hinted broadly that she should adopt the garb of a cowgirl. In his fancy he saw the two of them whirling through a Virginia reel, gay in fringe and buckles, easily the handsomest couple on the floor, and certainly the most talked-about.

Dolly recognized his longing, but felt it wise to be a little perverse. She wondered sometimes if she were not too acquiescent in her social relationship with Ben Steele. Constantly she had accepted his overtures whenever he made them, despite the physical weariness that tied her down, and at certain periods caused her to cry in bed at Mrs. Kristensen's as she contemplated the horror of her past and the stony riddle of her future. Only in a few braver moments was she completely confident of her ability to enmesh Ben in the coil of matrimony. After all, he had not yet proposed marriage or even less sanctified intimacies.

Dolly spent one evening with another man in a direct effort to bring about a positive reaction from Ben Steele. Mr. Ely Masterson, whose father owned the Lexington *Daily Ledger*, on which publication the son served as an affable but incompetent reporter—this same Mr. Masterson who was a friend of Ben's, and whom Dolly had met with Ben at the band concert, came to Miss Cook's to pick up a hat purchased by his mother. It was at an hour when both Floss and Agatha were absent, and Masterson hovered about, joking with Miss Hessian, trying to tease her a little about Ben. With a red face he asked then if she would go with him to a lecture offered at the Methodist church that week by a gentleman who had accompanied Teddy Roosevelt on his African venturings, and had the stereopticon slides to prove it.

Dolly accepted, and sat dutifully in the clammy auditorium for one hour and fifteen minutes, while fuzzy pictures of hartebeests, wildebeests and gazelles slid across the screen. During the homeward stroll which followed, Ely Masterson caught her in his arms in the black shadow of some big trees, and tried to kiss her. Her hurt and plaintive, "Why, Mr. *Mas*terson! Please. Oh, please, don't . . ." was a rebuke nearly as effective as a whipping to the inept man. She endured his mumbled apologies the rest of the way to Mrs. Kristensen's.

Ben Steele had heard about the date, of course, before he saw Dolly the following day—before he lounged with assurance into the millinery shop a few minutes before Dolly was ready to go home, and offered to drive her to her boarding-house—because, as he informed her with pitying humor, she looked played-out.

He chuckled once or twice on the way home, and Dolly, disturbed, wondered why he was laughing but dared not ask.

He inquired, "Did Ely try to kiss you last night?"

Dolly said she didn't think that was really any of his business. She thought, "At least, if he did try to kiss me, that's more than you ever tried to do!"

Ben persisted. "Under those box-elder trees, past the German Lutheran church?"

"Well—yes."

"He always tries to do that." Ben laughed tolerantly. "That's his favorite place," and then with real enthusiasm he began to recite the wonders of a light driving-harness—expensive harness, made to fill a special order—which had been completed that afternoon in his shop. Dolly went into Mrs. Kristensen's house despising Ben Steele cordially though briefly.

She was quite past her annoyance when the matter of the Hallowe'en party costumes came up, but firmly she decided against donning the habiliments of a cowgirl to match Ben's costume. First, she feared that such attire—with a short fringed skirt and mannish hat and perhaps a revolver at her side—would be a little too daring and tough for her to assume in Lexington, especially when people were telling stories about her. Second, work at the milliner's would prevent her from preparing an elaborate costume for herself if indeed she expected to see anything of Ben in the meantime.

So she said coolly that she had decided to go as a witch. Black sateen was cheap and plentiful—easy to sew. She could contrive a witch's garb in an hour, and a steeple-crowned hat in half that time.

At Lexington masquerade parties most of the participants usually wore false faces—masks sold in cheap variety stores—made out of stiff enameled paper or painted mesh. They were horrible contrivances designed to cover the entire face of the wearer—things with pointed noses or flat apish nostrils. The mouths were always too small and had to be cut out so that you could talk or breathe through them. Such grotesquerie was not to Dolly Hessian's liking. No dominoes were to be had; she made one herself—clipping and sizing it neatly at her work-table—a delectable slab of silky jet, concealing only the upper portion of her face. And her delicate eyes peered mysteriously through the apertures when she regarded herself in the mirror.

On October the 31st a tall cowboy escorted a slim witch up the noisy stairway leading to the Elks' lodge-room. Corners of the hall were stuffed with cornstalks, jeweled plumply with pumpkins. There were bowers of oak leaves above the piano and refreshment booth; there were a wishing-well, a Gipsy fortune teller, and a three-piece orchestra to play harvest-time airs.

Dolly looked with annoyance on those few of the younger women who feared to detract from their civilized charm by appearing in some sort of "get-up." She knew that her own dress of blue silk, now concealed by somber draperies, would have given her a power to exceed any prettiness offered by the others. Anyway, these black sateen folds had a gloss, and they were gathered more daintily about her waist than the rags of a legendary witch.

Through tiresome moments at the start of the party, when the hall looked too big and barnlike, Dolly found herself struck by a chill she did not wish to admit. She felt exasperated, annoyed with herself and Ben . . . was this all that her future might offer in Lexington—granted that she could manage to secure it there? Hopeless festivities in a barren room, with no one dancing or playing games—with people clustered in strained little groups, and the noisy buffoonery of the few determined gay spirits blasting painfully among the cornstalks?

But the fiddle-scraping and banjo-tinkling had their way in time. Red Devil Sylvester Cohen permitted a folding chair to collapse under him; there were shrieks . . . Clown Doctor Conger lost a makeshift trouser leg during the dance . . . more howls arose. In a rear cloak-room several bottles circulated busily. Soon the men were beaming and importunate; women yielded to the mood, embraced it; jollity began to wrap the throng.

Cold doughnuts were succulent, stiff with sugar and grease. The meat sandwiches were toothsome, the apples shone in generous red-and-pink piles. Dolly had never participated in a Virginia reel or a square dance before, but she was gracefully adept at any dance step. She found herself delighted as she was whirled from hand to hand, or dragged skippingly down the length of the line. And when the old-soldier tailor who called the dances shrieked, "Get your partners for a cotillion!" she and Ben were among the first to respond.

The official unmasking which came later was an anticlimax; everyone knew everyone else by this time. Everyone had indeed recognized everyone else when everyone first appeared in the hall, except for the few sheeted ghosts who paraded in spectral anonymity. But most of these were identified before long: the step, the voice, the mannerism, the company sought and maintained—these were infallible clues. In the end, only a traveling man from Des Moines who chanced to be staying at the Wildwood and who had attired himself in a burnoose of chintz provided by the Eckersalls—only this madcap Elk and one or two docile female spooks had defied detection.

Tripping alone through a dim side hallway on her way back from the washroom, Dolly Hessian met with an experience which accelerated her course in existence most certainly, if indeed it did not alter it.

She saw a big man standing with his back to her and apparently observing the frolic through a rear doorway which opened at the end of the ballroom. Dolly passed hastily; she gave the shape of this man no more than a glance, for at that moment her whole intention was centered on Ben Steele. . . . There was a further doorway giving on the middle of the lodge-room opposite the orchestra. There she could make an entrance not so palpably tied up with reëmergence from the toilet. . . .

"Miss Hessian."

His words reached her in a firm whisper . . . she could recognize instantly the owner of that voice.

Senator Newgate took her hand and drew her back down the hall, and then through a rear doorway which led to a landing above the dark stair. Still holding her hand, the Senator smiled down. "I have seen many witches in my time. Undoubtedly you are the prettiest."

She said that she was glad to be a pretty witch.

"Where's your mask?"

"Everybody took off their masks about fifteen minutes ago. But where's *your* costume?" she demanded chidingly.

There was something romantic and satisfying in the posture of Newgate as he waited before her now—his loose black topcoat flung over one shoulder like a cape, his wide-brimmed hat in his hand. Light came from the ballroom and found a diamond stick-pin in the man's necktie. The diamond flamed coldly.

"Oh, I merely dropped in to give my blessing to the young folks."

Subscribing to his mood, Dolly lifted the sateen of her skirt and curtsied. "The young folks thank you for your blessing, sir." She turned as if to leave him—although, despite her desire to rejoin Ben as soon as possible, she found herself affected by the spectacle of this ponderous older man—so alone in his pride and his power, remote from the multitude, exuding the dark compulsion of his physical vitality.

"Please," he said, and that one word held her where she stood. "Tomorrow is the first of November. I suppose that you will be leaving soon. I mean—leaving Lexington?"

Dolly lowered her gaze. She looked sadly at the dimness of the floor. "Sometime soon."

"I remember the date when you first arrived—the day we met at the hotel. As a trimmer, I knew you wouldn't stay in town always. . . . I watch you," he said, "sometimes when you don't see me. I watch you on the street, and other places."

She whispered, without lifting her glance, "I'm glad you do, if it makes you happy. I still have the mesh-bag. It's beautiful. I haven't had much chance to carry it, and tonight—I suppose witches shouldn't carry mesh-bags; they might lose them when they ride their broomsticks."

Newgate drew out his cigar case and slid the upper section loose. He took out the single cigar remaining, and replaced the empty case in his pocket. "I've been thinking," he said. "You know, I shall go to Des Moines next week, and will be there some time. It occurred to me that after leaving Lexington you, also, might visit our capital city."

Dolly's eyes met his blankly. "Why did you think that, Senator Newgate?"

He had his penknife out, he was cutting a circle from the stem of the cigar. "There are millinery wholesalers in Des Moines, aren't there? It occurred to me that you might have business in Des Moines. When there, my headquarters are at the Hotel Kirkwood. If I can serve you in any way I wish that you would call me at the Kirkwood, or perhaps write a note. Will you do that?"

Dolly said, "If I go to Des Moines."

"Will you promise, my dear?"

"Yes."

"Then all I can add is: I shall hope and pray that you come to Des Moines."

She went away from him down the hall toward the party.

His suggestion, the invitation imparted therein: these were completely obvious to Dolly Hessian. She found herself consumed with admiration for the weighty but effective assurance with which he had managed to convey his meaning. Word for word, look for look, Newgate had not committed himself in any way. His remarks might have been transcribed by a court stenographer, and yet they would never constitute acceptable evidence against him. He had said kindly things, he had made a helpful and generous gesture, that was all.

He might as well have said to Dolly, "I long to sleep with you. I shall treat you generously. We will be at least momentarily happy. Both of us will profit from the experience in many ways."

And yet the mere fact that Newgate felt that he might calmly say the things that he had said, and thus convey in ulterior fashion the assurance of his intentioned advance—this realization filled Dolly Hessian with a dread.

The man had watched her, estimated her, and made his decision. However much she had integrated herself into the community life of Lexington during her brief tenure of a job there, she was still a rootless thing, unclaimed, unclothed in security.

An alternative opened before her: the same dreary vista of train smoke, hotels, toilsome endeavor; the planning, the weighing, the weary scheme and plot. A lone woman needed to yield herself—she needed to embrace the loose tenets of the males who had constructed her civilization—or else she must shrivel, she must dry like a leaf in her self-enforcement. Alone she was only a female thing, never a social entity, and forever vulnerable to attack.

There was still the possibility (she counted it in each tap of her heels against the hardwood floor) that Newgate might let his life be shaped to her need. It was a desperate chance that she would take, if she joined him in Des Moines after the cold-weather trimming season was over, after the women of Lexington and nearer Dodge County were hatted against the winter. There was every possibility that once she had succumbed to external pressure, and to the even stronger persuasion of internal desire, she would be loose again in existence, uncraved, a bit more bedraggled, and perhaps with only a new watch or a breast-pin as the solitary material souvenir of her adventure. . . . No, she cried angrily, Not that again.

Eighteen

She said to Ben Steele, "Please take me away."

He had been munching an apple in solid contentment. "What's the matter? Got a headache?"

"Maybe it's just— All these people and everything."

She thought she recognized something new in his expression: a flash like the diamond of Newgate's stick-pin, but a younger, brighter fire. "All right. I'll get our coats."

In the street, with fiddle music still whining out of the stairway behind them, Ben reached over to wrap more tightly the folds of the cloth coat on Dolly's shoulders. "Gosh, you're shivering. Don't feel sick or anything, do you?"

"Oh, no. Sometimes—I guess I get moody and restless. Sometimes—people, parties and things—" She managed a weak mirthfulness. "Maybe I'm just bored."

"Not with me?"

"Of course not, silly." She added in a hidden whisper, "I'm never bored with you," and she was pleased when Ben squeezed her arm in reply.

He took her halfway up the block where Nagger was hitched and blanketed before the buggy. Dolly had suggested that they walk to the Elks' club from Mrs. Kristensen's; but Ben said No, it was too far, it might rain.

In this hour there was no hint of rain. The chilly wind had

blown away the shredded clouds which lingered at sundown. Stars were spicy and frosty.

In the buggy Ben settled the robes carefully around them, and Dolly snuggled deep beside him.

"I got out the old buffalo tonight. It's one Long Dan used to have. You need that when winter comes."

"Is winter here?"

"Pretty darn near. Let's give Nagger a little trot to warm him up." He slapped the reins, and the black horse swung eagerly up the long western cavern of Sixth Street with its ranks of trees arching and bare. Some spots in the road were littered with debris left by the imps of Hallowe'en. Ben slowed the horse.

A new plan was forming in Dolly Hessian's mind: a project born out of her desperation. She trimmed the pattern carefully, picked it up, examined it, found it good. The mere broaching required every delicacy which she could muster. But with Newgate's remarks still resounding in her ears, the girl felt herself nerved by necessity.

"Oo, I'm hungry."

Ben smiled through the cold gloom of their journey. "I don't wonder. You didn't eat hardly anything at the party."

"You know how it is. Kind of funny—you get just one thing in your mind, and you want that and nothing else. I didn't want any apples or sandwiches or doughnuts or things; I just wanted this one thing, and I can't have it," she ended plaintively.

"Well, why not? We could go down to the Greek's. He's open real late; we could get a tenderloin sandwich or— What was it you wanted?"

"Fudge."

"Fudge? Chocolate fudge?"

"Umhum."

"I wonder," he speculated, "if old Gert Garrett's candy store is open. No, I guess not—she usually shuts up pretty early, except on Saturdays."

"Pooh," said Dolly. "I don't mean that kind of fudge. Not candy-store stuff. You know"—and impulsively, or seemingly so, she crept closer to Ben beneath the heavy robes—"nights like this, it makes you think of when you were little. I remember at Aunt Edna's: sometimes she'd be gone to church or club meetings, and the cook would be asleep. And do you know what I'd do? It was awful naughty, but I used to do it. A cold night in the fall like this, I'd find myself positively *craving* fudge."

She told him what she used to do, embroidering the fictitious recital with gaudy stitches . . . a great dark house, crammed with old furniture and portraits, and herself in nightie and wrapper and slippers, creeping down the staircase. In the silent kitchen she would find a pan; she would turn on the gas flame and secure necessary ingredients from the larder. Secretly, joyfully, like an eager brownie, working in mischief and silence, she would cook her fudge above the blue gas flame. She would pour it carefully upon a buttered plate, and then just as stealthily clear away the evidences of her lark. She'd smuggle the plate of fudge back up to her lonely room, and there—rejoicing in chocolaty, sugary comfort within her satin comforters—she'd turn up the flame of the light near her bed and lose herself in a wonderland of fudge and tales.

"I'd read," she said, "fairy stories and— And *Little Women.*"

Not only did Dolly's description of the fudge provoke a

physical hunger within Ben, but there was something else in the legend—a reflection of his own scolded childhood—that warmed a new fondness. He found Dolly's hand and held it tightly.

"We could do that."

"Do what?"

"Sneak off and make fudge."

"How? Where on earth—?"

"My house."

For a time there was only the solid striking of Nagger's hooves against the roadway.

"But you said Mrs. Fachter goes home every night."

"Yes. There wouldn't be anyone else there."

"But— All alone—the two of us—I mean—in your house—?" And then her false protest resolved itself into the age-old query of Lexington and a million other towns: "What would the neighbors say?"

"Nobody'd know anything about it."

"But the horse and buggy? Folks might see Nagger in front of your house, when they were on their way home from the party. They'd know we were there. Oh, Ben, really it would be so much fun, and I can make the most *wonderful* fudge. But—do you really think—?"

He was headed back to the livery barn. "We can be very careful about this. There isn't anything to it. I'll just leave the rig at the barn, and if Maxwell or Uncle Em is around I'll say that we decided to walk home instead of driving. Then we can walk right up Fourth Street, and cut through the vacant lot next to Pryors' place, and go right in our back door. I'll even pull the blinds down before I turn on the light. Nobody needs to know we're there alone or anything about it."

Ninety minutes later Dolly Hessian, her face flushed and delighted, was beating a dish of fudge to its final creamy consistency with a big wooden spoon. She was alone with Ben in the solitary den of the Steeles, and gratified to find herself there. She was cautioning Ben to hold the nutmeats ready . . . now it was time to pour them in . . . oo, look out, hold the platter over here, it's all starting to harden . . . oo, I hope we get it out before it sets in the pan. . . .

They chortled together as the last quick scraping of the spoon carried a thickening mixture over the old willow-ware platter. There it was: a brown luxury studded with lumps of walnut.

Dolly did not tell Ben how she had learned to make such fudge. She had been taught this art by the wife of the second man with whom she ever had a love affair, and this man was a Chicago beer-wagon driver.

A silver knife marked off the squares and cut them deeply. Dolly made Ben close his eyes as her fingers conveyed the first oily rarity to his mouth.

"Golly—"

"Good?"

"It's wonderful." Then his eyes had opened and he was looking down at her with the quizzical air which had affected her when she met him at the railroad station. Ben lifted his hands and put them gently around her arms above the elbows. "You're wonderful."

"Why?"

"Oh, you can do so many things."

"Just make fudge."

"Hats, too. Beautiful hats. I guess you're just— You're a wonderful girl."

He bent forward to kiss her. Restrained by a peculiar shyness ever since their first date, it was the first time he had ever attempted to caress her thus. Dolly had decided just what she would do.

She turned her head quickly to one side, and closed her eyes and breathed more heavily than before. "Oh, no," she whispered through half-open lips, "Ben, please. Don't."

The clutch of his hand stiffened. She could feel his breath against her cheek. "Why not, honey? Why not?"

"I wouldn't have come here alone with you, if I had thought that you were going to try to—take advantage."

His hands fell away, and she looked up to find him shrugging as he regarded her with a wry smile. "All right, I'll be good. But don't talk about going home yet. I want to show you the house. And we've got to eat our fudge."

"I don't want much," said Dolly, as he led her toward the dining room. "Just a little bit. I thought I was so hungry for fudge—and I was, too— But I can't eat too much."

(On their arrival at the house, and with only the electric light in the rear entry turned on, Ben had gone ahead, drawing down the faded green blinds of the downstairs rooms. This interval, following which he came back and turned the switch of the kitchen light, had served for Dolly to remove the witch's garments which she had worn over her favorite dress of Persian-blue silk. She had lingered long enough—had waited stiff-necked and with arms above her head—in order for Ben Steele to observe her last little feminine wriggle out of the voluminous dark folds. She had heard his sudden, "Oh, pardon me," and then she faced him—the sateen gown in her hand, her face flushed, her hair a little tousled. She said, "I hope you don't mind. I thought it would be easier, if

I was making fudge, not to have all this extra costume on." He provided her with a white frilled apron—an old apron which had belonged to his mother and was kept in a neatly ironed stack along with other aprons and many doilies in the bottom drawer of a chest in the dining room.)

Now she untied the strings of the white apron as she left the kitchen, and with Ben saying, "Well, here's the dining room," she folded the apron and placed it on the oblong dining table.

Ordinary monstrosities of that period and of the previous generation cluttered every corner of the Steele house, together with many objects completely extraordinary and personal to the Steeles. Dolly's eyes (politely appreciative though they appeared to the young man) were nevertheless studying every piece of furniture and bric-a-brac in sight. She decided that if she were ever mistress of that house, the first thing she would do would be to get rid of the huge glass-doored china closet with its flaked mirror and veneered turrets.

She saw gilded cattails, crayon enlargements, a steel engraving of two little girls terrified by a flock of sheep, overstuffed cupids with bows and arrows. And horses everywhere.

In front of the dining room was a living room; beyond that, opening through wide doors, loomed the front parlor. Walls of these rooms were decorated with many photographs, some of them faded brown. Mad Steele and his father sat stiffly in sulkies; Civil War veterans beamed amid reunions; knobby-kneed colts strained at their halter-ropes. The fireplace was backed with tan tiles and crowded with an ornate black-painted grate.

On the mantel were the last pictures taken of Ben's father, mother and grandfather; and offending the corner of the parlor was a divan built out of an old buggy seat. The metal work had been gilded. This seat was the most loathsome piece of furniture Dolly had ever seen.

"What's that?"

"That was Long Dan's favorite buggy—the seat, I mean. After he died my father had it reupholstered and fixed up a little. I used to like to curl up on it when I was a kid, and read, sometimes—you know, the way you did in bed. I'd eat crackers and read the Alger books and things. If my mother wasn't around."

"Why? Was she cross, Ben?"

Ben looked her straight in the face. "My mother was just about the crossest woman I ever met. I don't even like to think about her. My father— He was a regular prince. He was pretty quiet, but when he said anything he meant it. My mother practically nagged him crazy. That's her up on the mantel."

He said, after Dolly had perused the photograph of the challenging, bitter-faced woman with her high-piled pompadour, "When Dad died I took that picture down. Then it kind of seemed as if I shouldn't— You know, after all, she was my mother. So I got it out of the drawer and put it back up there."

There was ferocity in the way he told these things, but Dolly was glad she recognized this implacability in Ben. It gave him a strength undiscerned previously. She was confident that he was a man who, once having made up his mind, could not easily be swayed. If once embarked on a venture he was bound to proceed with it. Too, there was an innate honesty about the way he confessed his abomination of his mother (it was the first time he had done this) and it seemed to mark an accéptance of Dolly as one to whom he might turn in confidence.

She reached out her hand. She grasped his fingers and squeezed warmly. "I'm sorry."

"Sorry?"

"I'm so sorry you were so unhappy when you were little. Maybe that means you'll be happier later on. Oh," she cried, breaking away from him, "what are those things on top of the piano? They look like arrows."

Thus she examined with shudders four Indian arrows, while Ben explained about them: three were of Cheyenne manufacture, one was a Sioux. These were relics brought from Nebraska Territory by Long Dan Steele, back in Civil War times, and had been treasured by his descendants ever since. Also there was a cavalry saber belonging to the old man, and Ben drew this weapon from its scabbard and acted a vengeful assault against Dolly, who squealed and ran to safety behind the platform-rocker.

"Well, that's about all. I guess you've seen the downstairs. I guess," he said after a moment's awkward silence, "that there isn't any point in going upstairs." With Dolly still silent before him, Ben felt his face growing hot.

He went to the table and helped himself to fudge from the platter they had carried along with them.

"It's late."

"Here, have another piece."

"No, thank you, Ben. It's late. I think you better take me home."

"Well, if you say so."

"But first we must wash up those things."

"Oh, heck, we can leave those for Mrs. Fachter tomorrow."

"Would she expect that you would be making fudge, here alone?"

"I guess not. But don't worry, I'll wash them up when I get back."

"Nonsense," said Dolly, "I'll do them now. You're just a man after all—just a clumsy old thing. Come on, show me where the towels are," and she sped before him down the side hall into the kitchen.

Standing before the sink, with hot water pouring from its faucet, Dolly knew the most urgent demand of her life to date. This was the opportunity she had sought to make . . . she must not lose it . . . she must not . . .

She must resort—and hastily—to the strongest compulsion of sex. Oh, she knew that she had been right: she should have turned her face away when he tried to kiss her . . . yes, she should. But not the second time. Not if he tried again. He must try again. He *must.*

She managed it well. The enamelware kettle placed on the edge of the sink, soap suds and chocolate froth foaming therein, the laughing request for a washcloth to be handed to her, Ben's responsive gesture, her body turning, her elbow flung out . . . she contrived it well: he thought that he had done it. Yes, he actually believed—

The kettle rolled off across the floor . . . there was a splash, a cry. Dolly's gown hung wet against her leg.

"Oh, God! Dolly, I'm sorry."

"It—it doesn't matter."

"Hell! Your dress . . . here, I'll get a dry towel."

She murmured, "No, Ben. Cold water—please—a clean towel—"

Together they scrubbed at her gown. Ben made a few rapid swabbing motions with the towel in his hand, then gave it up. They could both see the shape of Dolly's garter through the drenched fabrics . . . Ben stood aside and let Dolly do the best she could.

"You certainly were right. I'm just as clumsy as an old mule."

"It doesn't matter." With her face turned down, she worked at the task. Finally she straightened, smiling tremulously.

He asked, "Will it come out? Without spoiling the color and everything?"

"Maybe a cleaner could take it out. I don't know. Ben, it was my fault: I didn't put that apron on again."

He said abruptly, "I'm going to buy you a new dress."

"Oh, you *couldn't.*"

"Who the hell says I couldn't?"

She still faced him—so helpless, so endearing, so determined to be a good sport about the whole thing, so pliably feminine with the beauty of her skirt bedraggled, and with the skirt wet and clinging a little against her silk stocking, against the shoe-top—

She stood before the sink in his own kitchen, alone with him: a female thing, a woman in his house. They were alone—they were together—he needed her now—he needed her wildly.

And oh, the lace: the blue-black treasure which had first stricken his eyes with its incitement . . . this very hair on whose wild beauty it had pressed and been pinned. . . .

She had not worn the hat tonight—only the sharp tall crown of masquerade absurdity—and she had taken that off on entering the buggy for a drive which had led to his home instead of hers. She had not put it on again; her hair was loose and tousled; it needed no adornment but itself, and yet he might always place the imaginary frilled coronet upon it. That hat, hanging high at Mrs. Kristensen's now, screamed its promise to him. In some way he must now insert himself within this girl, within the permanency of her life.

She would wear the hat again. He would crumple her in his arms when again she had it fastened to her blondness, he would love her thus . . . as in the intensity of rape he would take the dim, dark web as being part of her, and part of the mystery she shed, and he would love and crush it, he would bedew it with nectar. . . .

His urgency . . . he should have known it all along; he should have hauled her close, strangling her wonder until each protest that rose against him was stifled.

And now, and now, and now—

"Oh, *Ben,*" she murmured.

"Oh, God. I love you. For God's sake let me kiss you!"

His mouth was over hers, his voice begging, he was dragging the very breath from her lungs. And she tried to play delicately for a time with the passion she had heated; but then she felt resistance draining from her, and a turbulence began to leap within her own body in response.

The next thing she knew, he had turned out the light, he was kissing her remorselessly. His arms had lifted her up. For a moment she dangled against him, and then he slid one arm beneath her shoulders and passed his other arm behind her thighs.

Dolly heard the kitchen linoleum and the boards beneath, crunching under Ben's tread. With a last quickening of resistance, the girl tore her mouth from his. "Ben, dear, where —? You're carrying me. Oh, darling, put me down—"

He croaked, "Upstairs. Dolly—" His mouth was over hers again.

She twisted away. "No," she gasped, "no!"

"I love you, Dolly." He began to sob dryly. "Dolly, I've got to. You're beautiful. I want— I want—"

Again she had turned her face from his. She heard her voice go singing remotely under the tall ceilings, past the ugliness of golden oak and distant lights of other rooms mirrored in the burnished wood. "Ben, we can't. We *can't.*"

"Why not? Oh—"

"Don't you understand? Please try to understand. A girl just can't just— A girl—" She wailed, "Some day I might want— I might meet someone else— Want to marry and have children — We can't do this."

He told her, of course, still wrapping her in his arms, in the hall below the stairs up which she refused to let him bear her —he told her what he would do—what they would do. My God, he loved her. Dolly—married? Of course he wanted to marry her . . . oh, Dolly, sweetheart, please marry me; please let's get married . . . oh, Dolly, I love you; I want you with me always.

He cried it all, consumed with the violence of his need. She stood at last affianced, his clutch around her with pride, his mouth coming down to kiss sacredly the yellow hair of her precious head. She stood, serene in knowing, planning what she would make of his life and hers, even while she felt his maleness pressing near her.

Nineteen

Much as Dolly Hessian might have wished to luxuriate openly in having achieved her engagement to Ben Steele, she wisely forebore. Until Friday she did not even tell the news to Floss Mahanna and Miss Cook. She had that feeling of collapse which follows any rigorous ordeal, no matter how happy its result.

The morning of November 1st, and with her mouth still bruised from Ben's attentions, Dolly lay wanly in bed until a late hour. She missed her breakfast. Mrs. Kristensen relented when she saw Dolly's pale face; she broke her firm rule against giving boarders any food at outside hours, and she regaled Dolly with apple sauce, cold toast and hot coffee at the kitchen table. Dolly didn't reach the millinery shop until after ten o'clock. Miss Cook and Floss "mothered" her, and made her promise to go home by five o'clock at least—earlier if she wanted to.

The black pebble-grained traveling bag with its rose-silk lining which Dolly fetched from Chicago had been bought late during the previous summer at a second-hand store on Clark Street. Dolly looked at bags in the department stores, but the ones she wanted were far beyond her reach. As often before in her life, she turned to a second-hand source. In the fourth cluttered store that she visited she found her bag: it showed only moderate signs of wear, and had been expensive in the first place. She haggled with the proprietor, who wanted fifteen dollars; finally she paid eleven.

But before completing this transaction, Dolly acquired also a picture of her own family. There were baskets of miscellaneous junk arranged along the floor in this store: books with scuffed covers, paper-weights, an old clock, pictures framed and unframed; and even some children's toys were there. These articles were included among the personal effects of an unhappy invalid who had died in poverty on the near North Side. The woman boasted no relatives, and everything in her room had been claimed and sold by the landlady in an effort to realize something on unpaid rental.

One photograph in particular caught Dolly's attention. This picture was turned slightly yellowish now; it was at least twenty years old: a group photo of a family gathered on the porch and steps of a comfortable brick house surrounded by well-tended shrubbery. There were two little girls in the group, and one was a blonde. The child held a rag doll, and might without much stretch of imagination be regarded as a picture of Dolly herself at an early age.

Three women, well-dressed and impressively hatted, became respectively Aunt Edna, Aunt Ellen and Cousin Mildred. The erect man standing beside them was promptly named Uncle McConnell; and the two Dalmatian dogs—one with his head blurred as he snapped at a fly—were Spot and Spike.

There exuded an ease, a warmth and satisfactory opulence from this family which Dolly adopted as physical evidence of her genealogy. She did not know who the people were or where the picture was taken. There was a photographer's stamp on the back, *Ernst for Good Photos*—that was all.

The junkman sold the picture to Dolly for a dime, and wondered out loud why she wanted it. She told him that it was because of the dogs: one of them looked exactly like her own precious Major who had been run over by a coal wagon the year before. She told the dealer that she was going to cut out the picture of that dog and keep it always, because she had unfortunately no photo of the defunct Major.

Nowadays this unmutilated picture leaned in front of the mirror of Dolly's dresser at Mrs. Kristensen's. At one time or another during the previous weeks Floss Mahanna, Agatha Cook, Mrs. Kristensen and two or three resident school teachers had all been in Dolly's room, and all had admired her family. She told them, with a smother in her tone, that one couldn't carry many pictures—traveling about the country as Dolly did—but this one she always took along with her. It called to mind those carefree infant days when she was happy, playing with her little Cousin Hazel . . . the warm jolly times when Uncle McConnell was alive . . . she lowered her voice even more . . . before Uncle McConnell lost most of his money and suffered a stroke and died.

Dolly had, with succinct remarks in proper season, built a menacing tradition about Aunt Edna. Of course she loved Aunt Edna dearly—she had been the only mother Dolly ever knew, really—because her own mother had died when Dolly was three weeks old. Her father had been killed in a Milwaukee railroad wreck soon after that, and Dolly couldn't remember him either.

Yes, she loved Aunt Edna, but found her prim old-fashioned severity a painful, a stifling thing. Aunt Edna had retained enough money to keep the fine old house in Lake Forest. She had a cook too. Of course she could no longer afford to keep up her stables, though Aunt Ellen and Uncle Bert had enormous stables at their home in Virginia. But Aunt Edna wanted Dolly to live there with her—to do nothing, to be idle—a polite parasite, really. Dolly had longed to study art, but Aunt Edna refused to let her go to college after she left the convent in her teens. Aunt Edna thought that art was very unladylike—almost (Dolly chuckled shyly) immoral.

Secretly Dolly had worked in a millinery shop in Lake Forest, while Aunt Edna thought Dolly busy with anonymous charities; and when the girl announced that she was going away to earn her own living, Aunt Edna nearly died.

None of the Hessians, Tavishes or Randolphs had ever done a thing like that before.

"But I bet you're a lot happier," her acquaintances cried.

"Oh, yes, much happier—even working so hard. It's wonderful to feel independent. But Aunt Edna doesn't understand, even yet. She's really furious. She doesn't write to me very often; but when she does her letters are cold." Dolly sighed.

"Well, I guess there's no help for it, honey. You just have to do what you think is right."

"Oh, I know. But sometimes— I don't want to be a baby, but I really do cry myself to sleep." Dolly sighed again.

On the Thursday evening after they became engaged, Ben appeared at Mrs. Kristensen's at seven o'clock. He was grinning all over his face; he was planning to take Dolly for a drive to continue certain delectable plans and discussions of the previous evening.

Dolly came down with a coat around her shoulders. Ben must understand, she said, and not be worried. But she did have such a headache; she had worked very hard all day and her head was just splitting. Mrs. Kristensen was going to make her some hot lemonade soon, and she'd go right to bed. But Ben must not be worried. It was nothing, really—just one of those things.

Mr. Steele, confused into helpless embarrassment at being confronted with such evidence of feminine fragility, mumbled of his love behind the bare lattice on the Kristensen porch. He said, "You know what, darling? We've got to get married right away, so that—so that I can take care of you. I don't like to think of you—you know—lying around in an old boarding-house, not feeling well. I mean— Oh, hell, Dolly, let's make it real soon. Won't you?"

"As soon as possible," she whispered. "I want to, too. Oh, Ben, I want to; but you know it all happened so quickly and everything." She tried to brighten her tone with a spritely humor. "I really think that's the reason I have a headache, as much as anything else."

Ben kissed her good-bye. He kissed her good-bye four times; and then went to drive furiously out the nearest country road all the way to the Catholic cemetery and back. The buggy bounded wildly over loose clods as Ben whooped and sang to the November breeze.

Dolly went back to her room and continued with the task she had begun the moment she was through supper. She was writing a letter to herself, writing it with her left hand. She was very nearly ambidextrous, so the script she formed in this fashion was round and large—the consonants all looped, and she made little circles for the dots over the i's. She wrote on pale-blue stationery with a white edge: writing-paper she had brought from Chicago. Finally she inserted the letter in the envelope, sealed it, put on a two-cent stamp and a special delivery stamp as well. She addressed this letter to Miss Dolly Hessian, c/o Cook Millinery Shop, Lexington, Iowa.

About ten o'clock she slipped out of Mrs. Kristensen's house and went by way of back streets to the region of the Illinois Central railroad track, and then down its bleak and lonely course to the station, where she waited briefly in nearby shadows for the ten-twenty-three eastbound train.

There was a mail car on this train, with a metal slot for the posting of first-class mail at wayside stations. Her letter thus filed into the care of the government, Dolly fled back to Mrs. Kristensen's, unrecognized, undetected, triumphant.

The letter would be examined with scorn and annoyance by some itinerant clerk aboard the car. He would stamp it with a smeared, nearly illegible circlet of black ink (a letter mailed through a slot aboard a train never bore a direct clue as to its origin) and he would send the letter back to Lexington again in some other westbound mail-pouch, from the next point where mail was distributed.

Late on Friday afternoon a little boy rode his bicycle up to the millinery shop, leaned it against the front window, and went in with this same letter and an accompanying slip for Dolly to sign.

There were only the three of them in the shop, for the services of the two extra girls had been dispensed with as of the previous Saturday night. The autumn season had passed its peak. Customers were fewer now, and normally Dolly's stint in Lexington would be nearly done. . . . She was working with a mound of red velvet and silver gauze when the letter came. She had put the metallic gloss on that stiff gauze herself, and she accepted the letter with fingers still clammy with silver paste.

Both Miss Cook and Miss Mahanna watched with interest as Dolly opened the letter, and they saw her pale face bent above it, and saw her lips half-moving as she read the lines.

Dolly had never received a special delivery letter before—not there at the shop, anyhow. What on earth—

With a half-strangled gasp, Miss Hessian arose, clutching the blue paper in her hand.

"Dolly! What—?"

"It isn't anything."

"But, Dolly. Look, Miss Cook—she's so white. Dolly, sit down, dear. Sit—"

She said in a flat voice, "It's from Aunt Edna."

"Is anybody dead?" demanded Agatha Cook.

"No, no. I don't care," she cried with a little sob. "I *don't* care. I'll do it anyway."

"Do what?"

She faced them, she swallowed softly before she let herself speak again. "I'm going to marry Ben Steele."

There were outcries, giddy shrieks, alarums and clamour, much hugging.

The letter Dolly had crumpled in sudden blind fury was smoothed out and appraised.

"I wash my hands of you," Aunt Edna had written. "Really, to think of my own niece marrying a livery stable man! Dolly, come to your senses at once. Though you are of age I consider myself to be still your guardian. My dear child, I forbid it. What would your poor mother think if she were alive? I don't care who he is or how well he is thought of in his own community—I would as soon see you married to the driver of a garbage wagon."

Florence Mahanna lowered the letter incredulously. "Oh, Dolly, isn't she mean?"

The forlorn Dolly said, "I guess she can't help being a snob."

Twenty

The wedding Floss Mahanna planned for Dolly and Ben was far different from the wedding which later became a fact. But at least it was noisy, crowded, and with a completely romantic fulfilment.

Floss planned that wedding all the way home in the darkness from Miss Cook's. It would be held in the Methodist church, in the early winter or late autumn. Whatever this cold season might be called, miraculously it turned to a perfumed June. Little Helga Kristensen—granddaughter of Dolly's landlady—was the flower-girl. She came tripping down the aisle—her glasses gone from her face, her clumsy legs miraculously graceful—treading the old red carpet with a fairy touch.

The Rev. Humphrey Kurchner was resplendently decked in a surplice or cassock or something. He became an Episcopal priest, and his voice rang portentously through the church, and all were hushed to hear it.

Floss wondered who should give the bride away. She decided finally on Senator Newgate—though she was not, in truth, aware that Dolly and Abie Newgate had ever more than nodded on the street to each other.

Dolly's relatives were there . . . Aunt Edna with a crust of rich lace about her throat, and a bejeweled chatelaine watch. Aunt Edna had come from Chicago, with Aunt Ellen from Virginia and Cousin Hazel from Scarsdale, New York, following in her train. They stood—a little cluster of prim, petticoated antiquity—aloof and annoyed, hating the entire process, foolishly blind to the radiance that shone in Dolly Hessian's face.

Ben Steele was serene in what the *Daily Ledger* might call "the conventional black." But Dolly's gown was a marvel of ivory satin, and she wore a wedding veil that had decorated the hair of her sainted mother twenty-odd years before.

The best carriage in the Steele barn waited outside to bear the newly wedded couple to a splendid reception at the Wildwood Hotel (Floss was rather vague about who gave that reception; but there it was, complete with ice-cream in the mold of doves) and thence to a Pullman car attached to the Chicago train—a handsome yellow-painted Pullman which carried the young Steeles directly to New York, where they rushed to board a steamship for Paris, France.

Oh, yes. Miss Cornelia Ritchie sang two solos: "O Promise Me" and "I Love You Truly."

Floss herself, seated at the pipe organ, played the wedding marches. Actually she could play no organ except the parlor variety—just the piano for the B.Y.P.U. where they sang "Joy Bells Ringing in My Heart"—and she could not play that very well. But in excited fancyings she exploited Wagner and Mendelssohn with celestial fortissimo.

Tonight there was a drabness, however, greater than that which ordinarily lay over her existence, as she passed the lights of houses that came before her own, as she saw the painted-glass shade of their own parlor lamp coming out through the window of that small white house where she was condemned to imprisonment. She had hoped to have Dolly for a chum, and to some degree she had enjoyed that relationship. For two weeks she had turned her face away, had Florence Mahanna, when she encountered Elizabeth Butterfield. Now, she supposed almost savagely, Bet would have to laugh on the other side of her face. There was some solace in this—not much.

For Florence had lost, or was soon to lose, the mystery, the proximity, the flavor of Dolly Hessian's presence. Floss pursued her dream even further (she was flagellating herself with every stroke of her imaginings, yet she flailed away). The honeymoon . . . there was that picture on the wall in the Mahanna living room: "Great Moments in a Young Girl's Life" it was called, or something like that. The proposal (they were on shipboard); the wedding gown; the wedding; the honeymoon; the young couple at breakfast; the baby at last. It was drawn by Charles Dana Gibson or some such illustrator—or was it Harrison Fisher or Howard Chandler Christy? Florence couldn't remember. She saw the pastel tints before her eyes; she dipped her brush therein and painted the same travesty across the future of Dolly and Ben.

Ah, she would continue in her affection for Dolly; she was with her constantly. She and Dolly had little snacks together when Ben was gone away on business. Dolly gave all sorts of giggly confidences to Floss . . . she showed her the tiny kimonos, the infant shirts and flannel bands she was stitching secretly until ready to surprise Ben with them. She whispered happily to Floss (the woman felt a hotness in her blood as she hurried home, entertaining these thoughts) of physical intimacies with A Man.

But it was Dolly's life, not hers. And there were all those hours Dolly would spend alone with Ben—the secret jokes and munchings they would have. Their life together: young married folks with the smugness and clubby assurance of their kind. . . .

Floss glanced through cold dusk, across the distortion of withered plants in a neighbor's garden. She saw lights in the Butterfield house beyond. Was Bet home yet from the courthouse? She wondered.

Her mother was especially petulant this night. She said that her eyes hurt; she had been reading the *Yeoman Shield,* which still came to them in the mail though Caleb Mahanna, Yeoman, had been dead a long time. Maybe there was a mistake; the magazine still came regularly. Mrs. Mahanna's eyes hurt, and she said that she got so tired sitting there all alone, and she wanted Floss to read *Freckles* to her. She wouldn't admit that she liked the story (she wouldn't admit liking anything) and yet she always asked Floss to read *Freckles*—even though Mrs. Mahanna usually went to sleep in her chair after the third or fourth page.

Having attended to certain needs of her mother's, Floss went into the kitchen. She shook the fire in the little coal range. She drew out the corncobs which she had set to soak at noon, lifted the soggy things out of the bent tin can with its kerosene, and tossed them gingerly onto the live bed of coals. They roared into flame. Floss poured in some coal, and the stove began to warm.

She cooked pork chops and opened a can of corn and another can of cherries. She fetched the butter, the bread. She made tea. Mrs. Mahanna ate hungrily, and she left a rim of brown crusts—a squared half-circle surviving from each piece—because she would not eat crusts, and Floss had neglected to trim them off. Florence was not a good cook, her mother declared.

Supper done, Floss washed the dishes and put away the leavings of food carefully. In response to her mother's insistence, she began reading *Freckles* again. They had reached the point in the story where Freckles has a terrible fight with a huge, brutal slugger in the wilds of the Limberlost. The description of the fight seemed bloody and revolting to Floss, and still completely unreal. Her little voice capered rapidly as she read . . . sometimes she would leave out whole sentences and even paragraphs—her mother didn't know the difference—and soon the older woman began to snore heavily. Floss put down the book and turned the lamp to a lower, steadier beam. She took an old cape-bonnet of her mother's out of the rear entry, and stole across gardens and backyards to the Butterfield house.

When she came softly up on the rear porch, she saw Bet inside, washing a few dishes in the sink. Probably Bet had worked late at the courthouse and had come home to eat a solitary meal. Her parents never waited for her; in fact there was little conversation exchanged in the Butterfield home at any time. Floss rapped timidly on the rear door, and Bet swung around almost angrily. She opened the door.

"It's just me," Floss had shrilled at her before the door was opened.

They stood in silence for a few seconds.

"Oh," said Bet.

"Had your supper yet?" Floss tried to make her tone easy and casual, but there was a nervous flicker in her throat very nearly bordering on hysteria. These were the first words she had spoken to Bet in more than a fortnight.

"Yes, just got through with it. I'm putting the stuff away," said Bet hoarsely.

"Mamma went to sleep while I was reading. She's pretty tired. I guess she'll go to bed right away. I just wondered— I thought—" Florence Mahanna hovered like a little hen, with the old brown cape around her.

The Butterfield girl said nothing. She put away the last piece of kitchenware and then slammed the damp towel upon a rack above the sink.

"I just thought maybe I'd make some marguerites pretty soon," Floss said. Thus she referred to a confection which she and Bet had both enjoyed before: the whites of eggs beaten into a thick cream, flavored with sugar and vanilla and spread on salted crackers to toast to a caramel brown in the oven. "I just wondered whether maybe you wanted to come over a while. I thought maybe we could play Flinch or something, or maybe you've got some fancywork. We could talk . . ."

Bet said firmly, "You know I never do any fancywork. All right. I guess I can come over a while." She went away to get her coat, and while gone she bellowed up the front stairway, "Mom, I'm going over to Floss's for a while," and there was a faint and answering mutter.

Mrs. Mahanna was awake again, fretting by the time they reached the house. Florence assisted her mother to the bedroom and endured again the labor of helping with undressing; she endured all the ugly detail of her mother's going-to-bed-toilet, the while Bet waited patiently in the living room. Bet had started the talking machine. It was an old model with cylindrical records. First Bet played the one new record Floss had bought that year: "We Were Sailing Along," with a whistling chorus; and then she put on a comic sketch about Uncle Josh going to the city.

"Tell Bet not to play that thing so loud," pleaded Mrs. Mahanna from the bedroom, and Bet snapped the switch as if in a rage.

Later, with the mother snoring again in stuffy distance, they did make the marguerites in the oven that was still hot, and they did play Flinch. They sat with knees touching slightly under the little table they used for their cards. Florence told Bet about Dolly Hessian's engagement to Ben Steele; the Butterfield woman merely grunted.

"I was wondering," said Florence at last with nervous reluctance. "I was wondering, Bet— You know, you talked about us maybe going down to Des Moines and going to a theater or something."

Bet stopped shuffling the cards and sat looking steadily at Floss. "You said you didn't think your mother would let you go."

"Well, I've been thinking. I thought maybe I could get Auntie Turnbull in to stay with her. You know. While I was away."

"You said your mother didn't like Auntie Turnbull."

With a slow gathering of venom within her, Florence Mahanna lowered her head and her voice, and spat the words out directly across the table. "I don't care if she doesn't. I'm going to go."

The black imitation-marble clock ticked its rusty notes across the room. Bet Butterfield was looking now, not at the girl opposite her, but at the clock on the shelf, the old clock with gilt posts at the corners. Then slowly across her big dark face there spread a rare and fatuous smile.

Twenty-One

Throughout the following week Ben Steele importuned and begged. Once committed to the project of matrimony which he had scorned or avoided theretofore (and which he had not regarded as even possible until that evening in his kitchen) he became ardent and reckless.

He spent so much time thinking about Dolly that he neglected many demands of his business. The November bills that should have been sent on the first of the month were not prepared until the sixth. Ben missed two appointments merely because he forgot—and one of those would have brought him an order for two wagons and a double buggy.

Furthermore Hilton Maxwell, the livery stable manager, was really ill with gall-bladder trouble, and might have to undergo an operation. The best workman in the carriage shop—Pete Stieger—was showing unmistakable symptoms of truculence which would assuredly end in a prolonged drinking bout, with Pete's skill lost to Ben Steele until Pete dragged himself back to work weeks later.

Usually by this time of the year Ben had all the sled-runners brought down from the barn, where they reposed during warm weather, to be checked against the possibility of an early season of snow. But Ben thought wisely that his marriage to

Dolly was more important than the consideration of any sleigh that ever slid.

Ben went into Fairchilds' jewelry store feeling bold and shy by turns, and keeping his hat pulled low over his eyes to shield his identity from the little country girls who whispered together over cards of bluebird pins. He bought from Abner Fairchild a fine diamond solitaire for sixty-five dollars, although local rumor soon set the price at twice that amount.

This concrete evidence of their troth was placed upon Dolly's finger, where its advent was greeted by fresh hysteria at the millinery shop and Mrs. Kristensen's. Secretly Dolly was a little miffed at what she considered the unnecessarily small size of the stone itself; but she demonstrated sufficient self-control and shrewdness to chide Ben prettily for his extravagance.

Her fiancé could not understand Dolly's reluctance to set an immediate date for the wedding. He supposed vaguely that it would be necessary for her to marry in her aunt's house at Lake Forest, Illinois, or at least in a church or chapel where her relatives and friends could attend. And for this he was prepared to journey to Chicago at the drop of a hat.

It he had but known it, Dolly was often sleepless among the problems that faced her immediately. Most certainly she wanted to make sure of the wedding to Ben: it would be a realization of the primary important step in the ascent she had planned for herself, although she had not known Ben Steele's name or even guessed of his existence when first she made her vows.

But if, according to Lexington idea, she "rushed him into marriage," many formless but thorny social obstacles would be set before her in the town. She was bound to make enemies, whatever occurred; but she saw no reason for making more than the minimum requirement of enemies. It was Ben who must be eager, who must be straining at the leash of single blessedness—not she.

Also there was the complex impediment of formal announcements, wedding invitations, the ceremony itself. In standard procedure a young woman who came to Lexington and achieved engagement to a man of the town would surely march him back to her own bailiwick for the nuptials. Dolly had observed this in the retrospect of gossip heard at Miss Cook's. And there seemed no logical reason for an elopement out of town.

She squeezed every resource of her craft to find a solution which would not too seriously impair her dignity.

The mendacious letter from Aunt Edna, delivered into her hand at the millinery store, had been a preliminary gun fired in her campaign; but its shot was not heard round the world, nor even around the municipality where she dwelt. Unfortunately Miss Cook and Miss Mahanna regarded Aunt Edna's abhorrence of Ben as disgraceful, and their admiration for Dolly stilled their mouths as effectually as adhesive tape.

When Ben, in the chaotic sessions of their talk, urged again and again for a date to be set, Dolly was forced into some kind of co-operation. She murmured, "Well, before Christmas, anyway," and Ben had to make the most of this uncertain assurance.

"But look here, sweetheart. I've got to know, so I can get things in shape if I have to go to Chicago."

"Oh, Ben. It's all so sudden and . . ."

"Sweetheart! You do love me, don't you?"

"Of course I do."

"Well, why couldn't we maybe run off to Fort Dodge or somewhere—maybe over to Webster City—and forget all about Aunt Edna and everybody?"

"It would look funny."

"Hell, I don't care how it looks. I want *you.*"

Very nearly he reached his bliss on a Sunday night, when Dolly, more physically weary and still more physically unrealized than she had felt in a long time, yielded to his comforting hands and mouth until these caresses stimulated her close to frenzy. It was a complimentary reflection on Miss Hessian's self-discipline that she did not visit the Steele upstairs then and there, and perhaps in some degree (the existing moral attitude of males being as duplex as it was) jeopardize her marriage.

But she brought herself into the decency which she was growing to detest, by a summoning of all restraint. She whispered to Ben that they must "wait until afterward," and the sulky young man stammered his apologies while Dolly smoothed down her gown and put her hair to rights.

She took no more chances after that. She said that she must not go to Ben's house alone with him; she didn't want to be talked about. If the element of haste were made too apparent, people would swear up and down that it was a shotgun wedding, and such calumny could not be disproved until many months had passed.

There was also the complication of Dolly's job with Miss Cook, or rather the cessation of it. In their original agreement Miss Cook had offered employment for a minimum of six weeks, and that period had elapsed before Dolly's engagement was a fact. Dolly knew that Agatha could not afford to retain a trimmer much longer, nor did she wish her to. Dolly Hessian now owned a nest-egg of over two hundred dollars which would serve to buy the articles she needed for her trousseau, and she wanted to place no strain on her friendship with the cotton-haired little milliner. She would need Agatha Cook's friendship in her new career, at least for a time.

Thus surrounded by the devils and deep seas of civilized dictates, Dolly drifted until nearly the end of November. There came a late-season flurry among the hats; the news of Dolly's engagement (officially unannounced, but made into fact by every machination of telephones, sewing circles and whist tables) had much to do with this last animation of Miss Cook's business. A few ladies, weak and low in the social system, crept fearfully into the shop in order to have their hats decorated by her who would soon be the wife of a prominent man.

But by the middle of the month Dolly had been able to take care of all this belated custom, as well as to build a backlog of merchandise with which her employer might face with confidence the sporadic occasional demands of winter. It was agreed mutually that Dolly's services should last be rendered on Saturday, November 18th. Thereafter she lingered at Mrs. Kristensen's as a solvent though unemployed boarder of indefinite tenure.

Dolly sewed for herself a new dress of peach-colored silk, with a draped skirt caught up with little flowers. Some deep-buried instinct which she would neither admit nor recognize told her that she could never be a spotless virgin, gliding altarward in purest white or even in egg-shell or ivory. If this breath of peach-bloom was to be her wedding gown, the representation she presented to the world was not wholly honest, either; but at least she would find satisfaction in the frock, since no corporeal Aunt Ednas or Cousin Hazels seemed indicated, and there existed no heirloom wedding-veil for her to don.

Dolly bought some black satin gloves of opera length, and, seated once more at the table in Miss Cook's rear room, she gave free advice from the sidelines and found the opportunity to make herself two delectable little hats: a toque, and a sailor hat—black, with a wide checked band. These would be ideal if she and Ben journeyed to New Orleans on their wedding trip, as they had talked of doing.

During the following week, when Ben Steele was in the courthouse on some matter pertaining to a deed, he found his interest and then his steps straying toward the office of the county clerk. He broke away, got as far as the front steps, and then went back into the clerk's office.

He said, "I want a marriage license."

He was a little annoyed with the clerk throughout the procedure. The old man seemed to think that it was necessary for Dolly to appear in person, too, along with Ben, and he acted as if only Ben's sound integrity in this community of his birth made the transaction legal or even plausible at all.

At first Mr. Steele thought that he would produce the license that very evening. He would unfold it before Dolly's gaze, and pray for immediate and salubrious results. But he felt abashed. It had not been fair of him to do this thing, and perhaps he would get Dolly talked about after all. Also the license was not valid in Illinois, whither they would probably go for the ceremony; Ben felt inclined to tear the paper up when he got home that night after taking Dolly to Mrs. Kristensen's. He did not do so. He read the license over again, including the finest type thereon; and wondered what his father would have thought. . . . He tossed uncomfortably, and to his annoyance had an unforgettable dream—not about Dolly at all, but about the hired girl who used to work for them before his father died.

On November the 29th, the afternoon before Thanksgiving Day, Ben left the harness store suddenly, cried for a horse and buggy, and drove rapidly about town hunting for Dolly. She was not at Mrs. Kristensen's. He walked the length of Sixth Street twice, entering stores where he thought she might be shopping, and then explaining his presence lamely when he found she was not there.

At last he went to Miss Cook's. It was dark by this time; and he should have gone there all along. He found Miss Cook in the act of departure. Warmed with relief although knowing the chagrin which he must soon admit openly, he spied Dolly busy at a table in the rear; and he made intended-to-be funny jokes about the gray weather of that evening.

Florence Mahanna fled jabbering at the advent of Ben. The lovers were left alone, with a last admonition to Dolly to be sure that the spring-lock was fastened tightly when she went out.

"I've been looking everywhere for you!"

"What for?"

"I've got to talk to you about something—"

"You ought to have looked here, silly."

"Dolly. Damn it, something has happened."

She looked up, startled. "You mean—" and the faltering note in her voice was honest without her making it so. "You mean some kind of—bad news?"

"Yes. They took Maxwell to the hospital about three o'clock this afternoon."

"Oh."

He stood above the opposite side of the table, frowning down at her. "Don't you see what that means? We can't have any wedding trip. It's that damn gall-bladder thing again, and Doc Conger says it's really serious this time. There'll have to be an operation, and even if he gets along all right he'll be out of the picture until January or maybe later."

"But I don't see why—"

"What can I do? I'm stuck. You see, every time I've gone away—I've only been away twice since Dad died—Hilton Maxwell was there to take charge of things. You know he's the livery stable boss and all that; but he's got a pretty good business head on his shoulders, and he could look in on the other stuff too. There isn't another soul I can trust who's capable of bossing the works. And now, with Pete out of it, the work will just pile up in the shop. We've got all this winter stuff coming along—sled bodies, repairs and things. The stable doesn't mean too much in the winter, except for boarding; but I can't forget that I'm still running a wagon and harness store. God *damn* it!"

Dolly said, "Don't swear. I got some bad news, too."

He gazed down at her weakly, his anger quieted by the tragedy in her tone. "What?"

For reply, Dolly rose and went to the sewing-machine near by, where her big handbag lay. In that bag reposed the photograph of Aunt Edna, Uncle McConnell, Spot, Spike and the rest. Dolly had visualized a scene something like this, but she had not known just when it would come about. With the only degree of preparation of which she was capable, she had carried that photograph in her bag for nearly two weeks.

She brought the picture to Ben, and he perused it, squinting under the green shade of the electric light over the table.

"Who's all these folks, honey?"

"My family. Of course Uncle McConnell's been dead a long time; but I always liked this picture: it brought back happy memories every time I looked at it."

Ben asked after he had swallowed delicately, "Is this one—Aunt Edna?"

Dolly came to peer past his arm. "No, that's Aunt Ellen. Aunt Edna's the one in the rocking chair." Her words fell soft beside him, but they seemed charged with a disagreeable menace. "Ben, darling, take a good look—"

He turned to her in perplexity.

"Because it's the last time you'll ever see this picture!"

She snatched the thing from his hands, ripped the cardboard across its middle, tore the two pieces again as Ben uttered a yelp of protest.

Dolly Hessian carried the pieces to the little stove in the corner of the room, lifted the lid and dropped the fragments on orange-hot coals. She watched them flame for a few seconds, and then replaced the lid. She stood, not turning to face Ben; and once she lifted her hands in front of her face, and then dropped them limply.

"My God," said Ben, "why on earth did you do that?"

"The letter's in my bag," whispered Dolly. "She says—I can't be married there. And she won't come here for the wedding."

Ben found the letter among crumpled little handkerchiefs. It was in the same envelope in which the first missive from her elderly relative had come to Dolly; but he would not know the difference—the mail-car cancellation was black enough and smudged enough . . . this letter had been written on the evening when Dolly decided to carry the photograph about with her, trusting that proper opportunity would occur for her to destroy it in Ben's presence.

There was no date on the letter, except "Tuesday" at the upper right-hand corner of the first page.

". . . I shall try to find the strength to mail this to you, my dear niece," said Aunt Edna. "No protests you can utter will sway me in the least. I cannot, with respect to our family, allow you to get married here, and certainly I will not come to Iowa to witness the event. I ask you again, how do you think your dear dead mother would feel if she knew that you were marrying a livery stable man? I would as soon see you married to a groom in a riding academy. You must realize, Dolly, that if you continue in this course, there can be no more love between us, and I shall not wish to see you again."

As she stood facing the stove (getting a little too hot at its proximity, scorching her face, but afraid to move for fear of injuring the dramatic effect) Dolly could feel Ben reading the letter; she did not need to see him. She could almost follow the words, her eyes mingled with his.

But she was not prepared for the roar with which he blasted the silence of the room and made her jump.

She turned swiftly. Ben hallooed again. His face was scrolled with laughter, his eyes were slits, his wide mouth was wider still with incontinent joy.

"Honey, you're just a little fool!"

Dolly tried to whisper, "It's really very serious, Ben," but he didn't hear her.

"Of course, you come by it naturally: she's an old fool and you're a young one. Livery stable! Good night, doesn't she know who I am? After all, I'm not a tramp, and I've got a few shinplasters in the bank. Does she know that I employ seventeen people—more than that, sometimes, when there's a rush on? I bet you never told her *that*. No, I bet you never did."

He stuffed the letter back into Dolly's open reticule, and then came round the table to take her in his arms. "Don't you worry about Aunt Edna. I've got a way with old girls like her. Say, why don't I call her up on the long distance? I'll bet ten dollars I can talk ten minutes and make her promise to let us be married in her best sitting room."

Dolly could only shake her head.

"Won't you let me try?"

"No."

"Aw, come on. Let me send a telegram, then?"

"No."

Dolly was affrighted mortally. She had not expected this reaction in Ben. She had thought that he would be insulted and furious . . . and now the whole construction of her scheme was trembling uncertainly in the wind of his humor, as it had swayed from other causes in the past, as her schemes would sway and tremble again.

She told Ben, distinctly and with solemn malevolence, "Ben. Listen to me, darling. Stop laughing. I repeat: you don't know Aunt Edna."

"No. But I bet—"

"You—don't—know—Aunt Edna. I hate her for saying these things. She deserves to be hated. I never want to see her again."

"Oh, come on! Remember she's an old woman, and she probably thinks a lot of you, and she has a lot of fussy flummy-duddle old notions like a lot of old hens around this town and—"

Then she was quiet for so long a time that Ben himself became a little alarmed. He put his hand under her chin and turned her face up to his.

"Ben. I mean it. Please don't mention Aunt Edna to me again, or—or any of them. Cousin Hazel or anybody. They're all alike."

"Well, I think you're being foolish."

She shook her head. Her eyes had grown somber.

"All right," said Ben after a while. "The question before the house is: what do we do now? Get married anyway—wedding trip or no wedding trip, Aunt Edna or no Aunt Edna?"

Dolly's gilt hair nodded against his chest. She dared not trust herself to speak.

"When do we get married?"

"Any time," she whispered. "As soon as we can."

Grown rough with incredulous delight, he shoved the girl away from him and whipped out his big leather wallet, to unfold and display the license carried there.

There was no longer any delay, no wish for any. Speed, haste, a whip lashing them to the gallop . . . they became busy with the telephone. Ben called the Methodist minister; then he told Dolly he didn't know who he wanted to "stand up" with him. He didn't have any particular friend among the men. There were several of the boys he liked a lot; but if he asked one, then some of the others might be peeved.

Who did she want?

She hesitated; then said, "Well, Miss Cook, if she isn't busy. After all, if it wasn't for her, we wouldn't have met."

"All right. But let me tell you one thing, darling."

"What?"

"Poor old Floss Mahanna. You'd better call her, too. She'll

feel pretty bad if she isn't there. Come on, call her; and then we'll go down to the Greek's and get something to eat. Then I want to go home and change my clothes."

"I want to change, too," said Dolly. "I don't want to get married in this old thing I've been wearing all day."

"All right. While you're calling, I'll run over to the barn and tell somebody to harness up. It'll take too long to run back and forth and everywhere on foot."

They did eat at the Greek's, though each went away leaving a steak only a third or a quarter consumed. Ben toasted Dolly solemnly in black coffee. . . . She began to reel in a daze, a kind of whirling lightness she had never felt before. It was as if she discovered that the fruits of her own sordid planning could be as real and luscious as any honest apples; and yet she scarcely dared reach up to pluck them.

At Mrs. Kristensen's, Dolly changed into the new peach silk. She took her gloves. . . .

"The hat," Ben had begged. "Please wear it tonight."

"Which one?"

"You know. The one I'm crazy about: the one you wore when you first came to town."

"Oh, that. But, Ben—with my new dress? I've got that little gray toque with the mother-of-pearl and the pink—"

"No, no. Do it to please me, Dolly. Please!"

She wore the midnight lace again, and she managed to smuggle out her pebble-grained traveling bag, scuffed corner and all. She held the wide folds of her coat to conceal the bag when she came down the stairs, and she could not have concealed it very well, but no one was in Mrs. Kristensen's living room or hallway just then.

They drove to the Methodist parsonage. Agatha Cook and

Florence Mahanna were waiting for them in the living room, the latter in a severe state of squeaking.

(Floss wondered what Bet Butterfield would think of all this—it was so romantic! Probably Bet would just growl. It was funny the way she acted about romantic things. Bet could get a lot more excited over the trip to Des Moines that they were going to have, than over a delicious match: a run-away elopement this was, almost—or it seemed like it.)

The Rev. Mr. Humphrey Kurchner accepted the license, examined it with formidable calm, and waited only on his wife and daughter to make up the balance of the wedding party. But a few minutes before the ceremony began there came a scuffling on the porch outside, and a peal of the big gong that operated by push-button through the door. Uncle Emory Buckland from the livery barn appeared, quite out of breath, and he was shocking in an old brown jacket with a stained sheepskin collar, and two of the buttons missing. His Grand Army hat was pulled tight on his head, and his hairy ears were pink with cold.

"I heard it," he kept chortling. "Alfy told me, down to the barn. He said, 'I got reason to think Ben's getting married to-night,' and I figured there was only one parsonage where a good Methodist like you would come!" and he brayed loudly, and jabbed at Ben with a dirty-nailed finger. He snuffled his nose during the ceremony, and his asthmatic breathing vied with the hollow accents of the Rev. Kurchner.

The happy couple stood in front of a false fireplace—before the mirror which lined the mantelshelf, opposite a large green and purple hand-painted plate—the artistic product of Mrs. Kurchner—and it was hung by gilt chains.

Dolly fastened her eyes against those chains. The roar of

her earliest impoverishments rose around her as she listened to the minister's reading of the service and gave her almost inaudible responses. Dolly Hessian was being hurtled at high speed into an existence long desired and suddenly almost frightful in prospect. . . . Ben had no wedding ring. A black cameo which had belonged to Miss Cook's mother was squeezed upon Dolly's finger. She was Mrs. Steele.

Floss Mahanna streamed her tears and made some spots on Dolly's dress which would never quite come out, though Dolly tried cleaning them with chloroform later on. There ensued a mild delirium of chatter and congratulation. Uncle Emory Buckland stabbed his finger squarely at Dolly's lip and told her that she had got a mighty fine young man; he went limping off toward the livery barn as the little party left the parsonage and hesitated on the short grass of the parking.

Ben said, "Let's all go down to the Greek's and get an oyster stew."

"I couldn't eat a thing," said Dolly, shivering.

"Let's all go to your house," said Miss Cook.

Floss said, "Hee-hee! That's right—let's go over to the house—Ben's house. It's only a block. I can make some marguerites or—"

Ben sent out his whistle, and stayed Uncle Em at the other end of the block. He called him back; the old man took the buggy and drove away to the stable.

The four people walked the short distance to the Steele house in silence almost complete. . . . Dolly's traveling bag creaked as Ben carried it. Florence Mahanna was almost overcome by the sound of the crunching leather handle . . . the presence of that bag conveyed such suggestion of intimacies and—and love and things—

The house loomed dark and tall. Ben had turned out all the lights when he left, although he had not locked the door (very few doors were ever locked in the town of Lexington).

They came into the house, and then shouts detonated around them. Lights were turned on. Faces seemed leering, hands gesticulating—the women shrieked shriller and louder than the men.

Surprise, surprise!

There were Congers, Cohens, Paisleys, Croys, a Duckett, a Lester. There was Ely Masterson (a bit nonplused as he thought of that attempted kiss under the box-elder trees), and also the two friendly young schoolteachers, and Mrs. Kristensen herself: practically all the people of her age or immediate association whom Dolly had known in Lexington, and those whom Ben had known best and longest and in the most comradely fashion.

Also enthroned in chilly sweetness on the buggy-seat bench was Miss Cornelia Ritchie, seeming no whit disturbed by Ben's marriage to this outlander—though her father was visibly disgruntled about it for a year at least. Miss Ritchie sang, "Somewhere a Voice Is Calling," and "I'll Take You Home Again, Kathleen" before the evening was over, accompanied on the piano very badly by Naomi Cohen; but this night her squawks could not penetrate the trance in which Ben Steele was walking.

"The guests," according to the newspaper account which followed on Friday, "brought well-filled baskets." It was a good thing that they did so: there was not much in the house to eat, and very little to drink.

A headline above the article said: *Popular Local Young Couple Steal a March on Their Friends.*

"How about sending a clipping to Aunt Edna?" Ben suggested jocosely on Friday.

"Please, Ben. Don't . . ."

"Oh, all right. I still think you're being childish."

But he didn't think her childish on that Wednesday night of their union, when the last guest had trampled vociferously from the porch, when empty pop bottles stood abandoned in odd corners, and the mound of paper plates and picnic leavings waited to complicate Mrs. Fachter's Thanksgiving Day.

He did not think her childish when finally they waited in his bedroom—their bedroom—where Ben had longed so often to bring Dolly, and where now he saw her turned ruddy in the dull light of a little lamp with ground-glass shade and clusters of frosty cherries.

"Ben."

"What is it, baby doll?"

"There's something I've got to tell you."

The laughter faded from his face. He seemed momentarily sadder, but also more adult and somehow more satisfying to Dolly the longer she looked at him. . . . This was no mistake. It was right. She had done these things deliberately, and had little conscience about it all. But this was right. She would be good for Ben; she would make him a wonderful wife. They would do things together. She would make him do them.

"Ben. It's one of those things: a girl— Can't you guess? Don't make it difficult, please, angel."

He sat solemnly on the edge of the bed. "Are you trying to tell me something about your—your past?"

"Yes."

"Was there another man?"

"Yes." She closed her eyes, thinking of all the men she had known in a Biblical sense, but considering them with rare repugnance. "Yes. There was a man. I was just a young girl. He took advantage of me. I ought to have told you before but—"

When she opened her eyes, frightened a little at not hearing Ben's response, she found that he was smiling drolly, and she had never taken such hearty assurance in anything before in all her life.

"Well, I guess maybe a wedding night is the best time for confessions, Dolly. I ran around a little, too—at college. Oh, I know how the fellows talk; they think it's all right for them to—to do some of the things we did; but they want the girl to be spotless."

"It's not fair," sobbed Dolly.

"Maybe not. But it doesn't matter." He watched her a while longer, and then whispered, "Put on your hat, hon."

"Now? My *hat*? Why, that would be silly."

"Put it on."

She obliged him in the end . . . she obliged, she gave unto him and he gave unto her. They found supreme and savage satisfaction undreamed or unimagined before. As she went to sleep in the exhaustion of Thanksgiving morning, Dolly turned to the young man lying beside her, and pushed her cheek against the hollow of his arm. She felt a strange timidity. She thought she was face to face with—a part of, a participant in—a circumstance so fragrant and compelling that it bordered on the bizarre.

Ben was comparatively untutored; and yet, driven only by the spur of his jolly lust for her, he had taught her things undreamed, unexperienced in previous encounters.

She thought idly, "Is this really love? I wonder." Could she have maintained such acquiescence throughout her existence with him, there would have been little complication and no tragedy.

Twenty-Two

Item from the Lexington *Daily Ledger* of Friday, December 1st, 1911:

> Miss Elizabeth Butterfield and Miss Florence Mahanna of this city are enjoying a pleasant Thanksgiving holiday vacation in Des Moines. They went down on the afternoon train, and tonight will witness Clyde Fitch's famous play, "The Blue Mouse" at the Princess Theater. Saturday they expect to witness another show, "Il Trovatore" presented by the Meridian Opera Company at the Coliseum. While in the Capital City the local young women will be guests at the Kirkwood Hotel.

Twenty-Three

In the conduct of Dolly Hessian's life as previously described, the attitude which she evinced in the preliminary stages of her marriage might be deduced easily. She was as self-conscious, as willfully crafty, as constantly scheming for a desirable effect, as she was before she married Ben Steele.

But a kind of softness grew within her at times. In the transport which she enjoyed with her husband, she yielded to a strange and comforting languor. It was difficult for the woman to convince herself that by this process of matrimony she had become economically more secure than most people —and solvent spiritually as well, if she wanted to be. Her prickling ambitions were lulled in winter nights by the activity of Ben Steele's body, and the good-natured generosity of his spirit.

Little boyishnesses, such as most men of his kind display in secret with women of their adoration—things like these were completely new to Dolly. They had not come into her experience even vicariously, except through the most casual acquaintanceship; and that was when she worked in other towns, and occasionally worked beside some honest young woman who was pressed into a relationship with Dolly that she believed to be friendly, and thus offered a confidence which Dolly had matched with lies.

The cousin with whom Dolly had been reared was a contemptible beast. The men with whom she had been associated later on were sometimes ardent, but through all such illicitness they were fencing as Dolly fenced. They, too, had their secret selves to guard from her.

She had not expected to possess a husband who, when the spirit moved him, would lope naked from bedroom to bathroom to bedroom, making sounds which he described as a perfect imitation of a dog after a rabbit. She had not expected that he would use words like "comfy" and "cuddly"; that he would, empowered by stray suggestion, launch into a detailed monologue about something that happened to him in the first grade of school; nor had she expected to hear him recite the virtues of a tomcat he owned when he was five.

There was a lack of dignity about a man so severely and permanently in love with her, which theoretically Dolly compelled herself to describe as absurd. But in actual practice she was charmed by the maudlin, endearing little things he did. Drowsily she felt herself tempted again and again to yield—to give the complete truth to him, to let his mercy, and his alone, determine what her future should be.

If she had trusted herself, she might have trusted Ben. Trust was something she had never known. Despite the tenderizing of her affections, she still did not recognize the existence of an honest and complete faith between two people.

There were minor frictions; not all the hours sang for them. Their first quarrel had its inception within twenty-four hours after the wedding ceremony.

The element of Mrs. Fachter in their domestic life brought an immediate abrasion. The woman had appeared early Thursday morning, while the young couple were still asleep;

and not having yet heard of the marriage, she regarded wonderingly the litter left through downstairs rooms by skylarking friends. Ben had not given a party since his father died. Two or three times he had had half a dozen men in to play poker in the dining room, but the other rooms had never been disturbed before. . . .

Awakened by the sound of carpet-sweeper and of dishes being rattled, Ben put on a blue cotton bathrobe and traipsed belowstairs to visit the tidings upon Mrs. Fachter.

The woman was a widow. Her only daughter lived nearly three hundred miles distant, and willingly Mrs. Fachter had volunteered to prepare Thanksgiving dinner for Ben, since apparently he was not invited out anywhere, not even to the Ritchies'. She was a woman incapable of demonstrating much surprise about anything. She smiled, she said, "Well, I never!" and then offered a doughy kind of congratulation, and went on with her cleaning.

When Dolly appeared, toward the noon hour, she was duly introduced; to Ben's mind the amenities had been well taken care of. They were all now embarked on a pleasant domestic journey, with Mrs. Fachter as chief engineer, stoker, and mess officer.

Dolly came back upstairs while Ben was shaving.

"Ben, who else is coming?"

"Nobody," he said through his lather.

"Well, she's made a mistake. I'd better go and tell her."

"What do you mean—a mistake?"

"She's got the table set for three."

Ben stood, razor in hand, regarding his bride with astonishment. "Why, sure. There are three of us."

By this time, Dolly knew just what he meant; but she was

determined to seem opaque before his simplicity. "No, you silly little boy— Not yet, anyway," she added, archly. "Just the two of us."

"Three. You, and me, and Mrs. Fachter."

"But, Ben, does she *eat* with us?"

"Why, sure. Like everybody else. Heck, she's a nice woman." He was frowning now. "What do you mean, anyway? She's a hired girl—I mean a hired woman—a kind of housekeeper; but she's always eaten with me. You know—like an aunt or something."

Dolly's gaze was the innocent stare of a kitten set down in a strange basket. "But, darling, does everybody do that in Lexington? I mean, do their cooks eat with them at table? Their servants? Why, it just isn't done."

He turned back to the lavatory basin in growing annoyance, and there was silence between them as he stirred his brush against the soap in the cup. "Look here, Dolly," he said (trying to instill a little humor into his tone, but being deadly serious in spite of it), "maybe you've picked up some funny ideas from your Aunt Edna and all those folks. I don't know how they worked those things in Chicago and places like that. As you well know, I've never been around in high society, or anywhere where they have butlers or stuff. Not many people here in town have hired girls; but, my gosh, I've been to the Pittengers' lots of times, ever since I was a kid. Their hired girl always eats with them; and *he's* president of the bank."

Dolly said, "I only thought— You see, you'll be working so much—you'll be busy all day. We'll be separated, darling. Oh, just think of it . . . separated for hours and hours. How will we ever get a chance to talk at meals? What could we talk about with—with another woman present?" She hesitated, and then asked, "What on earth did you talk about with her at meals, all those times?"

Ben regarded himself in the mirror, and seriously tried to remember just what he and Mrs. Fachter had talked about. He realized that they probably didn't talk about anything much. He might have told her about something that went on down at the carriage works or the livery barn; or maybe he had been silent, thinking over some matter of business; or probably—this last month or two—thinking about Dolly.

"Listen, snookums. I've got to shave."

Thus ended inconclusively the first round in the Battle of Fachter.

The Thanksgiving dinner was excellent, judged even by the high, homely standard of Mrs. Kristensen's table. It was, however, a sporadic meal, punctuated by frequent telephone calls from Ben's old friends and from Dolly's new ones. There was no soup; there were roast chicken with sage dressing, mashed potatoes, cranberry sauce, cubed turnips, the inevitable celery and olives, two or three kinds of pickles and sauces which Mrs. Fachter had "put up" late the previous summer, and both mince and pumpkin pie as dessert. The somber but bustling servitor had even made hot baking-powder biscuits to go with the chicken gravy.

Ben ate largely, between telephone calls, and talked with vociferation. Dolly observed that Ben's rigid table manners of their restaurant encounters underwent a rowdy alteration at home.

She was careful not to address Mrs. Fachter directly at any time during the meal. When she praised the chicken Dolly did so to Ben. She did not think that he would recognize or resent her attitude immediately; she wished only to suggest to him an austere disquietude—a pained experience of social degradation—perhaps the attitude evinced by the Duchess of Devonshire on finding herself compelled to lunch with a party of painted Zulus. Stolid as she was, Mrs. Fachter was still a woman; the patent frigidity of acceptance displayed by Dolly did not go unperceived by her.

All in all the first full day of this married career was crowded, confused, and not too satisfying to anyone. It would have been pleasant to loll about after the Thanksgiving dinner, to bask stupidly in cigar smoke, and Ben kept thinking of many personal treasures he would like to reveal to Dolly: things to point out, old family photograph albums to show her. There were relics she had not yet observed: two candy boxes filled with bullets, arrowheads, military buttons, faded and frayed pin-cushions which had a history, and the portable inkwell carried in his coat pocket by Long Dan's father, Thomas Steele, when first he came to America. It would have been pleasing if Ben could have spent the afternoon showing Dolly the little gold football of his recent college days, and the lash from the first carriage whip his father ever gave him.

But such ancestral worship was never theirs on this Thursday. Dolly fretted with persistent serenity to have her belongings brought over from Mrs. Kristensen's. Also Ben had to go down to the livery barn to look after things, because of Hilton Maxwell's enforced absence; he felt compelled to drive to the hospital to see Hilton. The sky was clammy, threatening snow for the whole of Lexington and Dodge County. And Dolly grew soggy inside, as she thought of the wedding trip to New Orleans which would never be hers.

She walked to the boarding-house while Ben was busy with

his other errands. She had asked him to bring an extra suitcase or two in the buggy when he came, so that she should not have to squeeze her clothes so tightly into the confines of her luggage. At Mrs. Kristensen's she met with raptures from other of the female boarders. They greeted her as a bride, and her sky grew proportionately brighter.

When Ben came he was downright worried about Hilton Maxwell's physical condition, and he was upset because Uncle Emory Buckland had had a violent disagreement with one of the stable boys, and the stable boy had quit. Now the barn was one man short until Monday.

Circumstances seemed to have been particularly venomous in allowing Dolly and Ben no dreamy surcease from the problems of the world at large—no protracted echoes of their first melodious mingling, no honeymoon worth having, no honeymoon at all.

They drove to the huge brown house on Third Street, and the light was already failing. Winter gathered around them.

"Ben. What about Mrs. Fachter? Does she go home on holidays like this, or does she stay to get your supper?"

"I don't know exactly. See, she's usually never there on Sundays or holidays. Let's see . . . Fourth of July . . . oh, I went on a picnic. I guess she didn't come at all that day. Of course Dad was still alive last year at this time. What does it matter, anyway?"

He put his hand around her knee, and pressed the little mound of flesh and bone and satin, happy again in his legalized lechery. "We don't care about her, do we? Anyway, I'm not hungry after that big dinner. We can get something out of the icebox."

"I was thinking about our room."

He regarded her with shock. "That isn't another notion you picked up from Aunt Edna? Don't you want to stay with me in my room?"

Dolly bent low and kissed his hand, and thus left no doubt of her intention. "That isn't what I mean. I wondered if you would consider moving into the front room? It would be larger for the two of us."

"That was Dad's."

"Yes, I saw his clothes in the closet there—I guessed they were his. You see, darling, it's such a little teentsie-weentsie bit of a closet in your bedroom—you hadn't thought about your wife's clothes, had you?—and there are two closets in front. I looked."

Ben meditated. "Guess you're right—that would be the sensible thing to do. I've been intending to give those clothes of Dad's away, but I don't know anybody they'd fit. Probably Reverend Kurchner would know somebody who was—you know—deserving. I'd hate to just give them away at random."

He regarded Dolly with conviction showing in his face. Several times on this day she had exclaimed to herself, aware of new powers of personality that lived within Ben. Perhaps there was something about their relationship that made him more able, more adult. Perhaps really and truly she was good for him. Again she put her face against his hand. Her little tongue came briefly out between the borders of her lips and touched his skin.

Ben drove up and stopped in front of the house. He was still prospecting the vein of emotion to which he had turned a moment before. "Seriously, Dolly, here's the way I feel. You know I was pretty crazy about my father—"

"I know. . . ."

"Well, it sounds funny, but that room of his—it was something like a shrine that the Catholics have. Once in a while last year (funny, I don't mind telling you this) when I was mixed up, wondering about things, I'd go in there and just stand quietly for a while. I wouldn't sit down on the bed or anything; just stand. Sometimes I'd go and open that closet—the one in the corner where you saw his clothes—and I'd look at his old coats hanging there, and think about him."

Dolly said in a faint voice, "Then I won't mention it again, if you really feel that way about it. Maybe," she added, reverently, "we ought to keep that door closed all the time."

"Now, listen. That isn't what I mean at all. I mean—Well, now we've got a household again—I mean now there's a Mr. and Mrs. Steele—maybe we ought to be in that room. It just hadn't occurred to me before. What do you think about it, hon? Of course you never knew Dad; but from the little things I've told you, do you really think we ought to? I think maybe we ought to. I think maybe Dad would like to have us in that room."

"I think so, too, Ben."

So within the hour, they moved bag and baggage into the larger room where Madison Steele's wife had berated him through all of Ben's infancy—where Mad had slept sternly, at last peacefully in the virtue of his widowerhood, and where an odor of moth-balls would linger for long unless exorcised by Dolly's perfume.

Mrs. Fachter had not approved of this abrupt change of sleeping base. She was still at the house when they arrived with the suitcases, and while Ben carried the relics of his father into the attic, Mrs. Fachter came up to the second floor, ostensibly to help in the moving, actually to make her resentment felt by Dolly.

"This was always Mr. Steele's room," she told young Mrs. Steele lugubriously.

"So my husband told me."

"The other one—Ben's room at the side— That gets the morning sun first, because it's on the east," said Mrs. Fachter. "Where do you want this here bag put down?"

"Just anywhere."

"Because it's on the east, it gets the sun first. That's a lot more healthy."

Dolly disciplined herself, cramming back her antipathy. She spoke with brightness of the two closets and the extra dresser in this larger chamber. "And there's that little balcony on the front. Isn't that cute? There's room to walk out there, too."

"Those timbers ain't safe. I heard the man say so when he was patching some new shingles on the roof. It ain't safe."

"Then we'll have them fixed up, and a new floor put in the little balcony. I love the idea of—"

"Cost you a lot of money," said Mrs. Fachter. "Money don't grow on trees." Poor soul—she knew.

Dolly did not pity Mrs. Fachter for her poverty; she had known plenty of poverty of her own. It was well that Ben was in the attic, stowing away the last lot of his father's clothing against the day of charity. Dolly's face was suddenly as hard as a rock, and so was her voice as she addressed this stocky, disgruntled woman before her.

"If you please, Mrs. Fachter, I am the lady of this house.

I am not interested in your opinions about what rooms we occupy or anything like that, or how much money is spent, or if repairs are made. Those matters are none of your concern. Now, do we understand each other?"

Mrs. Fachter made an explosive sound, something between a gulp and a growl. She left the little bag which she had just brought, and moved abruptly away—away from Dolly, away from the front room, away from the menace now disrupting her workaday existence of many months.

She called up no good-bye to the young people. She did some light chore or other in the kitchen . . . the water was running for a minute. Then she went away, slamming the front door loudly.

Ben came clattering down the attic stairway. "What was that?"

"What?" asked Dolly, her arms full of princess slips.

"That bang."

"It must have been the door downstairs."

Ben went to the head of the stair and called down for Mrs. Fachter without result.

"I think she's gone," said his bride.

"Well, holy gee! She doesn't have to break the house down when she goes. She—" He returned to the bedroom to survey Dolly with curiosity. "Say, I never heard her slam the door like that before. Did you have a row with her, or anything?"

Dolly's voice was muffled in the darker reaches of her clothes closet. "She was impertinent."

"Impertinent? What—"

Dolly told him. A written transcription of her testimony

would have been substantially correct, but she managed to convey a picture of a Mrs. Fachter grown somewhat more rampageously defiant than a Yaqui Indian.

Ben opened the front door and tested the balcony cautiously with his foot. "That floor does give a little. Guess I better have it fixed. Oh, well, Dolly, I suppose it won't work. I guess maybe she is a bossy old woman."

"She doesn't know her own place."

"Well, what on earth is her place?" cried that embattled democrat, Ben Steele. "I tell you, you'll have to get a lot of these Lake Forest upper-crust ideas out of your head. You're not at Aunt Edna's—you're in Lexington, *Iowa.* And the hired girls *eat with the folks.*"

When Dolly did not reply, Ben fell into worse temper than ever. By this time he was disgusted with himself for raising his voice at Dolly at all. He was angry because he had not comported himself in a more coolly masterful fashion; he was hurt at the mere imagining of the hurts he inflicted on Dolly. Thus he yelled the louder.

Presently he heard a little whinny. His wife stood in the closet after she had hung up her last batch of dresses. She remained there, with face turned away from him. His impulse was to rush and snatch her into his arms and cover her face with kisses, and her neck too, and . . .

While still he fought a losing battle against affectionate impulse, Dolly came back out of the closet. She touched her eyes briefly with her handkerchief and didn't look at Ben when she spoke. "Darling," she said evenly, "don't you think you'd better get dressed? After all, it's getting late. What time are we due at your friends'?"

A hasty reception for bride and bridegroom had been arranged by the Paisleys, to be held in the home of Mrs. Paisley's father—Mr. Alfred Pittenger. There the Steeles would see the majority of those persons whom they had seen the previous night, with the exception of Florence Mahanna. Floss had indeed been thought of—her name had been put down upon the list temporarily, so to speak—but in the long run it was thought that Floss would not "fit in." In this the arbiters were quite correct, though Miss Mahanna waited hopefully all that day for a call—she was sure that someone would give a party for Dolly. The only communication she received was one in person from Bet Butterfield, who wanted to talk again about Friday's excursion to Des Moines. It seemed that Bet just couldn't talk about anything else.

In the Pittenger home on Thanksgiving evening, Dolly and Ben would have a strain between them. Because of the argument over Mrs. Fachter, they would be uncomfortable when the eyes of one found the eyes of the other in unrevealed exchange. They would laugh mechanically at jests made by Sylvester Cohen; they would eat turkey sandwiches and oyster stew. Several of the men would enjoy "snifters" in the kitchen, and would then nibble Sen-Sen in order to kill the odor of their breath. This would be a postnuptial celebration in which the honorees found the least joy of anyone.

All these things occurred as might be expected. Also, as might be expected, a not-too-late hour found the young Steeles bedded before the gloomy headboard of old mahogany which had reflected the unbalanced hysterics of Ben's mother in her time. Once more they were together beneath sheet, blanket and comforter. They had their taut moments. There was Ben's blurted apology, Dolly's small-voiced acceptance of the same. . . . Then they were disporting again, forgetting that they had been exhausted by animal antics of the night before, believing again that they had found something unique—something wholly remarkable—a secret which no demand of generosity might ever permit them even to hint to the rest of the world.

Twenty-Four

Before the next week was out, the corrosive threat of Mrs. Fachter was removed from their presence, and Dolly made sure that there should be no repetition of the unfortunate contretemps which had arisen in the table set for three.

She advertised—not locally, because everyone would know who was advertising—but in the Webster City *Freeman-Tribune* and the Fort Dodge *Messenger*. Letters came in response. Toward the end of the week Dolly entrained for Fort Dodge, ostensibly on a shopping tour, looking winsome and pale-eyed under her new gray toque.

When she returned that evening, Dolly was leading a spindle-shanked young Negress, with straight black hair and bony shoulders. This girl rejoiced in the name of Valeria, but said that the lady she worked for had always called her Larry. She was installed in a small rear room at the head of the back stairs, and turned out to be a cook with skill inferior to that of Mrs. Fachter. But she knew all about finger bowls; she served with grim determination from the left side even if she had to walk all the way around the long table to do so. And when Dolly gave her first tea party, Valeria—in a pink uniform, white apron and large pink bow at the back of her head—nearly frightened the other women into fits. There was a discomfort which might attend the infliction of liveried servants on those unaccustomed to them. When Valeria entered the room with a tray of sandwiches, conversation ceased abruptly, to be resumed only on her departure.

Ben took the banishment of Mrs. Fachter with humor; quite unknown to Dolly, he awarded the lady an honorarium of twenty-five dollars for her faithful service, and in whispers suggested his regret that things hadn't worked out the way he had hoped. The woman went away to her square cottage in Shoetown, and proceeded to eke out a precarious existence as a practical nurse. She slipped on the ice long afterward, and lay for months suffering with a fractured hip which did not mend properly. Three people, of the dozens she had served in Lexington, came to see her at the hospital. Dolly did not visit Mrs. Fachter, but she alone sent flowers—six carnations. They wilted in a horrid green vase beside the patient's bed in her ward, and were removed by the nurse one by one as they grew repulsive. At last Mrs. Fachter was conveyed to the home of her daughter in South Dakota, where she lived a long time—partially crippled, playing Lotto with her grandchildren—a burden to all except the Lotto players.

On Saturday the 16th of December, 1911, Dolly Hessian Steele became a woman of substance for the first time in her life.

Financial arrangements had been makeshift and furtive in the earliest days of their marriage. To tell the truth, Ben had not thought about money for a week at least. And then, when Dolly brought home some material for pretty house-dresses and aprons, he asked her where she had got the money.

"Don't be silly. I have money."

"Well, anyway, I hope you charged it. I mean, to me. Where did you get it?"

"Spillman's. I never thought about charging it. I paid cash."

"Well, don't do that. Say, look here. I'm pretty thoughtless. I hadn't thought about it at all. You just charge anything you want, anywhere, and they'll send me a bill. But I guess women have to have pin-money or something."

He looked in his pocket and found only three crumpled one-dollar bills and some change. That afternoon he sent an employee to the bank, and later Dolly found a fifty-dollar bill tucked into her purse. She spent the money joyously on three new lamps to replace some of the more particularly hideous objects in the downstairs rooms.

Ben praised her choice dutifully, aloud. Secretly he would miss one lamp he had always admired: the box-shaped shade was made of stitched buckskin, and had ears of corn painted on it, with other corn shocks in the background, and a big moon coming up. He hunted this lamp, found it on the back porch where Dolly had dumped it to be carted away, and Ben smuggled the lamp to the attic, in the thought that some day he might furnish up a den for himself or something.

But she would need money of her own—no denying that. So on that Saturday of importance, with Christmas looming ahead, he came home in the evening so obviously possessed of a happy secret that Dolly was far ahead of his realization in her imaginings.

Larry had set the table already, but Ben turned the plates over on their faces, and when Dolly lifted hers, she found a green bankbook bearing the imprint of the Dodge County Savings Bank, Alfred E. Pittenger, President. Inside, Dolly's name had been inscribed together with the amount of the deposit.

"Ben! What—? I never dreamed—"

He grinned across his bowl of too-salty beef soup. "Remember I said something about pin-money?"

"But, Ben! A thousand dollars! You know I told you I had some money of my own." She had, too: exactly seventy-six dollars and thirty-five cents left in her Chicago account.

"Well, let's call it salary—your wages for being a wife. 'A laborer is worthy of her hire'—at a salary of a thousand dollars per something or other."

"But I don't want you to go broke."

"Oh, I kept a shinplaster or two for myself."

With the precious green book in her top bureau drawer among powder-boxes and hair pins, and with folds of currency in her new red purse, Dolly thought with scorn of her former impecunious self, as she walked the bustle of Sixth Street bound on her Christmas shopping. Not all of the money, however, was destined to be spent on Christmas presents, or to repose cherished safely in the coffers of the bank. Some thirty-nine dollars went into a pair of greedy hands, and quite unexpectedly.

Only a few evenings before Christmas, Dolly was hastening homeward up Hazel Street, tripping carefully in her new overshoes across the puddles of forming ice, and progressing more slowly through the unshoveled snow of the vacant lot north of the Methodist church. A man stood behind one of the huge elm trees in front of the Steele house and watched her as she approached along the clearer distance of Third Street. He recognized Dolly, and put himself carefully back into black shadows again.

When she came opposite the tree, he stepped out, calling softly, "Hello, Dor," and putting a firm hand on her sleeve.

Dolly fought back a scream. She stared through gloom,

and made out the wan face of that same young man who had hurled a grape-juice bottle after her on the Chicago West Side.

"Don't you recognize me? It's Rick."

"What are you doing here? Let go my arm . . ."

"I want to talk to you a minute."

"How did you know I was here? How—?"

He said, "Oh, I was riding the blinds. You told Ma you were coming out here. We hadn't heard anything, and I thought I'd stop and take a look."

"Where are you going?"

"Out west. Maybe California. I know a gink in Oakland, California, that I think can get me a job out there."

"But how—?" She might have screamed if Ben were home. She might have whipped Ben on with her yells to pursue Rick to the boundaries of the town, to beat him into a senseless pulp . . . if she cried that Rick was a tramp, perhaps Ben would shoot him. But Rick might say something first, and anyway, Ben was still in the harness store. She had seen him inside, busy with customers, when she came past. She waved to him through the frosty glass, but he did not see her. She had smiled and hurried along. . . .

Into her contentment, into the smoothness of her Lexington life and all the violent ambitions she held, this ugly pollution was now injected . . . she wanted to scream. . . .

She demanded in a fierce whisper, "How did you know I lived here?"

The thin voice said, "That never bothered me much, Dor. It was easy. I've still got a little change in my pocket. I found a kid and gave him a dime to go into the millinery stores and ask if Miss Hessian worked there. The first place they just said No. I gave him another dime. The second store was it. They told the kid that you weren't there any more—that you were married to a gink named Steele—and where you lived, and they wanted to know why he wanted to find out. But I guess he didn't tell them anything. He was a pretty smart kid."

"How long have you been here? Where have you been hanging around?" She wondered with impotent fury how many people he had told about her. Oh, God, who had he talked to? Who—?

He said that he had talked to no one, he taunted her with his laughter, he gloried in the fright he put upon her soul. All the time she was staring past his shabby shoulder, his thin shoulder, now grotesque in a dirty overcoat too large for his body. She was gazing down the block against the lights of distant Hazel Street, and hoping and fearing that she would see Ben coming there.

"Oh, I just hung around in the pool hall. Got something to eat and— Well, I guess you know, Dor. I'm pretty flat. I need a little money."

"No!"

"Come on. Nice lady like you, married to a nice guy, probably— Can't you spare a few nickels? I was looking at your house. Pretty nice. I saw a nigger walking around inside—there in the front room. That's pretty nice. You got a nigger working for you; you don't have to work like a nigger yourself. So how about it?"

"If you don't get out of town on the next train," said Dolly, "if you ever come back— God damn you, Rick—"

"Suppose I go downtown and bust a couple of window-lights, or get in a fight or something. Then maybe I get arrested, then maybe I say, 'You call up Mrs. Steele. She'll get me out of trouble. She—' "

Dolly contemplated this frightening possibility; but she was not particularly frightened by it after a moment's thought. Her mind was defter than Rick's—it was rising far beyond his fabled invention.

"No, I guess you won't do that."

"Why not? I might."

"I know why. You wouldn't want the police to pick you up. You probably got in some trouble in Chicago. You'd never have left there in the middle of winter—riding on freight trains and things, or baggage cars. No, not you. You'd hang around some nice warm—"

Now it was Dolly who put her hand on the man's arm, and he gazed down at her stupidly, though she could not see the expression of his face in the shadows. She said, "Rick. Quit your kidding. Do you know what I'll do? If you try to go to my husband or anyone else in this town, and try to tell them about me, and where I came from and who you are, and—and try to tell them things—I'll shoot you."

He looked at her in silence. Not in all their years of feud and mutual hatred had Dolly ever threatened to kill him before.

"I've got an Iver & Johnson revolver. My husband bought it for me. He taught me how to use it, because I was afraid about burglars. I'll shoot you. I'll shoot you dead, and then I'll say that you were a neighbor boy in Chicago, and that you raped me. That's what I'll say. How would they know you didn't"—she got the words out again—"rape me?"

"Don't try to buffalo me," Rick snarled.

"I'm not kidding, either," she said quietly. "You ought to

know I'll do it. You ought to know I'll do anything I say I'll do."

The look which he gave her was frantic—although there could be no discernment by Dolly through the chilly darkness. Swiftly the man reached forward, snatched Dolly's purse from under her arm, and ran away carrying the purse, fleeing down the block toward the Methodist church, slipping on the ice and nearly falling again and again.

"This time," Dolly thought as she watched him go, "I am the one who ought to have a bottle to throw."

When he had passed the corner, looking back only once, she went slowly with hesitant tread along the path he had taken. She passed a man she did not know, coming her way. The man was looking back. He had seen Rick running.

When Dolly rounded the church corner fearfully, she saw her bag before her, plainly discernible on a snow-bank. Little things were scattered all around. The money purse had been ripped out; the ribbon which fastened it was torn in two and Dolly's mirror was broken. She retrieved the bag, wiped away the dirty snow, and never told Ben what had happened. She lived in worry until after Christmas, but Rick was gone. He must have ridden away: she heard nothing of him around the town, nor saw him again.

Twenty-Five

The winter, spring and summer of 1912 went down in Lexington history as an era when more change befell in manners than at any similar time. Recording angels may have written the facts in their ledgers; but no concrete cross-indexed notations were kept by anyone locally concerning the direct and indirect effect of Dolly Hessian Steele in their midst.

As assuredly as the young lady made her alterations of the decor in the Steele house and in her husband's subsistence, so did she have her deliberate and sometimes relentless way with the structure of Lexington itself.

There were more parties given during December, January and February, for instance—that is, large-scale, dress-up parties—than had generally been held in any twelve-months period before. It was incumbent upon all of Ben's old friends to attempt elaborate entertainment of the newly wedded pair. Dolly fired back such suppers with reciprocal determination as fast as they were offered. In addition a number of families with whom Ben had never enjoyed much personal contact and no rapport whatsoever, felt themselves turned plastic beneath the social manipulation of the wide-eyed, daintily spoken companion of Ben's bed.

Mr. Steele had not thought that his married life would be quite like this. He had imagined evenings (looking happily ahead into the apple-pie-scented, fire-warmed domesticity portrayed in advertisements and cartoons) when he and Dolly would be contentedly alone, perhaps popping corn or stirring batches of the same perfect fudge which she had created for him on the night of their engagement. . . . There was really very little opportunity for such cosy kitchen adventures. The few nights when they were home alone, Ben was usually tired out, and went to sleep on the sofa in the living room; and one evening actually slept for two hours doubled up on the old buggy-seat divan in the parlor.

This same buggy-seat divan served as a symbol of the stalwart ugliness with which Dolly knew Ben's life had previously been encumbered. Uncle Emory Buckland was another symbol. Dolly had not been aware before her marriage (or, if informed, had no recollection of the fact) that on every Friday night Uncle Em ate his supper at the Steele home. This rite had been instituted by Long Dan Steele, and not even the ferocity of Ben's mother had served to extinguish it: it happened that Ben's maternal grandfather and Uncle Em were comrades-in-arms and both had been wounded at Jackson, Mississippi, on July 12th, 1863.

Each Friday afternoon Mr. Buckland put on "his clean shirt" before coming to the Steele's and Dolly was compelled to find some gratification in this, though the old man never wore a necktie. After all, Uncle Em put on only one clean shirt each week; Ben told Dolly dryly that she should feel honored to be the first to see him in it.

In the beginning Dolly had hoped that the veteran might be frightened away by the presence of a full-fledged maid in uniform; but she soon saw that this was not to be. Uncle Em persisted in calling Valeria "Dinah." He teased her about her hair-bows, and threatened to sell her into slavery when she burned the biscuits. Dolly feared that Larry would be furious, would resign and go back to Fort Dodge; but nothing of the kind occurred. Larry called Uncle Em "that funny little old grandpa," and tittered constantly while he was in the house.

The young Steeles ranged busily through the reorganized life of Lexington—Dolly leading on, Ben following gamely for the most part, but occasionally balking and hauling back against the halter-rope by which he was led.

The calendar chronology of a few weeks in late spring or early summer of that year would suggest, better than lengthy exploitation, the pattern of events:

Wednesday, May 15th. Meeting of the Wednesday Whist Club at the home of Mrs. J. J. Van Dorm. Mrs. Ben Steele, chairman of the recently instigated bridge committee, reports on progress in auction bridge lessons. Sixteen of the twenty members now proficient at auction bridge. Moved and seconded that name of club be changed to Wednesday Lily Auction Bridge Club. Touching protests from minority group. Mrs. Ben Steele suggests prettily that vote be postponed until next week. This is agreed by extra-parliamentary procedure.

Thursday, May 16th. Dusk. Mr. and Mrs. Benjamin Steele, riding behind Barnum, visit site of new Lexington Country Club along banks of Inkpadutah River and Blacksnake Creek, north of town. Mr. Steele gloomy over country club prospects: thirty-two per cent of group's stock still unsold. Steeles encounter Mr. and Mrs. Wayne T. Croy, also driving to explore region, but in motor-propelled equipage. Barnum disturbed at approach of vehicle: Dolly frightened. Ben, restraining horse, mollified to hear enthusiastic report from Mr. Croy: two new memberships sold that afternoon. Party repairs to Croy home. Gentlemen engage in game of Seven-Up; ladies discuss combination corset-cover and open petticoat drawers in process of construction by Mrs. Croy. Dolly makes delicate suggestions as to embroidery. Suggestions adopted.

Friday, May 17th. Dolly appears on Hazel Street in new hobble-skirt—the first seen in Lexington, excepting those worn by actresses visiting city during previous March. Hobble-skirt discussed lengthily by entire population witnessing garment. Miss Elizabeth Butterfield makes sneering remark to Miss Florence Mahanna. Miss Mahanna in tears. Mr. Steele astonished on arrival home to find wife clad in hobble-skirt. Protest uttered, but Dolly suggests certain old styles now outmoded, certain new ones coming in. Uncle Emory Buckland, arriving for supper, appealed to by Ben. Dolly resents appeal, points to buggy-seat divan as shocking example of antique object undesired in modern world. Buggy-seat divan defended bitterly by gentlemen. Ben sullen at supper; Dolly martyr-like; Uncle Em reminiscent concerning battles participated in by Third Iowa Volunteer Infantry.

Saturday, May 18th. Relations between Mr. and Mrs. Steele somewhat strained during daytime encounters. Buggy-seat divan defended once more by Mr. Steele. Spouse silent. Mr. Steele apologetic, later ardent in nighttime encounter. Relations no longer strained.

Sunday, May 19th. Many members of recently-born Lexington Country Club Association foregather on banks of Blacksnake Creek to observe and discuss alterations being made in terrain, foundations being laid for rustic club house, projected golf-course, etc. Mr. Steele states determination not to engage in "sissy game." Plays One-Ole-Cat valiantly with friends while ladies prepare picnic lunch amid lumber and log-piles. Cold fried chicken, potato salad, cole slaw, baked beans, sandwiches, olives, etc., etc. consumed in quantity by party. Discussion of country club improvements leads to discussion of proposed municipal improvements. Ben Steele makes effective if impromptu speech in favor of suggested curb-and-gutter construction on West Third, Fourth and Fifth Streets. On way home, Mrs. Steele timidly comments on husband's fitness for public office. Husband amused.

Monday, May 20th. First attendance of Mr. and Mrs. Benjamin Steele, newly elected members, at Monday Supper Circle. Supper held at home of Mr. and Mrs. Bernard Ritchie. Mrs. Ritchie hospitable and kindly to new female member of club; Mr. Ritchie chilly. Vocal solos following supper: "Somewhere a Voice Is Calling," "I'll Take You Home Again, Kathleen" and "Just a' Wearyin' for You," sung by Miss Cornelia Ritchie. Mr. and Mrs. Steele later compare opinions as to Miss Ritchie's interpretative art, in bedtime session; rejoice to find opinions identical and unalterable. Love-passage of enthusiasm between Mr. and Mrs. Steele.

Tuesday, May 21st. Florence Mahanna encountered about 6 P.M. by Mrs. Steele, near Methodist church corner. Mrs. Steele admits to pitiful sense of loss because Miss Mahanna has not been more frequent in attendance at Steele home. Miss Elizabeth Butterfield observed waiting grimly beside courthouse steps. Miss Mahanna weeps, kisses Mrs. Steele in hasty departure, runs away to join Miss Butterfield. Ladies retreat in southerly direction through courthouse park. Mrs. Steele, observing departure, is contemptuous, disgusted, also soothed at being rid of onerous social obligation.

Wednesday, May 22nd. Wednesday Whist Club votes officially, during afternoon session at home of Mrs. R. A. Lester, to change name to Wednesday Lily Auction Bridge Club. Bridge played by four tables; whist by one. Terrific rainstorm before evening, approaching proportions of cloudburst. Mrs. Steele arrives home in liquid condition. Mr. Steele, arriving late and equally drenched, relates gloomily how freshet is reported to have washed out preliminary construction of dam on Blacksnake Creek where Lexington Country Club planned to construct private swimming pool. Mr. Steele bitter in affirmation of wasteful expense of country club idea; declares it was not his idea; declares country club in town size of Lexington complete nonsense. Mrs. Steele weeps in bedroom. Mr. Steele apologizes later, also in bedroom. Mr. and Mrs. Steele reunited in affection, and in bedroom.

Thursday, May 23rd. Splendid dinner party given by Mr. and Mrs. Benjamin Steele. Duke Laidlaw, local popcorn merchant, retained for evening and disguised as family servitor in white coat. Guests confused; do not know whether to ignore Duke when he opens front door for them, whether to shake hands quietly, or whether to say, "Hello, Duke—where's the peanuts?" Ancient social institution (division of dinner party by sex immediately following end of meal) revived by charming hostess. Ladies ill at ease in parlor; men ill at ease in dining room. Miss Cornelia Ritchie obliges with two delightful musical readings: "The Two Marionettes" and "In the Usual Way." Guests depart. Certain ladies discuss Mrs. Steele in uncomplimentary fashion during homeward journey, but all admire table decorations. Duke Laidlaw, no matter what his age, seduces Valeria at late hour among lilac bushes in backyard. Seduction unwitnessed, unchronicled by contemporaries, but wholly satisfactory to participants.

Friday, May 24th. Mrs. Steele worried, fearing pregnancy.

Mr. Steele unappraised of condition, but would have been delighted. Mr. Steele entertaining paternal ambitions. Uncle Em puts in early appearance at supper; Dolly retires, pleading headache, still fearing pregnancy. Reminiscences of campaigns of Third Iowa Volunteer Infantry at supper table. Uncle Em departs. Weary Mr. Steele goes to bed early and sleeps heavily; weary and frightened Mrs. Steele doesn't sleep until late hour.

Saturday, May 25th. Death of Mr. Hilton Maxwell after long illness. Mr. and Mrs. Steele call on bereaved widow. Mr. Steele affirms that surviving son and son-in-law may have employment at livery barn if necessary. Mr. Steele, stricken into serious frame of mind by circumstances, later recites views to wife on man's responsibility to fellow men, to nation in general, to family and community in particular. Mrs. Steele suggests public office such as member of county board of supervisors, or possibly even mayoralty of Lexington. Mr. Steele silent and thoughtful.

Sunday, May 26th. Mrs. Ben Steele definitely *not* pregnant. Mrs. Ben Steele definitely relieved. Mr. Steele blissfully ignorant of facts. Picnic supper at country club grounds, where dam repairs proceeding well, and framework of rustic lodge now handsome. Cold fried chicken, baked beans, cole slaw, potato salad, olives, etc., etc. Mrs. Steele feeling frail; Steeles retire at early hour.

Monday, May 27th. Funeral of Mr. Hilton Maxwell. One of horses drawing hearse frightened while casket being removed from church. Near runaway. Later Mrs. Steele speaks mind to husband about danger of horse-drawn hearse as compared with motor hearse. Mr. Steele, miserable as result of obsequies, returns savage defense of all horse-drawn vehicles and horse-drawn activity as compared with stinking, greasy, expensive, explosive, unreliable, dangerous automobiles. In absence of proper consummation of mutual affection, Steeles find slumber in sad condition, back-to-back.

Tuesday, May 28th. Buggy-seat divan enters Steele conversation again. Relations strained.

Wednesday, May 29th. All five tables play bridge at meeting of Wednesday Lily Auction Bridge Club, held at home of Mrs. E. I. Masterson. Evening reception given by Senator and Mrs. A. B. A. Newgate to members of Dodge County Bar and a few carefully culled friends. Mrs. Ben Steele ravishing in white taffeta gown with Robespierre collar. Senator Newgate again plans ravishment of Mrs. Steele. In private discussion near vines of side porch, Senator Newgate again tells Mrs. Steele that latter reminds him of defunct infant daughter who would have been just about her age. Senator Newgate asks permission to bestow fatherly kiss. Tête-à-tête interrupted by approach of other guests. Situation unresolved.

Thursday, May 30th. Memorial Day. Decoration of graves of departed Steeles by Ben and Dolly. At 2 P.M., Memorial Day procession, with Uncle Emory Buckland prominent as color-bearer of Grand Army Post. Convocation at cemetery marred by runaway. Steeles discuss horses again—Mrs. Steele discussing horses with especial disfavor, and also prophesying day when Lexington will be overrun by garages. Mr. Steele unconvinced and hurt. Mrs. Steele declares only her affection and loyalty prompted remarks. Mr. Steele embraces Mrs. Steele.

Friday, May 31st. Mr. Alfred E. Pittenger and two other distinguished men of prominence call on Ben Steele in harness store. One candidate for city council in June elections has withdrawn suddenly from race. Mr. Pittenger rings appeal to Ben to serve as candidate. Ben says he hasn't time. Mr. Pittenger says, "I've got a notion to talk to your wife." Ben says, "For God's sake, don't!" Mr. Steele and Mr. Pittenger unaware that suggestion of Ben for city council post emanated from Mrs. Steele, promulgated through Mrs. Paisley to Mrs. Pittenger to Mr. Pittenger. Mr. Steele goes home feeling relieved but slightly guilty; meditates on possibility that after all he might be damn good on city council. Mr. Steele, brooding and abstracted, considers these things during supper. Uncle Emory Buckland offers vivid description of encounter with rebels during Confederate retreat from Corinth, Tennessee, in October, 1862. Mrs. Steele patently unresponsive. Uncle Emory Buckland offers detailed description of skirmish with overwhelming force of rebels at Monroe, Missouri, at earlier date; Mrs. Steele still unimpressed. Uncle Emory retires to livery barn; drinks remainder of hidden-away bottle of rye whiskey; goes to sleep in horse's stall, luckily untrampled by horse.

Saturday, June 1st. Late in evening—annual midnight smoker at Elks' club. Mr. Steele, excited by growing-pains of maturity, of family and community responsibility, absorbs quantities of liquor. Mr. Steele, called upon for recitation by other gentlemen, obliges with, "Down in the Lehigh Valley, Me and Me Old Pal Jim." Mr. Steele requested to offer encore. Mr. Steele offers, instead of recitation, vocal solo beginning, "There Was an Old Farmer Who Sat on a Rock." Mr. Steele's contribution to entertainment highly appreciated by brother Elks. Senator Newgate, chewing cigar in sobriety, estimates Ben's community popularity, thinks well of him as possible political timber. Senator Newgate, in even more secret discussion with himself, considers delectability of Mrs. Benjamin Steele. Senator Newgate plans to discuss with Mrs. Steele possible political future for Mr. Steele. Benjamin Steele assisted to residence by brother Elks with very little ambulatory control. Benjamin Steele offers post-concert revival of, "There Was an Old Farmer Who Sat on a Rock" in family bedroom. Mrs. Benjamin Steele indignant.

Sunday, June 2nd. Mrs. Steele still indignant. Mr. Steele, suffering headache, remains in bed until late hour. Mrs. Steele quietly, firmly refuses to converse with husband. Mr. Steele, horrified at own wicked behavior, offers sun, moon, stars to wife if she will forgive. Mrs. Steele extracts reluctant promise from Mr. Steele to dispense with buggy-seat divan. In late afternoon Steeles visit country club grounds and find assorted Ducketts, Paisleys, Cohens, Croys, etc., etc., striking furiously at small white balls with steel-headed clubs. Onetime Gus Olthoff pasture land in process of conversion into golf course: fresh earth bunkers scraped up, ditches filled, etc. Ben Steele, still stubborn, still suffering from slight headache, roundly jeers participants in "sissy game." Is challenged to strike small white ball with steel-headed club. Mr. Steele strikes, misses, strikes again, misses again, etc. Mr. Steele remains with mates to assault elusive small white ball, while wife retires to hammock and female company near partially completed rustic lodge. Mr. Steele vengefully pursues small white ball until dusk.

Monday, June 3rd. Buggy-seat divan conveyed to office of Steele livery barn—pathetic emptiness in Steele parlor resulting.

Tuesday, June 4th. Dolly gives tea party for select group of lady friends, including Miss Agatha Cook, whom she sees seldom these days; Miss Cook included in guest-list at instigation of Ben. Dolly serves hot chocolate instead of tea; offers delicious surprise to delighted guests in form of individual marshmallow toasting—guests all toasting own marshmallows on toothpicks over individual flames at prettily arranged tables. Dolly complimented by guests on originality and cute idea. Dolly neglects to mention idea suggested by article in recent though obscure household magazine. Hopes no one else has read same magazine.

Wednesday, June 5th. Stableman kicked by horse in Steele livery barn, leg badly bruised. Ben Steele reports disaster to wife at dinner table, thus provoking discussion of gasoline engines vs. horse-power. Mrs. Steele expresses doubt about economic future of livery barn, wagon works, harness store. Mr. Steele cites statistics concerning horse population of Dodge County. Painful argument resolves into angry discussion of personalities. Reconciliation delayed until at least an hour after Steeles retire to bed on this evening.

Thursday, June 6th. Dolly worried about package from Chicago which should have arrived and has not.

Friday, June 7th. Steeles receive last-minute supper invitation to Pittengers' to meet officer of Iowa State Bankers Association. Ben disinclined to accept because of previous commitment to Uncle Emory. Fervent debate between Steeles as to advisability of putting antique sentiment ahead of social and/or professional necessities. Ben capitulates to Dolly, departs with her for Pittenger mansion. Uncle Emory disconsolate at receiving second-hand explanations and apologies offered by Larry, but brightens considerably after appearance of meat loaf, mashed potatoes and gravy. Gives lengthy description of battle near Blue Mills Landing in Missouri, and vividly recounts rescue of six-pound cannon saved from enemy through gallantry of Private Emory Buckland, Captain Trumble, Lieutenants Crosley and Knight, and a few others less noted. Larry not exactly overwhelmed by reminiscences but willing to listen. At distant Pittenger home, Dolly Hessian Steele still worried because package secretly ordered from Chicago has not yet arrived.

Saturday, June 8th. Package arrives. Dolly enraptured. Package hidden.

Sunday, June 9th. First official country club picnic to christen newly constructed swimming pool. Bottom of pool very muddy, one man cut on clam shells, one lady scratched by submerged stick, several other ladies frightened by water-snake. Entire assemblage, including Benjamin Steele, stricken dumb by dramatic appearance of Mrs. Steele prettily clad in new black bathing suit—*man's* bathing suit—with no wide skirt or bulky bloomers and no sleeves at all. Women confess privately to shock and dismay, but before day is over Dolly receives seven requests for name of firm from which she ordered bathing suit. Ben Steele necessarily pretends to prior knowledge of bathing suit; is jealously but pridefully aware of glances of men turned on Dolly; tries in weakness to admonish her on way home. Dolly innocent and appealing. Historic love-encounter between Steeles at late hour.

Monday, June 10th. New golden-oak, leather-upholstered divan delivered to replace departed buggy-seat divan. Horse of delivery wagon team steps into flower bed adjacent to porch, destroying plants. This act leads to further review of merits of horses vs. motorcars.

Tuesday, June 11th. Mr. and Mrs. Sylvester Cohen, plus infant son Clifton, appear in street in front of Steele home at early hour before Ben has left for work: Cohens uproarious with delight, demonstrating new Everitt "Six-48" touring car acquired by them, equipped with self-starter, top, windshield, speedometer and Prest-o-Lite tank. Ben, politely complimentary but still basically hostile, tells Dolly later he would be damned before he would waste eighteen hundred and fifty dollars on a crazy-looking thing like that. Dolly decides to abandon motorcar vs. horse, garage vs. livery stable campaign until more propitious season. Wonders why she ever married Ben in first place.

Wednesday, June 12th. Dolly now delighted that she has married Ben, when he initiates conference on vacation plans. Ben proposes fishing trip to remote Minnesota lake; Dolly professes inclination to visit New York City instead. Destination unselected in preliminary discussion. Private but mutual opinions of stubbornness, heartlessness, lack of appreciation of other's desires.

Twenty-Six

As a matter of fact they went to Chicago instead, and very late in the summer. Senator Newgate was indirectly responsible for the decision made. It seemed that the Senator was worried about the health of his beloved wife who had been bedridden—or at least houseridden—through most of the hot weather. He voiced his fears to Dolly at an evening picnic party at the Lexington Country Club, where Japanese lanterns were hung on wires across the unpainted veranda of the rustic lodge, and where too much wind blew throughout the evening, and three of the paper lanterns were whipped to exciting conflagration as a result.

"Where are you and Ben planning to go on your vacation?"

"We haven't decided yet. I," said Dolly, "would love to go to New York, but Ben . . . Oh, dear, he keeps talking about fishing. I just don't like to fish—it seems so *cruel*. And then he says he's got some men he ought to see in Chicago: a wholesaler and some horse-breeding man he wants to see about—about something or other."

Newgate said with jocularity, "Possibly he wants to see him about breeding horses!" but he regretted his jest when Dolly turned away delicately. "My dear," he told her with haste, "I have been praying that perhaps you and Ben might visit Chicago while I am there. My wife—" He paused heavily.

"Perhaps you have heard. Mrs. Newgate is ill. I must take her to Chicago to seek the best of medical attention."

Dolly whispered, "I'd like to go to Chicago, too. It has many happy memories. Although I became estranged from my family when I married Ben," and she waited for Newgate to utter the sympathetic sound which indeed he uttered.

"My dear child, I will be at the Caxton in Chicago beginning next week. It would be wonderful if we met—"

Another lantern caught fire, and the resulting hurly-burly brought this interview to a close.

There was a final encounter on the street that week. Again Newgate, looking upon Dolly as he might have looked upon his own golden-haired little daughter, spoke touchingly of the ambitions he entertained for Ben. "A fine young man. I become more impressed with him the longer I know him. Do you know—sometimes I feel that he is wasted, with his sole activity concerned in business—"

"I think so, too," Dolly murmured. "But you know how it is, Senator Newgate: a wife just can't come out and—and tell him—"

Newgate said, "One of these days I shall tell him myself. I do hope that you decide to vacation in Chicago. I would enjoy seeing you there. It would brighten what I fear may be a very lonely ordeal. Remember, if you come, I shall be at the Hotel Caxton."

To do justice to Dolly, she was not at all enamored of the Senator. She found her emotional and physical companionship with Ben a happier thing than she had ever dreamed it might become. But she had been in Lexington nearly a year, with only one out-of-town trip to Des Moines, a weekend at Clear Lake, and a few sorties to Fort Dodge. She was bored by the flesh and bones of Lexington—even with the novelty of the country club which she had procreated in the barren social womb of this raw village. She was sick unto death of the Wednesday Lily Auction Bridge Club; she was nauseated by the regularity of Uncle Emory's visits on Friday nights; she had heard every one of Sylvester Cohen's "parlor stories" until she wanted to scream.

There was a spice of deviltry in acceding to Newgate's hidden appeal. And Chicago would be fun. She could shop; there would be some theaters to go to, even in summer. A vacation in Chicago . . . a luxurious whirl among cafés and stores: such triumph she had promised herself long before, and this seemed a proper season in which to achieve it. And there were the hints which Newgate gave about Ben's future career. . . .

She suggested Chicago to Ben, and to her delight found him not uninclined. He thought that he could combine business with pleasure; and in solitary mind he was gratified to learn that Dolly did not hold out for New York City any longer. They began to make plans at once.

In Chicago, the Hotel Caxton was an institution both antique and self-assured. Its old red cornices and cupolas marred consistently any beauty which the skyline of Michigan Avenue might struggle to achieve. The Caxton was not quite so expensive as the Blackstone; not so filled with people from small towns as was the Palmer House; nor so crammed with businessmen as the LaSalle; nor did it tingle with sparks cast off from the Stage, like the Sherman House; nor did its halls and shafts resound with the piercing *ah-ah-ah-ah-ah* of opera singers, like the Auditorium. But moderately the Caxton partook of the nature of each of these hotels, and it was famous for its food.

It was famous in the mind of Dolly Hessian Steele as a blissful, baroque, gingerbread-loaded pinnacle to whose elegant attainment she had long been dedicated. And for a particular reason. There were only two or three other people now extant (and none was a part of Dolly's modern world) who knew that once upon a time, years before, at the age of fourteen-and-a-half, Dolly had worked for five dispirited, greasy weeks as a dishwasher at the Hotel Caxton.

Her economical husband talked pleasantly about a room (yes sir, a corner room if she insisted, although that would be a little more expensive than just a room) but the adroit Dolly, managing reservations by hasty correspondence in her best hand and verbiage, and on the newly engraved linen stationery which had been part of her Christmas spoils—Dolly secured a small sitting room to adjoin their bedroom.

Ben whistled. "How much extra?"

"They didn't say. It won't be much, darling. And we do have to have some place to entertain our friends—you know, it would be embarrassing in a bedroom, with clothes around and everything."

"Guess maybe you're right. But who on earth are all these friends we're going to entertain, come to think of it? I don't know anybody from Lexington who's going to be in Chicago next week—except Abie Newgate. He's taken his wife in there to the hospital again. I suppose you heard?" He looked at Dolly meaningly, and lifted his eyebrows.

"Yes, that's what everybody is saying. Cancer."

"That certainly is too bad."

"It certainly is. Poor, poor woman." Then Dolly smiled. She had an exalted courage within her—a courage which enabled her to rise above contemplation of the agony which Creation was now visiting upon Marguerite Newgate. "Well, we'll have to entertain him, of course. If he isn't too busy. And—and there might be somebody else around—some local people, I mean. I'm trying to talk Harley and Myrtle into coming in on the weekend—you know, we could all go to the theater and have a lot of fun."

"They can't afford it."

"Just as if Alfred Pittenger's son-in-law couldn't afford a trip to Chicago!"

"That isn't the way it goes, honey. You just don't understand. Harley and Myrtle: they live on what Harley makes."

"Oh, pooh."

"Well, they do—or try to anyway. Myrtle tries pretty damn hard. She doesn't like the idea of herself and her husband living off Papa. An assistant cashier's salary isn't—" He took another conversational tack. "How about your own friends? You know, from Lake Forest and—?"

Dolly offered him the gray-gold mysticism of her eyes. "Ben. I should prefer not to mention it."

"Why not mention it? There ought to be somebody: you're always talking about— Even if you still don't want to see Aunt Edna you—"

His wife's voice sounded tiny and remote, softly bruised: the plaint of a cuddlesome furry animal which has been severely hurt by being stepped upon but is not truly minded to complain.

"Not one of those girls has written to me, Ben—not one,

since our marriage. I don't know what Aunt Edna's told my friends, and—I don't care! I, at least, am *very proud* of my husband," and she walked around the breakfast table to bury her face against his chest.

Ben put his nose down into her hair, and decided that instead of carrying two hundred dollars' worth of traveler's checks to Chicago he would take two hundred and fifty dollars' worth.

The city was a mighty, noisy witchery when they arrived. A thin rain was spraying blackly, smoke was thick in narrow caverns of the Loop, and the hot electric signs on State Street were many of them lighted by mid-day. But no amount of tropical humidity and daytime darkness could cast a blight on Dolly's spirits. She sang her way through the little suite at the Caxton; she gave the bellboy fifty cents out of her own purse —to Ben's amused horror at such extravagance—and she flirted outlandishly with her husband while they were unpacking.

He had embraced her when they were snuggled in the Pullman berth the night before, but she whimpered affectionately away from him . . . oh, precious, not here! Think of all these people around . . . And the next day, freshly come into the excitement of an ornate place where there were satin puffs draped sensuously on each of the beds, and fat-bosomed courtesans provoking the attention of bewigged Frenchmen among the bedroom picture-frames—with this giddy honeymoon froth and quiver about them, Dolly was still slyly repelling him as she sprayed herself with toilet water. . . . Oh, no, darling. Not now. Wait until tonight. . . .

Ben made a couple of telephone calls. He was going to perform some business errands while they were there, as he had stated before. He made one appointment for the next day, and one for the day following.

The mist that wrapped Chicago began to intensify into a dashing rain, and coolness came with it. After they had lunched in the Caxton's coffee shop, Dolly changed into her black suit, because of the sudden clamminess that touched this weirdly climated city. Accoutered for shopping and for rain, she lured Ben to Marshall Field's and to a furniture store. There were so many things they needed for their home, she cried: towels and sheets and pillowcases were at a low ebb. But she demonstrated frugality, and stoutly shook her head when the salesgirl asked if these things should be initialed.

They had a mid-afternoon snack in a delightful little place on Wabash, where a Polish violinist from East Chicago, Indiana, played the "Flower Song" in a somewhat flat fashion but right beside their table. Chicago became the Paris of Dolly's gayest fancy. Her heart sang in the scraping of the strings.

The Steeles window-shopped a little wearily down Michigan Avenue and entered the Hotel Caxton through its east arcade—the main entrance was on the side street. Here were shops: a fruiterer's, a candy store, a lingerie shop, a haberdasher's and a jewelry store—each more remotely opulent, more politely unoccupied by many customers than the richest establishments which the visitors had seen on Michigan Avenue.

In the window of the jewelry store Dolly observed a thing which brought a new shine to her eyes and a dizziness to her being.

"Ben, look at that!"

"Where?"

"Right there. Isn't it wonderful?"

"It certainly is."

"Ben, look. It's all alone in the window. Look at it! It makes me shiver all over."

The lower portion of the narrow window was draped in folds of pale green satin; amid this luxury, placed funereally on a black velvet slab, was a solitary brooch. A gold rose in the center bore one stone of flashing green, and gold leaves radiated outward in a conventional whorl, where scores of tiny chips discharged their transparent blaze.

"Golly, that's really a piece of jewelry. Wonder what Abner Fairchild would—?"

"It's the most lovely thing I ever saw in my life," Dolly whispered.

"You know, my mother used to have something like that. I remember, when I was little, Dad gave it to her one time after they had a big fight. Of course she was always lambasting him, but . . . Anyway, he gave it to her, and the very next week she lost it up in the Eastern Star rooms somewhere. Never did find it. Mother claimed somebody had stolen it up there; she wouldn't go to Eastern Star any more, and that made Dad feel pretty bad."

"But it couldn't have been like *this*."

"Sure—sort of. I remember it was rhinestones, because I remember reading about the Rhine River in Germany in geography at school, and I wondered if that was where rhinestones came from."

Dolly said, her voice listless with admiration: "I don't think those are rhinestones."

"Well, they're just about as nice."

As Dolly held her face close to the window, she made Ben think of a child in front of a candy store. Suddenly he was overcome with appreciation of this woman, with thought of all the love she had given him—the cute little mannerisms, the comfort she exhaled—the thought of the devoted interest with which she viewed his life, present and future.

He contemplated the passion to be shared again in a night to come. This was a honeymoon . . . they had never had a honeymoon, really—had never gone on their trip to New Orleans. Hilton Maxwell in the hospital and—

She was so wonderful; she was like nothing else—like no other person who had ever put a small foot in the paths of Lexington. She had given up the love of family and friends to be married to him. She had given him so much: her body and her beauty, too. She would give again.

Ben cleared his throat.

"Dolly."

"Yes, Ben?"

"Do you want it?"

"Want what?"

"That thingamabob in the window."

"But, Ben! You can't mean—?"

"Do you realize something? I've never given you a wedding present—not really, I mean. We didn't even have a wedding ring. Oh, I know I went down to Fairchilds' the next week and got that little wedding-band, but—I don't know—I was pretty stupid about it—"

"This would be terribly expensive, dear."

"What's the difference? I don't care what it costs—not even —" He was about to say, "Not even if it costs a *hundred dollars,*" but he stopped himself in time. After all, another look at that brooch told him that it might well cost a hundred dollars—maybe even a hundred and twenty-five—and he didn't want to crawl out on a limb. Yes. Even a hundred and a quarter . . .

They went through the door of the jewelry shop in that same moment when A. B. A. Newgate entered the arcade from Michigan Avenue. The Senator saw them both. He quickened his pace, although it was no news to him that the Steeles were already registered at the Caxton. He had made certain of that; he had telephoned their room, but it was after Dolly and Ben were gone shopping.

Freshly come from the ether scent, the hard despondency of falsely bright hospital corridors, and with disintegration well advanced in a life neither admired nor endeared, but at least the only other life admittedly close to his own—freshly away from such calamity, Abie Newgate desired the stimulation of Dolly's physical presence with fervor.

He slowed his pace as he approached the jewelry store window and saw a man's hands reach down inside and lift the brooch respectfully. Through two layers of glass and amid complicated reflections, Abie observed the brief encounter of Dolly and Ben with the bitter riches of this world.

The interview was terminated abruptly. Newgate could hear no word spoken, but the expressions of those faces spoke keenly enough: the tremulous rapture of Dolly, changed to pitiful desire; the downright stricken dismay of Ben's face, flaming with confusion; the supercilious hauteur of the fifteen-dollar-a-week clerk as he withdrew into his elegance again.

With Newgate gone rapidly around the corner of the marble tunnel and up the steps into the hotel lobby, the Steeles retreated ignominiously from the jewelry store and followed unaware on his path.

"My God, Dolly, I didn't believe it was possible!"

"I said it looked expensive," his wife mourned.

"But, hell's bells! Eleven hundred and seventy-five dollars! Why, if Abner Fairchild ever—"

She said, almost pettishly, "Oh, Ben, please don't let's talk about it. It was really embarrassing."

"Well, hell! I'm sorry I embarrassed you. But, my God, I'm not a millionaire. Why, I never dreamed— That's criminal! What do those people think they—?"

"Ben, don't you realize it wasn't rhinestones? It was little diamonds and a great big emerald."

"I don't care if it was attar of roses. Eleven hundred and . . . !" Then he grinned down at her with his native jocularity already commanding. "I guess the Steeles have learned all about Chicago now! I guess we'd better go to a variety store —unless maybe you want to buy that brooch out of your own money," and he laughed.

"Sometime," said Dolly, "I might buy it. I might save and save."

"Guess you'd have to save a pretty long time on what I give you. Anyway," he added sturdily, "it still goes. I mean what I said. I'm going to buy you a wedding present before we're out of this town."

In the lobby they lingered for a time at the magazine and candy counter, and Ben was buying cigars as well. Ordinarily he smoked only his pipe, and that not too frequently, but there was something about Chicago which seemed to demand cigars. The time consumed in these minor dawdlings and purchases served for Abie Newgate to conclude a conversation in the telephone booth.

Newgate replaced the receiver slowly. Eleven hundred and seventy-five dollars, the jeweler had said. Well . . .

He wondered how long, actually, Marguerite would live. Not that it mattered; except that the hospital was expensive, and the doctor bills would be even heavier. However . . .

He waylaid the young couple as they crossed the lobby, and other people turned to see the kindly greeting which this pompous and obviously important individual with gleaming gray curls bestowed upon the younger pair.

"I thought you were always at the Blackstone, Senator Newgate," said Dolly. "You said—"

"My dear child, you must have misunderstood me. The Caxton—always the Caxton. For more years than I care to recall. Ah, well . . ."

Ben asked about Mrs. Newgate, and the Senator beamed happily. "I have retained the best specialist I could find, and already the results are most encouraging. Dr. Strothers is contemplating an operation which, he says, will in all likelihood restore Marguerite's health. He offers every hope." Dr. Strothers was, in fact, offering nothing of the kind.

Dolly said in the accents of Florence Nightingale, "I should like to go to her as soon as I can."

The big man shook his head with a pitying smile. "No callers, I'm afraid. Not just now. Very soon, however, she will be able to welcome you."

He stood humbly, his big left hand spread flat to hold a black hat of smoothest felt, his big right hand caressing the crown. "Do you know how you could both make me very happy?"

Ben's first reaction was, "Why should we?" and quickly his

eyes shifted to his wife, and back to Newgate's face again. Dolly had been regarding the Senator only with trusting fondness . . . gosh, thought Ben, maybe that's the trouble with Dolly. She trusts everyone too much. . . .

Dolly asked, "How?"

"By dining with me tomorrow night."

"That would be lovely. We could, couldn't we, Ben?"

"I guess so. Sure. Uh—thanks a lot."

Newgate let his gaze go above and beyond them. He seemed staring, not at marble columns beveled and chunky along the borders of that lobby . . . instead he seemed regarding the past with gentle superiority.

"Twenty-five years ago tomorrow, a very tired and frightened—but I will say earnest—a very ambitious young man was admitted to the Bar, out in a certain town in Iowa."

He thought this sounded well: sufficient excuse for any celebration which he might contrive. He would have said, "Dine with me *tonight,*" but he didn't know whether he could find sufficient guests to make a dinner party of substance in so short a space of time. He did not know more than twenty or thirty people in all Chicago, and he would be lucky if he could glean more than eight or ten of any acceptable social stature from this meager roster. He would try very hard; he would go to the telephone at once. Perhaps it would be more effective to send notes of invitation by messenger, and have the messenger wait for a reply in each case.

It was exactly twenty-eight years, four months and seventeen days since Abie Newgate had become a lawyer. Who would know the difference? A quarter-century sounded much better.

"Just a small party. A few friends. There are some people

whom I should love to have you meet: a few from the press, one or two from the stage. Would eight o'clock be all right?"

"Of course. We'd love to come."

Senator Newgate gave them the benison of his smile, he gave them a warm though dignified farewell, he went slowly toward the elevators though in his spirit he was sprinting. He spent the greater share of that day in summoning and finally securing as his guests an assistant freight agent of the Chicago & Great Western railroad—and his wife; a man from the advertising department of Montgomery Ward—and his wife; a Carson Pirie Scott & Company salesman—and his wife; a soubrette who had recently lost her job with a small stock company; the sister of a deceased ambulance-chaser whom Abie had known at college; and a lame bookkeeper from the *Drovers' Journal*—a man who had more courage than Richard the Lion-Hearted, more patience than Job, more single-purposed determination then Ulysses S. Grant—a man who had lived in Lexington briefly as Abie Newgate's neighbor thirty years before, who had struggled against pain and poverty with saintly fortitude, who had reared three orphaned nieces the while he tended a diabetic wife whom he loved deeply and whom he saw die most miserably—a man rusty of voice, nearsighted of eye, blemished of skin, bad of breath—a man who had never dined at the Hotel Caxton before and had never tasted either lobster or champagne in his life, and who would never do so again—a man ten thousand times more valuable to humanity than ten thousand Senator Newgates, but who in 1916 would perish of osteomyelitis—scorned by his fellow-employees, indebted to the Illinois Household Finance Company, forgotten soon by the nieces he had cherished, and totally ignored by the public prints.

Twenty-Seven

Abie Newgate's dinner guests assembled amid a collective and individual inferiority. They wondered at finding themselves feted by a man whom few of them knew well and whom none trusted completely. But, as at the Elks' masquerade in Lexington some months before, food and drink had a leavening and leveling effect.

Newgate had ordered a few cocktails and some sauterne, though the maitre d'hotel suggested champagne. The sauterne was at hand but not yet decanted when Dolly Steele appeared with her husband a little more tardily than politeness demanded. To the Senator's eyes she was a delectable flagon of aphrodisia in a new gown bought at Mandel's that morning, and altered during the afternoon. The gown was of frail, clinging black satin, with a pink yoke and fichu. The skirt was slit and slightly draped, and folds of that same appetizing pink appeared in the slit whenever Dolly moved her limbs. Abie pondered only briefly on this spectacle before summoning a waiter and whispering for champagne to replace the sauterne.

The other guests—two of the men at least in rented evening clothes—were parceled carefully in their seats after more cogitation by the host than was ever given by any ambassador's wife to a Washington function. Ben Steele was awarded the soubrette, a red-headed ignoramus (voluble; but also, to the unsophisticated Mr. Steele, fascinating in a worldly-wise manner). He sat between this woman and the wife of the Montgomery Ward man, a fat little brunette with a pretty neck and bosom and a persistent giggle. Dolly Steele was enthroned at the host's right, next to the Carson Pirie salesman, whose intemperate chatter contrasted miserably with the priestly charm of the Senator.

They reveled in a private dining room above the mezzanine floor, and two bald Germans assisted their delight with conscientious application of violin and piano.

From an adjacent exterior balcony could be obtained an excellent view of dark-fronted shops and a feebly lit dairy lunch across the way. Upon this balcony Dolly found herself escorted while the guests sipped their coffee. She heard the worthy host speak briefly of the great future which lay in store for this very Chicago beneath their feet, and for the younger men of the Mississippi Valley: men of vision and ambition, men not averse to building a midland empire of the honest materials within their grasp.

Yes, it was a good thing for Ben to come to Chicago, said the Senator.

"I think so, too."

For a moment the smoke of Abie's cigar obscured his face. He waved the smoke away. "I fear that he wouldn't have come, except for you, my dear. Perhaps he would do few things except for you."

"I am only a woman but . . ."

"Behind every man of accomplishment, there is always a woman. Perhaps"—he rolled up his eyes—"I could have gone further than I have gone, if only . . ." He smiled, he left the sentence uncompleted.

Dolly whispered against the rising chatter and the bleat of music inside, "You shouldn't really say that, Senator Newgate. You have done so much."

"But I am no longer young."

"You seem very young to me." Soberly she opened her little silver-mesh purse and drew out a tiny pink handkerchief with which she touched her lips.

"Do you like the purse—the little mesh-bag?"

"Of course I do. I told you: I'll keep it always."

He said, "I love to give you things. You know why . . ."

"I am happy to have this dear little bag—if it makes you happy."

Newgate took Dolly's hand and held it tenderly. She wanted to flash a glance back through the open French windows, but dared not allow herself that guilty observation over her shoulder. She wondered if Ben— He might be alarmed. She was sure that Ben didn't really like Senator Newgate. But—

The man whispered, "There is something else which I would love to give you."

"What?"

"I wonder if you can guess? It flashes," he said, "the way your eyes flash sometimes. Its gold is like another gold I admire."

Dolly inclined her head to let whatever light there was lay upon her hair. She murmured, "I can't imagine what you are talking about."

"A brooch. A brooch which lay in a window yesterday afternoon."

"What?" There was no fakery in the wonder which she gave to him then. "How on earth did you *know*?" she gasped.

"Perhaps it is my business in life to observe the things you want—the things you need."

"But— Oh, Senator *Newgate,* I—"

"I wish you would do something for me. I wish you would call me Amos. No one else ever does."

Marguerite had called him Amos for a long time, even before they were engaged.

Dolly said, "I'd love to, but it seems so—so— I'm so much younger than you, and— I mean you're not old, but—"

"But what?"

"Maybe I really shouldn't—Amos."

He felt sweat all over him.

"Dolly, please let me do something—"

"We must go inside. Please, Amos. People will *talk,*" she cried. Unwillingly he followed her into the room as she fled before him. But her eyes, her smell, her hair, her satin gown: the whole condition and reality of her. . . .

He spoke to the waiter, ordering additional champagne. He idled beside the piano, quietly requesting the musicians to remain for longer than they had originally been engaged, and accompanying this demand with an extra gift of folded currency.

Then he went to attend the sister of his old college friend; he plied her with the most gallant attention of which he was capable, in order to dispel any doubts which might have been born within Ben Steele's mind.

The champagne worked wonders, and so did the brandy and liqueurs which came along after the coffee. By this time several of the guests were dancing. The musicians, provoked to accomplishment by the application of frequent beers, were outdoing themselves with *Wiener Blut.*

Again Abie sought and made an opportunity for himself. "I want to talk to you. I must. I need to talk to you alone."

"But where? How could we?" breathed Dolly.

"Dolly, it's about Ben. I have things in mind for him—great things."

"So have I. I should like to see him"—she whispered the ambition which had formed even before she knew that it might with proper manipulation become a fact—"in the legislature."

Newgate had not thought of that at all. He had considered, rather, the city council of Lexington. He regarded the woman in momentary astonishment.

"That's rather a large order."

Dolly lifted her champagne glass and drank lightly. But her guileless eyes were regarding Newgate with faith above the rim. "You could make it happen, Amos."

"Perhaps. But not at this election. I . . ."

"Why not?"

"Because Charlie Ryder's already nominated," he explained almost angrily.

Dolly said simply, "I don't know much about these things. But wouldn't it be possible—that is, I mean if Mr. Ryder knew that you wouldn't support him—that you'd support Ben instead—that your whole—your whole organization would support Ben for the legislature—wouldn't it be possible to put Ben there?"

Newgate looked down at the hard pink tip of his cigar. He was breathing a little heavily. Liquor taken in quantity usually did that to him: it forced his breath, it made him fumble, and that was the reason he seldom drank to any intensive degree.

His brain was wheeling . . . he saw faces . . . he saw correspondence and ballot sheets, and the whole chorus of political chicanery welled to a yelling in his brain. . . . Man overboard? He had never been party to an outright political assassination before. Within the entire district, Ryder held little popularity. Of course a Democrat could never win a nomination nowadays; and yet the Republicans had had no one else to put up except Ryder. The man's record was weak and colorless . . . there was a way. . . .

"I might do it for your sake," he said. "Yes, it might be possible."

She whispered, "I wish you would make it possible," and her love went past him to caress Ben Steele, as Ben swung the red-headed and now red-faced actress past the piano in wide-flung gyrations of the waltz.

"The little brooch," said Newgate tenderly. "I bought it for you. Dolly, I want you to have it."

"I can't believe . . ."

"Yes, I bought it. I saw you both in the shop yesterday afternoon; I knew you wanted it." He tried to swallow, his throat was too dry for swallowing. "Dolly," he said, and his voice was hoarse and raw, "will you let me fasten that brooch . . . ?"

He looked at the fleckless softness of pink fabric above her bosom. "Let me fasten that pin upon your gown tonight. Oh, Dolly . . ."

Her pulse also was punishing her temples. She fancied the crash of a brass band blaring opportunely only a short distance away. Not this silly piano and fiddle music, but a great, marching band with the gold sunshine of open Iowa coming down, and voices crying praise for a new executive. Oh, in God's name, she thought, I wish . . . By God, it is possible, it could be. The Governor and his *Lady*.

"When?" she whispered.

"Afterward. After they're all gone. I am in Suite Eight-sixteen."

"But—but I'm afraid. If Ben ever dreamed . . ."

"Perhaps he might have another brandy or two." Newgate arose swiftly and, standing behind her chair, he said with lips barely moving, "Dolly, it's up to you. I can do anything for him, anything you want. There's no fake about it. He's got everything: brains, personality— He'll have to learn, but— Remember now: after everyone's gone, and when he's—well, asleep. It will be your responsibility. Can you remember the number of my suite?"

"Eight-sixteen," she said as if in a remote stupor, though she was in no stupor. She was seeing an emerald-diamond blaze—the flash of jeweled lights within her brain. And she was hearing again a roar of applause that burst from the future.

Twenty-Eight

Dolly went to Suite 816 about ten minutes after one in the morning, the guests now long departed from the private dining room, the music stilled; and tired people, anonymous in midnight slavery, clearing away the mess left by the pretended celebration of Senator Newgate's quarter century at the Bar.

She went scampering absurdly, a coat of light-weight black cloth gathered around her like a cape. And one part of her brain was wishing for an opera cloak trimmed with fur, and the other departments of her intelligence were seeking the shrewdest way to go—the slyest course with which to penetrate unobserved to the opposite, Michigan Avenue side of the hotel—to mount four flights of service stairs, to pass the red fire-escape warning that sizzled balefully because there was something wrong with its wiring, to forget the two women and the man who came out of that east-side fourth-floor room she passed, though she would remember for years the paltry things they said, the way they quacked behind her and did not notice her flight.

Dolly went, leaving her husband stretched on his side, the bed covers tossed off around him; and he looked ungainly in his underwear. She dared not put his nightshirt on him. He might awaken, he might—

She had had trouble enough leading Ben to his room. By

the time the party broke up, with Ben's intoxication simultaneously reaching its peak, he was determined to call up an old football friend in Berwyn, Illinois, whom he had not seen since they were at Ames together. All the way to the fourth-floor rooms, in elevator and in hallway, Ben spoke his thick-voiced affirmation of Lawrence Bessman's sterling qualities, and called to mind the occasion when Lawrence had run back a kick-off through the whole Iowa University team. These chronicles would have bored Dolly to some degree at any time; but coming when instigated only by champagne, brandy, and a moment of conversation with the *Drovers' Journal* bookkeeper who happened to know Lawrence Bessman's father, and stimulated above all by Chicago's proximity to the suburb where Lawrence Bessman now owned a butcher shop—these lusty reiterations tortured Dolly into a state of nerves which she could ill conceal even from her inebriated husband.

The varnish of guilt was over her as she had never imagined it might be. For years adept at petty intrigue, at marauding elegantly through more hotels than a few, she was now reduced to the terror of the innocent village matron who is afraid that Baby will wake up during her first extra-curricular encounter with her husband's friend.

Dolly managed to get Ben to bed. He went to sleep while she was pulling off his shoes. He resisted a little when she removed his trousers and shirt, he snored while she was hanging these things up, and thus she left well enough alone.

Already she had contrived an excuse in case Ben should rouse during her absence: she would say that the champagne and all the food had made her feel ill, and that she had gone down to stroll back and forth in front of the lighted hotel entrance, chaperoned by the doorman, seeking fresh air to restore her. This was a hasty improvisation, not especially sound except in a case like this where there were no palpable grounds for suspicion. It was only one of the many little anchors that the handsome barkentine which was Dolly Hessian Steele always had ready to cast to the leeward. She doubted mightily that she would need this excuse (nor did she need it when at last she returned from Senator Newgate's rooms. Ben had not awakened; he had only turned over and was lying on his face, his snores muffled by the wadded pillows).

So she approached the door of 816, feeling relieved that she had encountered no waiter or chambermaid in the halls or on the stairs—scornful of any woman who would have used the elevator in a case like this. The door was ready for her, standing slightly ajar. Senator Newgate was waiting.

He had removed his dinner coat, his stiff shirt and necktie, and he was wearing a red dressing gown with gilt fringe on the sash. He had tied a white scarf about his throat. He was in no way discomfited on recognizing that this costume was not sentimentally appropriate. The dressing gown had been bought for him one Christmastime by his spinster mistress in Des Moines; and in madness she had christened it in the first hour he put it on.

For so long Abie Newgate's life had been built of sophistries that he could not afford to be thin-skinned; it was impossible for him to be thin-skinned any longer. He had no sensation of shame as he stood anticipating Dolly, and as he reviewed briefly the spectacle of his wife in her room at the Blackstone Memorial Hospital, thirty blocks distant, and wondered whether she was awake or sleeping in her pain.

Newgate had prepared the physical appurtenances for this

tryst as painstakingly as he laid out the campaign to achieve it. He had found in experience with the majority of women (affectionate, domestic creatures, so appealing in their purity, as they waited to be seduced) that they did not usually prefer brandy. He had ready at hand a bottle of Cointreau and a flask of Benedictine, and waited only for Dolly to state her preference.

She said the usual thing as he made sure the door was fastened behind her: she said that she shouldn't have come. She didn't know what she was doing there; she must be out of her right mind.

"Perhaps," he said reassuringly, "you are not out of your right mind. Perhaps you have just found it," and he led her into the room and prepared for a common salutation *en liqueur*.

Dolly had consumed not more than two glasses of champagne during the entire evening, though to the best of the Senator's observation she had drunk at least eight. She was a slyer hand at this particular game of alcohol-versus-womanly-resistance than was Abie. He himself, not ordinarily given to over-indulgence, had imbibed heavily. The gate of reluctance, the bars of self-control had weakened and fallen as he contemplated his approach to a fulfilment which already had cost him thirteen hundred dollars in cash and a tremendous amount of mental effort.

Further investment faced him, no matter how much champagne Dolly seemed to have absorbed. Her mind returned tenaciously to that last conversation beside the dinner table.

"It's wonderful, Senator Newgate, for you to take such an interest in Ben."

"You called me Amos before."

"I—I'm just a little frightened, Amos. Please forgive me."

"Of course I forgive you. Now, which shall it be? Cointreau or Benedictine?"

"Oo, I know so little about alcoholic drinks. And all that champagne— It seems as if I were going round and around. Amos, maybe I ought to go back downstairs."

"Please don't leave me, Dolly."

"Someone might come. I'm scared."

"No. No one can possibly come. The door is locked. Now, please take something. Here, try this."

"What are you having?"

"This is brandy."

"Oo, but I don't like that. What did you say this other was?"

"It's Benedictine. It's made by monks—Benedictine monks—in France."

"Then I guess it must be all right if monks make it. Oo! Amos, it's so *strong*."

"Not at all. It's really very mild. Dolly, I—"

"Amos—about Ben. You know I was thinking, after we got downstairs— It isn't as if it were anything—crooked—or anything like that. Ben would really make a wonderful State Representative in the Legislature."

The Senator nodded. "Of that I am convinced. Believe me, I have encountered few young men of more professional honesty—men more community-minded, more seriously considerate of the welfare of their fellow beings, than your dear husband. I knew him as a child. I knew his father—yes, even his grandfather before him. The Steeles are typical of the sturdy American yeomanry who have made this country great, and who, in the future, will make it even greater."

Dolly whispered, "It sounds so wonderful when you say that. But how can you—? I mean how could he—? How could it ever be done? I mean the politics, the party and everything. What will the Republican wheel-horses think?"

Newgate poured himself a fresh glass of brandy. He was conscious of a pounding in his temples. He thought wearily that he had not drunk so much on any single evening in a very long time. But it was worth it.

He said, "Oh, those things have a way of being worked out. I told you that Charlie Ryder has no great—well, call it political charm—in the opinion of the organization and—ah—of the voters in our district. He hasn't been the man we needed down there. But who else did we have? Old E. I. Masterson—you know, Ely's father—he tried to run a time or two and didn't get very far." The Senator found himself fascinated by a bright buckle on Dolly's slipper and by the sleek silk stocking above that buckle.

He could not proceed just then. What was it he was saying?

"But, Amos, perhaps— Perhaps tomorrow you won't feel this way. Perhaps it's just a kind of temporary thing," Dolly whimpered. And her voice seemed like a mere bird rustling in this hot, ornate, midnight parlor. "I wish you'd do it now."

"Do what?"

"I wish you . . . I wish you'd take steps."

There came a jagged sword of clean lightning through the increasing buzz in Newgate's head. This woman . . . she really knew what she was doing. She was driving a bargain.

"You drive quite a bargain." He heard his voice coming back to him, echoing from the farther side of the room.

"I don't know what you mean."

"I mean—"

Here she was before him; he had wanted her so long. Here, with bright hair plaited about her head . . . the satin of her face, the fabric, the tantalizing substance of her pale hands, the satin of her shining new gown which she had bought especially for him. She had never worn it in Lexington; he was sure of that; she had bought it for his party and in his honor.

And he was more powerful than she in every way. He would take from her the mad response which she wanted, yet feared, to give.

"Don't you see what I mean, Amos? I'm afraid—afraid it's just the champagne and everything. If I could only believe that you meant it—"

He came back from the distant pole where he had stood examining her; his ears were ringing as he came. "All right," he said, "you shall see. Yes."

He got up from the chair where he had been sitting, and went to the telephone on the Japanese lacquered desk. Dolly gave a little fluttering cry as he lifted the receiver; he tried to smile reassuringly; it was a moment before his bulbous eyes could focus upon her. When the operator answered, Newgate said, "This is Senator Newgate. Suite Eight-One-Six. I wish to send a telegram immediately."

The operator's voice bickered back at him, but he kept on carving each word carefully, examining the syllables, the pronunciation, before he expelled them from his mouth.

"Mr. Harvey R. Winstrom, Lexington, Iowa." With his hand clamped down he told Dolly across the top of the telephone, "You know who that is, don't you?" He returned to his message: "After serious consideration have come to the conclusion that the incumbent discussed at—during evening conference last Tuesday is definitely unfit for the office. We must draft Benjamin Steele. Suggest you take preliminary steps to prepare present candidate for withdrawal and to groom Steele for the campaign. Am—am convinced we can win easily with Steele who will have enormous following among religious fraternal civic groups and especially in rural areas. My decision final so far as I am concerned."

He gave his name, he insisted that a boy be summoned at once, that the telegram be sent without delay. Then he hung up the receiver and came toward Dolly, stumbling against a chair on the way.

Her face floated before him.

"Dolly," he said, "I have something—I mentioned it to you before. Here it is." Taking her by the hand, he drew her to the couch, and he was a little rough about seating her there, although he did not intend to be.

"Oh, I am sorry. I didn't mean . . . Here. Here it is, right in my pocket. Look, my darling . . . I mean, my darling child. I bought it for you. I want—I want to pin it on you. Dolly, do you realize what this is? It's for you."

The glass bookcase doors beyond them—the black doors inlaid with their false mother-of-pearl—they seemed to sway and bend. Newgate's fingers were made of concrete. They were heavier and bigger than logs as he dragged the little parcel from the pocket of his dressing gown.

The thin fragility of this woman's tone . . . little female voice cheeping beyond the dissonance of bells and buzzers he wore in his ears.

"But how will I explain? Because Ben— Oh, I'd love it; but how can I ever wear it?"

Newgate thought weightily. He reached toward the brandy

on the little table; he tried to reach it, and then Dolly was up; she was tending him, she was bringing him the brandy he wanted, and he looked his gratitude and thought it was wonderful to have her serving him.

He said thickly, "Haven't you got money of your own?"

"Just a teentsie little bit."

"Does he know how much?"

"No, I don't think so. No, I know he doesn't."

"Well, then. You bought it yourself." Again he strove to make his hands behave as they worked at the ribbons binding the tiny box.

Dolly said, "I could . . . Amos, that would be the answer. But still—there's just one thing: I can't believe you're giving me this because— I don't want there to be any misunderstanding," and she may have said something else in between—some words, perhaps many sentences, that he did not hear. He could not tell. He heard the final words she said.

"There wouldn't be any misunderstanding." He thought his voice was roaring at her as paper fell away from the box in which the brooch reposed. "Open it. My fingers all thumbs . . ." He laughed.

She had opened the box, she was holding the busy flash of the jewels and hot metal . . . her fingers shivered as they lifted the sharp beauty of this instrument.

"Let me fasten it on—on your dress."

"But you said your fingers were all . . ."

He laughed and pushed his knees over against hers. Did she draw away? Maybe she just moved; maybe he only imagined that she drew away. She would not draw away much longer, she would not dare to.

"Here," and his hands messed against the yoke of her gown.

"Don't stick me." She was laughing when she said it. Then she cried "Ow!" in real pain as the gold pin scratched her flesh.

Away, away . . . all around the room, out among talkative stars and the smoke of the town, his voice went rambling and came back to him again. He heard it through the confluent racket of his ears. "Then you fix it on yourself, Dolly."

"Only if you're sure . . . Oh, Amos, I know it isn't right for me to take this. But it's so beautiful, and you did tell me the truth, didn't you? About the little bag and everything? It was only because—because I reminded you somehow of her?"

"Yes. Of her," the man repeated, bobbing his head. When at last Dolly had fastened the pin to his liking, he fell forward against her, gripping her with afflictive arms. She quivered and cried out. Why did women do this sometimes? But usually he hadn't had so much to drink . . .

"Dolly," he was mouthing, his face perspiring against her neck, his brushy eyebrows hurting her. "Just once, Dolly. That's surely not too much to ask?"

Drunk or sober, he knew his own strength, his ability to coerce. He had used his competence well and often with other women he sought, and he had not been disappointed. One kiss: that was all he needed. She would collapse before him . . . all that satin he would be stroking and possessing. . . .

But somehow she eluded him, she was up and swirling away, making little appeals as she rioted off. A queer phonograph record played on and on within the room. It stammered, repeating itself: the needle was stuck on the cylinder, the cylinder swirled in its greasy black, the needle was constantly at just about the same place, the voice talked on and on.

Why, Amos; why, Senator Newgate; you promised; oh,

Amos; please don't; I'll scream; you promised me; you told me it was just because; you promised me; reminded you of her . . . she flew and skipped. He'd think he saw her there, but she wasn't there—she was over here; and so he went pawing, stumbling, his mouth seeking, the flesh of his face now fallen into pathetic jowls: the jowls of a hound-dog that chased forever, that chased with all purpose and all devotion, the jowls of a hound-dog grown old and cumbersome; and so he could chase but never catch.

Dolly. He whispered it time and again; and then he thought he roared the name. He didn't know. His throat was swollen, there was no breath left to him.

Quite afar he heard the click of the latch, and he imagined that the door opened and closed. But what door, and where? And was that the safety chain swaying, touching lightly the panel for a time in its pendulous movement, and then remaining still? And he was here, alone.

A windy roar of futility played around Abie Newgate; the lamps flickered. And those chairs—they had been upset. He was sorry . . . but, my God, she was gone . . . and glasses upset . . . spoil the carpet, maybe. He would have to pay for it or have it cleaned.

He would have to pay for so much, so much, and he had already paid for so much. He wanted to halloo, "Oh, my God, what a fool!" Imagine, eleven hundred and—how many dollars? A fortune . . . he was hot.

This thing she had done—this fleeing away, this defilement of the fidelity that should have existed for them both . . . Subterfuge, the blatant hypocrisy of their conversation . . . This thing she had done . . .

His desire flew from him. He felt limp, but also stifled by

the thick air of the suite; and maybe he would be sick in a minute. He had been sick before.

"Air," he thought, and in a stumbling plunge toward a window, he pushed the heavy scarlet draperies aside, and tore one of them loose and heard part of its little gilt bracket strike the floor. The window stuck and came up slowly, and then with a jerk and a rush, and Newgate went forward across the low sill to breathe the thin revivifying rush of night. Thus he fell too far.

As, sprawling on and on, he plunged his way toward the empty concrete sidewalk of Michigan Avenue, he felt an unbelievable surprise. Again that white beam blistered inside his head and struck firmly against his memory. He had a precious scene in mind as he died. He was diving now; he had dived before; he felt a peculiar mixture of terror and outlandish satisfaction. For he recalled how he had stood upon a bending willow tree, knobby with rough bark, and looked at the brown water of a creek, and thrust his hands straight out above his head; and he had flung himself forward, and so he had dived (but with no dressing gown to flap like wings) and so he had gone through a seemingly endless rush of space, when naked he fell against that water—long before, when he was a little boy.

Twenty-Nine

Three principal questions concerned the police during their brief investigation of Newgate's death. The first was the fact that a struggle might have taken place in the living room of the Senator's suite before he fell accidentally—or leaped deliberately, or was hurled to his death—from that low-silled window.

Secondly, there was the matter of the midnight telegram to Iowa, which was brought to the attention of investigators by members of the hotel staff later during that same night.

The third possible clue, or cause for a consideration of murder, was a matter of which the police were not apprised until about ten o'clock in the morning; but Dolly Steele realized simultaneously a grave danger which beset her.

By the time when Abie Newgate's body smashed against the sidewalk, Dolly was safely back in her own quarters, and luckily had encountered no guest or hotel employee while in retreat down the closed stairway from that fatal eighth floor. The little bathroom suite which she occupied with Ben was Number 452-3—far on the opposite side of the hotel, well removed from the excitement which attended Newgate's precipitate appearance on Michigan Avenue.

It happened that Dolly (disrobing hastily but with care, and hiding away the brooch in a tissue-paper wad, secreting it temporarily in a box of Houbigant's powder in her toilet kit) did hear a remote ringing of gongs from municipal vehicles which rushed to the scene. Faintly there echoed a thin whooping of voices, a blowing of whistles, and the other muddled noises that attend upon unpremeditated excitement of this kind.

But she had no reason to imagine that Abie Newgate was now unbeautifully deceased, with oilcloth spread across the deflation of his ego and his body. She went to sleep in appreciation of a Providence increasingly beneficial to her. She thought that Newgate would apologize when next they met . . . she would offer to return the brooch to him . . . he would refuse to accept it. . . . Thus might begin another series of diplomatic or guerrilla encounters between Newgate's lust and her own professed virtue. It was not a wholly unpleasant prospect, and would serve to liven up the winter a little.

Dolly slept well, in spite of the slight headache she already owned. She was as horrified as Ben when, in the early morning and after members of the hotel staff had been quizzed, persistent knocks thudded against the door of Room 452, and the unhappy recital began.

Ben's astonishment when he was told the contents of the telegram sent to Lexington was obviously unfeigned, unrehearsed. He impressed the old detective who questioned him to such a degree that mentally and immediately the detective crossed Mr. Steele from his list of possible suspects in a possible case of murder. In a second interview an hour or two later, the officer came to the conclusion that Senator Newgate had been so modified by emotion, or opinion formed during the previous night's champagne party, that he had made a civic decision solely inspired by a mixture of alcohol and candid evaluation of an up-and-coming young man.

A re-examination of Suite 816 suggested that the disordered furniture and broken glasses might have resulted from the dead man's drunken meanderings as he wended his solitary way through additional bedtime libations. When he upset a small table he had smashed his own glass as well as Dolly's; he had left no suicide note; the night elevator operator declared that Newgate went to his suite alone, and Ben himself swore that he and his wife had retired simultaneously. This latter statement Ben believed, nor was he disillusioned throughout his life. He retained a distinct impression that he and Dolly had commingled in love before he went to sleep, perhaps because such pleasant ambition was in his mind at some moment while Dolly undressed him.

The broken bracket, the ripped window drapery in the Senator's parlor were silent evidence pointing toward accidental death; and indeed this verdict was rendered by a coroner's jury within a very short time, though all the other guests at the party were questioned before the case was closed.

A long-distance telephone call, received by Ben from Mr. Alfred E. Pittenger that same day, served to crystallize his latent political ambition, no matter what his state of shock.

"Of course," Mr. Pittenger cried across the miles of throbbing wire, "the Republicans are running around kind of crazy."

Ben yelled, "I don't blame them."

"What?"

"I don't blame them."

"I can't hear you."

"Never mind."

"People have been here in the bank talking," said Mr. Pittenger. "They say Winstrom and his crowd are completely flabbergasted by Abie's telegram. Then when word came on the heels of it that Abie was dead, Winstrom said—so they say, anyway—he said, 'Well, I don't understand this; but if Abie's dead I'm not going to try to back him up on this, and tell Ryder to withdraw—not if I have to resign from the county committee.' No, he won't resign his chairmanship, or even from the committee. Can you hear me?"

"Yes."

"Well, you see where that would leave you, Ben. You couldn't be a Republican candidate for representative—not with a Republican nominee already chosen at the primaries."

"I suppose not."

"What?"

"I suppose not."

"No, you couldn't. But what I wanted to say is this: with Abie dead, the Republican committee's going to lose a lot of strength in this county. I mean there's a lot of feud, and so on. Now, what I thought was this: Ben, do you want to be a candidate for representative?"

"How could I be? Just like you said—Charlie Ryder's still the candidate."

"Yes. But I've got a new idea. You may remember I didn't vote for Taft in 1908—I just didn't vote. I was a Roosevelt man in 1904 and, by golly, I could be one again! The Dodge County Bull Moose haven't got a candidate for representative in the fall—"

"Well, I don't know what to say."

"Ben. Your father was a Democrat and so was Uncle Danny before him. I don't know how you had thought of voting this year before this thing came up, but we could run you for representative on the Bull Moose ticket. I think maybe we could win. Ryder's never been very strong personally. He always ran behind the ticket."

"I don't know, Mr. Pittenger. I hadn't thought much about it. I still can't understand why Abie ever sent that telegram. I guess he just got drunk; we had a real good time at the party . . ."

"Ben, this call is costing me a lot of money, but you think it over. I've talked to two or three others just a while ago, and they feel the same way. You think it over."

"I don't know . . ."

After the call was concluded Ben sat in a chair drawn up by their open window, his shoeless feet in a chair opposite, and he tried to explain to Dolly the things which Mr. Pittenger had told him. Ben's conversation wandered somewhat; he had to keep forcing himself back to the point he was trying to explain. His main attention actually was focused on the window and the space in the street canyon opposite the window. He could not help thinking with pity and wonder of that big body which flopped heavily downward through nearby air only a few hours before.

He had never held much fondness for the dead Senator, but childishly he began to count Abie Newgate's virtues; he found many unperceived before.

His wife meanwhile was entertaining a particular panic in her own mind. It was something which had occurred to her that very morning, and was now substantiated by a vague hint in the afternoon newspaper. A reporter, overhearing some conversation at Headquarters, had written:

> "Although police are inclined to accept the theory of accidental death, one important point remains to be cleared up. A Chicago merchant is said to have reported that Senator Newgate purchased an expensive object, the nature of which is still undisclosed, yesterday morning. It is believed that an examination of the dead man's personal effects failed to disclose this recent purchase or yield any clue as to its whereabouts. Thus a police official who refused to allow the use of his name has suggested that a theory of robbery and murder is still tenable."

Consider the matter as she might, Dolly found herself entertaining a wholesome terror of the brooch which now lay in its wrapping within her powder-box. There was doleful regret in parting with it, but her agile resource soon suggested a safe course, and she followed it before the afternoon was over.

Determined to assume the character of a ministering angel, Dolly steadfastly refused Ben's willing offer to accompany her to the bedside of Marguerite Newgate. She must go, she said, as one woman to comfort another; and the presence of Ben might bring only an added misery to the invalid.

Thus when she entered the Blackstone Memorial Hospital, Dolly walked alone. Ben sat smoking in the shaded taxicab, waiting for her. She went sad-faced, the bearer of a secret tribute, the bearer of other wickeder secrets which she struck into oblivion as rapidly as they suggested themselves.

Marguerite Newgate lay dulled by opiates, her mind still normally receptive despite the tragic news and the more tragic, procrastinating fate which enveloped her flesh. Her doctor, a man blunter but more humane than most of his generation, had insisted upon recounting to Marguerite the tidings which others might have kept from her. This man had the bluff and practical hardihood to realize that one possible effect of the announcement might be to terminate the patient's suffering.

Dolly passed through a cordon of probationers and internes. When at last over professional protests her name had been borne in to Mrs. Newgate by the woman's nurse, Dolly was admitted to the chamber. She would never enjoy a bouquet of salmon-pink gladioli again. Such a bouquet stood up, flat and stark, on the dresser opposite Marguerite's bed. These were the only flowers in the room, and forever such gladioli would suggest a smell of medicines, a cheerless aroma of disinfectants and decay.

"Maybe I shouldn't have come, Mrs. Newgate." She held Marguerite's hand in hers.

The sick woman muttered unintelligibly.

"I can't tell you," said Dolly, her handkerchief before her eyes, "how Ben and I feel."

Mrs. Newgate gave a faint humming sound. She was, in the more murky moments of her drug-induced calm, given to consorting in imagination with butterflies which she had never caught or owned. A Spicebush Swallowtail . . . she had wanted one so badly, with its heavy blackness of wings and the small red dot near the margin of the after-wings. Yes, she had wanted a Spicebush, and a Buckeye too. Neither had ever come to her garden.

"Maybe in a clover field," she whispered to Dolly.

"What?"

Mrs. Newgate's nurse cleared her throat to catch Dolly's

attention. Her eyes narrowed behind her spectacles. She was indicating the door, but resolutely Dolly turned from her.

Dolly opened her bag and brought out the crumpled tissue paper from which she had already shaken powder carefully . . . and the crusty weight of gold and stones was inside. Heavier than a sewing-machine bobbin, heavier than—

"It was last night," Dolly said. "He asked me to keep it for him."

Marguerite Newgate fought with determination, and led her straying attention back from the chemical-scented pastures where it had been wandering. "I don't understand. He—Amos —gave you—?"

"It was a present. He was afraid to keep it. He said that he knew he was drinking more than he usually drank. And when we were having dinner he gave it to me to keep for him, so that he could give it to you."

Again the invalid made that whining . . . a scrape of a cello string, a resinous note of pondering unreality.

The nurse began: "I'm sorry. You'd better go, Mrs.—— She's going to sleep. The doctor—"

By this time Dolly herself was crying as sincerely as she had ever cried when she was a child, when she was hurt and frightened—as indeed she had been frightened and hurt with ghastly frequency.

She told the nurse (for all her tears, she spoke to her determinedly)—she said, "Here. You've got to help me. He bought this for her. He thought it would make her feel better."

The nurse yielded, and she came to the other side of the bed, and together they pleaded with Marguerite Newgate to understand, to observe, to come back from the strange vales down which she ran light-footed and girlish (unchewed by the pain of duplicating cells, unsick, unafraid of anything).

"Oh, Mrs. Newgate," they cried. "Look! See here. How wonderful! It's so beautiful. Look, it's an emerald. He sent it to you. . . ." and when Marguerite saw the thing at last she could not tear her lucent eyes from the galaxy. She could only disbelieve; and she put up an opal hand to touch the brooch when once they had pinned it onto the bedraggled lace bed-jacket, the cheap, tattered bed-jacket which no wife of so great a man as Abie Newgate should have worn. They pinned the soiled limpness together, and the brooch glared out from among those folds, though you could still see the coarseness of the hospital nightgown underneath.

Suddenly the moths were all flown out of the woman's mind. Her dreams were gone . . . the narcotic lessened and she would need more, for anguish was swelling through her loins and stomach again. "I can't understand it," she said clearly. "It just don't make sense. He never gave me anything like this before . . . he never gave me anything, I guess. Isn't it funny how I should get this given to me? I mean—oh, God—that he should have given this to me after he was dead?"

Thirty

For perhaps the first time in her life, Dolly Hessian Steele now wept with integrity when contemplating a misery other than her own. The salve of pity is not always an unguent; so, as Dolly felt a compassion she had not felt before, the spectral hands of her spirit were burned to the quick. The acid ate its way through outer skin.

A knowledge was staggering about somewhere in a lonely space at the back of her brain as Dolly descended in the slow-moving elevator and saw beside her an empty cart on which some other rag of mortal misery had been recently conveyed: there were horrors undreamed in this world, unperceived until now by her who believed stubbornly that she had tasted all the hot black dregs of frustration.

She had been striving, single-purposed as always, to find a safety for herself: a way out or a way in, a manner of achieving a thing essential. And in so doing, Dolly was staggered to find herself telling a lie of such Christlike charity that the angels sang in clean-swept corners of Mrs. Newgate's chamber . . . the fairies would dance around Marguerite as she died.

Sobbing when she came away from the hospital steps, Dolly was comforted by the tall man in the skimpy suit, who leaped from an open taxicab and put his arm around her.

"Ben . . ."

"Honey, what . . . ?"

"Oh Ben, she's dying."

"Now, honey, quit crying. Don't cry like that." He brought her into the taxicab.

"Ben, Senator Newgate never gave her *anything*."

"Dolly, quit it. Here, lean over against my shoulder."

"I don't want to," she choked. "It's too God damn hot," and he was surprised to hear her swear like that.

They drove in silence, fumbling their slow way up Wabash from the south side, halted often behind a phalanx of drays, a wall of tired horseflesh progressing beneath the smoky sun. Dolly left off crying, and sat staring at the driver's tanned neck where a dirty handkerchief was pushed between the collar and the man's skin.

"Honey," Ben pleaded.

She whispered, "What is it?"

"Honeybunch, I've got an appointment, but I'm going to break it. This has been too much for you—the whole business. What happened after the party and . . ."

She turned to look at him suddenly, her eyes blank.

". . . I mean Abie Newgate, and all that stuff. And then your going in to see *her*. You ought to have let me come. Honest to God, Dolly, is she really dying? Abie said—"

"I don't care what Senator Newgate said," came Dolly's dull voice. "He was an awful old liar anyway."

Ben shook his head. "Don't speak ill of the—"

"I don't care if he is dead. He was an awful liar. Ben, the world is full of liars. Everybody's liars, liars, liars. I am, too."

"Darling," he cried desperately, "what's got into you? You look awful. Now, look here, I've got that appointment over at the Peerless Wagon Wheel Corporation with Mr. Knowland, but I'm going to call him up and break it. I'm just going to sit around all afternoon and hold your hand. I don't want my baby to look the way she's looking now."

"Your baby's all right." But when the taxicab had drawn up in front of the Caxton's entrance, and even when the doorman had come forward to turn the big brass handle and open the rear door of the car, Dolly still sat motionless on the stiff leather.

Ben got out and extended his hand to her.

"I'm not coming with you now, I'm going on," she said.

He frowned. "What under the sun—?"

"There's somebody I've got to see."

He cast around in his mind, but not for long, and then he whispered (the doorman still standing ready behind him), "Your aunt?"

"Yes. I want to go and see her. I'm all upset."

"But that's away out in Lake Forest. You'll have to take a train."

"It doesn't matter. I want to go."

"Want me to go with you?"

"No. Please, Ben, I want to go alone."

"All right, if you say so. You got money?"

She nodded, exhibiting her purse and trying to smile. The tears had left dry patches amid the powder on her face, her hair was damp with sweat, her eyes puffed and reddish, but Ben's heart went out to her.

"Honey, it's hot as hell. I'm afraid maybe you might faint or—"

"Please don't worry. I'll be all right."

When unwillingly he had moved away from the car, she leaned forward and spoke a few words to the driver. The man nodded, champed his gears, and the taxicab grunted away west. Ben stood in shade of the hotel canopy, back in the cavern formed by iron grilles, and watched the cab go. It was held up for a moment by a traffic jam at the next corner; a policeman's whistle bubbled; the taxi went on west.

Dolly gave further instructions to the driver as they approached the boundaries of the Loop, and so they drove to a brick wilderness, out under the hard array of chimneys, gas tanks, warehouses that formed the awful wasteland of Chicago's summer. They drove with heat waves quavering around them. Whistles mourned perpetually; steel wheels pounded at every cross-track; the yellow smell of the stockyards came north and west to meet them.

In that same street where she had walked so many months before, and where the words "Feldstein" and "Plating" baked on the painted boundary, Dolly told the driver to wait for her. She rapped on a wooden door.

There was no answer from within, but soon a thin young woman carrying a fussy baby came out on the porch overhead and called down, "What do you want?"

"Does Mrs. Hesske still live here?"

"Yes. But she doesn't want to buy anything."

"I'm not selling anything," said Dolly. "I'm not a bill collector, either. I'm a relative."

"Well, she's up here setting on my back porch. You go on in. I'll tell her to come down the back way."

Dolly turned the knob of the unlocked door and closed herself into a room where the smells were less rancid than those of the stockyards but fully as persistent. She walked past a rumpled bed, on into a kitchen where unwashed dishes and kettles stood stewing in their own dirtiness.

Soon there came a creeping, a noisy breathing on the rear stairway that led down into ash-piles of the back areaway; and Dolly's aunt, Anna Hesske, came into view. She came as rapidly as she could. It was not rapidly at all: the woman's legs were frightfully swollen; it was hard for her to move. She wore a faded pink dressing-sacque and a dirty black petticoat. She had taken off her dress skirt because of the heat.

When she saw Dolly (almost before she saw her) the woman broke into the same high-pitched moan of affection and recognition—a wail that lamented the brutality and wickedness of the past, and dreaded the brief future that still remained. It was the same keening sound with which she had always welcomed her niece in their recent encounters. Those meetings were few and far between.

Mrs. Hesske said, "Oh, I thought I'd just about seen the last of you, Dor. You didn't write or nothing!" Her fat, freckled arms, with their unhealthy sweat and pallor, were embracing Dolly. The loose face was pushed close to the younger woman's. There was a stench . . .

"I was in Chicago, and I thought—"

"Oh, Dor. Rick's gone. My little Rickie's gone away and I don't know where he is!"

"I don't give a damn where he is."

"Oh, Dorry, don't talk that way about Rick. He's just had a hard time. He didn't have no chance at all."

"He had just as good a chance as I had. Maybe better."

The woman clung against her, and Dolly was compelled at last to push her aunt away.

"Dor, don't shove me. . . . He said he saw you that day, after you was here last summer or whenever it was. He said he wanted you to lend him some money so's he could redeem his tools. He had to pawn them; he got in some trouble, and he had to make bail."

Dolly said, "Of course I didn't give him a cent. I had just given you fifty dollars."

Mrs. Hesske collapsed on a kitchen chair among dirty underwear and dish-towels, and began to cry again. "I have such a hard time getting along, Dorry—an awful hard time. That family I got living upstairs: the man's been out of work; they ain't paid no rent in three months, and I'm behind on my taxes."

Dolly floated far and high, utterly removed, no part of this disgrace now, never a part again. "Rick came out to Iowa, where I'm living," she said, "last winter. He wanted some money and I wouldn't give him any. He stole my purse and took what was in it. I guess he got out of town then. I didn't see him again."

Mrs. Hesske whined on. "Well, I don't care how you talk about him . . . he was my baby. I just didn't have no chance to bring him up right. Dorry, I'm so sick. I tried to get down to the doctor—down to the clinic, on the street car last week; but it was just too much of a good thing. You just won't believe it, but I—" She related the physiological symptoms; they were doleful, disgusting. Dolly listened stonily.

She said, when her aunt had talked herself into a gasping collapse: "Aunt Anna, I'm sorry I didn't write to you. I guess I should have. I'll give you some money now. Here," and she pressed into the swollen hand the greater share of bills in her purse. "I'll send you more next month—every month—

as long as Rick isn't here. Not if he comes, though; not if he's here. I won't send a cent."

Mrs. Hesske blubbered, "Poor little Rick—he won't come here, Dor. They won't let him. The cops are looking for him all the time. He don't dare come home. Dorry, don't look at me like that. I done the best I could: there wasn't anybody else to take you in when you was little. Oh, Dorry, please forgive me. I know I didn't bring you up right but—"

Dolly overcame her repugnance; she bent down and kissed the oily hair on top of her aunt's head; she turned and walked away through the vileness of the living room, knowing in exhausted relief that she would never see her aunt again, alive or dead. It was not an idle promise Dolly made. She would send the money. She would. Maybe she had no right to use Ben's money in that way, but she couldn't help it.

When, in intimate confession of other seasons, Dolly had declared that her mother died when she was three weeks old, and that her father was killed in a wreck on the Chicago, Milwaukee & St. Paul railroad, she was telling the only truth she ever told commonly about herself. Her mother had died of puerperal fever; and her father, a news-butcher on the trains, had been crushed amid his candy packages on a rear platform.

What she had never related was the horrid factual narration of her earlier career; that other big gray house in a West Side suburb where her father's brother and sister-in-law managed their evil; the smelly kitchen, with cheap whiskey bottles crowding the table, and cases of beer underneath; the bottle caps and soiled feather boas she remembered as her first toys; and the aunts—oh, the aunts who lived upstairs: their shrill voices, their sleazy wrappers with spotted frills on them, the rouge, the high-frizzed hair, the corsetless harpies lounging in the front parlor (Aunt Edna? . . . yes, God knew there *was* an Aunt Edna, and she had red-blonde curls, and she was shot and killed on the front porch by a police sergeant with whom she had quarreled; and Aunt Myrtle, Aunt Ruthie, Aunt Gwendolyn . . . Dolly had known them all, and she had grown up to know the life they lived above-stairs, to know the life lived by every adult there); the officers who came to the door regularly with cigars in their mouths, and went away with money in their pockets . . . one of them used to give Dolly penny ice-cream cones, and he would shake his head and say that wasn't a very good place to bring up a kid in; and Rick—Aunt Anna's darling baby, who contained in his brutish little body every inclination toward mendacity, toward creepy vice—dear little Rick, who chopped the tails from the starved-to-death kittens, who sneaked in hiding beneath the beds upstairs, and retailed amid shouts of appreciation in the kitchen what he had heard and witnessed; the meager schooling Dolly had found freely; the wicked school of street and back-lot, offered with such profusion; other children, sainted by the decency of their homes, who followed her shrieking when she came from the parochial schoolroom, screaming, "Dorry Hesske's uncle runs a House! Dorry Hesske's uncle runs a House!" The dish-washing; the wandering away; the cash-girl years; the people who took pity on her; the grim-faced forewoman who had more than commiseration in her heart, and formed an ambition and a dream for Dolly, and gave her books to read, and magazines, and baked for Dolly the only birthday cake anyone had ever baked for Dolly, and it had sixteen pink candles on it. . . .

She cried no longer as she went up the steps from the front

areaway, staring unseeing into the hurtful heat. She had cried her last; she would never see that place or that woman again. Except for the obligatory charity she felt she must award, she would never think of Aunt Anna again if she could possibly help it.

The driver roused himself from his doze and opened the car door. Then a man came from an opposite doorway and crossed the street slowly. His face was strained, wondering. It was Ben.

He motioned her into the car. He got in after her and told the driver to take them to the Caxton.

"Dolly."

She did not answer, she did not turn toward him.

"Dolly."

"Yes?" she whispered at last.

"I followed you."

"I can see you did."

"For Pete's sake, Dolly, what was that place back there?"

"Why did you follow me? Oh, Christ—why did you follow me?"

"I was worried about you—I told you that. I thought I'd follow you, after all, to the train—you know, the station—and then I'd get on the train and surprise you, and ride out with you. I'd go out to Lake Forest or wherever it was. You know, just to keep you company on the way. . . . Dolly. Better tell me."

"I can't."

"Who was in that house? Why did you go there? You've got to tell me."

"My aunt." She got the words out at last.

"Your Aunt Edna? Does she live in a place like that?"

"I haven't got any Aunt Edna . . . Ben, it's all a lie. I told you I was a liar. It's my aunt; but her name's Anna Hesske. That was my name, too—Dorothy Hesske. I changed it."

Ben sat looking stupidly at his shiny black shoes, scraping long hard fingers against his seersucker knee. "What did you—?"

"I gave her some money."

He said after a while, "Is there anything else you want to tell me?" and then he lifted his eyes and looked at the driver and wondered what the man thought of all this, and what it would mean to him, and probably it would mean nothing at all. The driver was wise; he must be a generous and kindly man; he had not turned round to embarrass them, he had not been scornful or inquisitive. Laboriously Ben reached his hand into his pocket and got out his wallet as they approached the Loop again. He hoped that he had the proper change: he was going to give the driver five dollars in addition to all the accumulated fare.

"Honey," he said again, "is there anything else you want to tell me now?"

She said weakly, "Not now. Sometime I'll tell you the whole story. It isn't a—nice story at all. That's the reason I always lied: seemed like the only thing to do, to keep going." She sobbed for the last time, "Ben, do you still love me?"

"Of course I do." He meant it well.

Thirty-One

The Steeles did not return to Lexington until five days after Senator Newgate's death, and thus escaped the ordeal of his funeral. There was a little talk about this. It was thought that friends of Abie, such as Ben and Dolly, could at least have shown sufficient respect to the dead statesman to participate in the burial rites. Another school of opinion defended them as staunchly. Rumor told that Dolly sat hour after hour beside the bed of Marguerite, in the Blackstone Memorial Hospital, and gave her the spiritual succor which only womankind could offer. Dolly did in fact visit the invalid once more; but Marguerite was lulled, drowsing in a forest of morphia where even the most agile midnight moths did not choose to fly.

Dr. Strothers, encountering Dolly at the door of Mrs. Newgate's room, told her that he did not think the illness would be protracted; and within a month he was cited with appreciation by the Recorders in Higher Regions. He injected a measured overdose into the arm of the sufferer, thus performing a deserving euthanasia, as he had performed it before, as he would do again, as many other members of his profession have done before and since: the courageous and deliberate act of a worthy sergeant not unreluctant to serve as the delegate of Better Authority.

The campaign for Dodge County's representative in the

legislature boomed into resounding proportions by early October, and Ben Steele gave himself earnestly to his search for office. He was not a brilliant candidate, but one wholly acceptable, especially in rural districts. His opinions and the promises he made did not confuse the populace. They were, in fact, very similar to the professed statements of his chief opponent, the Republican candidate Charles P. Ryder; but whereas Ryder had served several undistinguished terms in the House at Des Moines, Ben Steele was looked upon as a kind of white hope of prosperity and reassurance.

This happened doubtless because he was young, because he had an energetic charm and salty humor, and a vigorous simplicity.

There were no thorny questions in that campaign to split the ranks of Dodge County voters into furiously opposed sections. When Ben spoke at rural schoolhouses, in an auction-barn, at a rally in front of the courthouse steps, and to the Bull Moose committee at the Wildwood Hotel, he pursued a safe and steady course among the few problems of which Dodge County was completely aware. His views on interstate commerce, on freight rates, on taxes, on governmental regulation of what the citizens chose to term their private affairs—these beliefs and resultant expressions caused little stir and no antagonism, though the entrenched Republicans waited hopefully for Ben to put his foot in his mouth.

He was as honest in his conservatism as most moderately intelligent men of his time and place. In the common parlance of Iowa, he voted Dry and promised that he would, but he was no fanatical Prohibitionist. He drank Wet with the Elks; everybody knew it; Abie Newgate had done the same thing.

Ben believed that woman's place was in the home, and said so. A campaign or two later he might have stirred up enmity among the distaff side of his bailiwick by this attitude; but in Dodge County the question of woman-suffrage was not yet sufficiently acute to cause any trouble.

Thus the campaign simmered down into a mere preference of persons and personalities. The Democratic candidate, formally nominated at the recent primaries, was a dreamy-eyed old physician residing in a village near by: a perennial aspirant for public office who doted merely on the brief limelight he achieved in this capacity, and did not expect or even hope for election. The Bull Moose party had only recent recognition thereabouts, and that among die-hard admirers of Theodore Roosevelt. By all estimation of political history, Ben Steele was a dark horse, a write-in candidate.

But he was a good one. He had the Republicans worried. Old Mr. Pittenger and the friends he had swept to Ben's support (following the cryptic and forever unexplained telegram from Abie Newgate)—these people found a zest in the activity, and Mr. Pittenger even fancied himself on the State Banking Commission. The Republican Committee, from the chairman down, had never been able to fathom the motives behind Newgate's amazing message. Ben himself was not able to throw any light on the mystery, even during the most earnest conferences with his colleagues. But the Republicans had no intention of reading their man out of the race merely because "Abie got drunk in Chicago and had a brainstorm." They took unkindly to the implication that Newgate should boss their fortunes from his grave.

Domestically Mr. Steele and his pretty wife seemed drawn closer together than ever before. Murmured confessions from

Dolly were bound to come in response to Ben's queries . . . they had begun to come, even before the Steeles left Chicago, in response to the husband's sympathetic questioning. The dreary tale which Dolly unfolded gave no cause for Mr. Steele to shun his bride. He had never pitied her before; he pitied her now. She had lied completely and insistently to him, but those lies were the only defense she had. Ben was smart enough to see that; and his generosity polished delightedly at the shining facets of his wife's heroism. He knew that few girls born and reared among such surroundings could have attained to the balance, the suave efficiency in human affairs, the sugary charm of this woman he loved.

He told her as much, and often—perhaps too often for wisdom's sake. In penitence though she might be, after the experiences in Chicago, Dolly was unable to abandon the conniving habits of a young lifetime. She was reassured by her husband's soothing, pleased that at last they held conjointly an important secret which concerned her; but she was just as much determined to continue in her management of his fortunes.

Adroitly at times, too painfully blunt on other occasions, she came back at him again and again on the question of his business career. She wished for Ben to give up all horsy affairs not only because she loathed the uncouth aspect, not only because she detested the ammonia smells, the manure flavor that saturated the entire enterprise. She insisted—and believed shrewdly—that there was no prospect in the business. She wanted Ben to have a well-sustained financial future—for his own sake, for hers, for the sake of children who might be born to them. There was not much money in politics per se. If Ben were to prosper in public office, and still remain as resolutely honest as before, he would need an adequate income.

On every street of Lexington, on every street in every town, the new automobiles rattled and chugged. There were twice as many cars in town now as there were on the day when Dolly first descended from the Illinois Central train. One machine shop and one implement company had been remodeled into motorcar garages and repair shops since the previous winter. The automobile owners already formed a persuasive lobby, affecting the decisions of the city council as paving plans were projected with renewed insistence. Ads filled the magazines . . . some manufacturers were producing cheaper automobiles and in greater number. Dolly was no prophet, but she believed the news she read and observed. She knew that she was right and that Ben was stubbornly wrong.

The Chicago tragedies had wedded them more tightly, but what remained of their natural conflict in marriage was focused on this repetitive disagreement. When they fought, they fought about the livery stable and its satellite industries.

They were to fight again, and bitterly, and soon. . . . Unknown to the town at large or to the victims of her malevolence, Miss Elizabeth Butterfield was responsible for the disagreeable event witnessed by the Steeles on the evening of Monday, November 4th, the night before election day.

In her capacity as assistant to the county recorder, Bet Butterfield enjoyed a dull but traditional comradery with men who came to the courthouse on business or who loafed there because they enjoyed the atmosphere. This afforded Bet an opportunity to strike at Dolly Steele by striking at her husband; she hurled her blow with dispatch.

Florence Mahanna was now devoted to Bet: the ties between them were as strong as thwarted emotion could make, and though their affection might be unestimated in its true light by the townspeople of that generation (who saw only two laughable old maids stalking about, a duet to be cartooned forever, to be lampooned in thought and in ludicrous gossip), they both felt with poignant secrecy that they were set apart from the rest of men and women at large. They lived, to themselves and in their spirits, in that bleak desert bordering the pastures of the blessed. They were in the life of the town and in the heterosexual world—they were not of it.

Floss, intrinsically feminine in thought and deed until decoyed by Bet Butterfield, felt her condition more keenly than did Bet. Hence Floss was apt to dissolve in tears on odd occasions, and was then viewed with resentful alarm by her partner. Bet feared that Dolly, by some act of appeal, by exertion of the glamor in which Miss Mahanna's gaze had dressed her so early, might steal a portion of the fealty which Bet Butterfield claimed. She never lost an opportunity to "run down" Dolly Steele.

When she recognized the esteem in which Ben was held, and when it was rumored that he had a very good chance of beating Ryder in the race for representative, Miss Butterfield was worse than annoyed.

Dolly, as soft-spoken queen of the Lexington elect, constituted a threat to Elizabeth Butterfield's peace. But ennobled as the wife of a State Representative, she would be a nightmare. Bet imagined Ben Steele and Dolly in temporary residence at a Des Moines hotel during a session of the legislature. When Bet and Floss went to Des Moines together, Floss would feel impelled by every power of previous admiration and of Lexington kinship, to call up Dolly on the telephone.

Dolly might in turn invite Floss to her hotel—perhaps even to a dinner where Officers-of-State were foregathered. . . .

As she pursued this frightened thought, Bet could see Floss returning to her own dubious charms with a newly engendered hostility.

It was dangerous. Bet did not like to think of it.

Casually, she appeared unimaginative; that was only because her angry face and body were large, ugly and dull. Bet had a highly developed imagination and a kind of sadistic humor. These combined to project an enterprise which she hoped would prove disastrous to the immediate political fortunes of Ben Steele.

In informal conclave with certain other people of Republican preference, Bet saw her opportunity. She had observed enough politics to know that ridicule was a barbed weapon in any campaign. . . . She spoke her mind, she laughed heavily, she made more suggestions; the younger and more purposeful of her hearers were entranced. Bet then occupied her whole intelligence with a design which had come to her merely as a fugitive thought. She contrived, she schemed now as effectively as Dolly had ever schemed. The grinning Republicans did their best, and their best was Elizabeth Butterfield's best. They worked with celerity. It was the Friday before the election when Bet conceived her idea, and there was no time to be lost.

Monday night, November 4th, the air of downtown Lexington was assailed by a medley of horrid blatting and tooting. Tin horns were used, klaxons, rattles, little wooden duck-calls, and every variety of toy with which cheap hullabaloo could be made. Routed from temporary headquarters in the Wildwood Hotel, the Bull Moose partisans, together with their earnest candidate and his wife, hastened to the veranda to witness the spectacle advancing up Sixth Street in a glow of red fire and gasoline torches.

There was a Bull Moose in the lead, but he was labeled largely, "Mr. Bull Mouse," and he was made of brown cloth and cardboard, and in his body and as his legs two anonymous clowns capered wildly. Behind this monstrosity moved an horrendous caravan not unlike the Calathumpians of pioneer times; they were accompanied by an array of broken-down animals and vehicles. There rolled every squeaking, grease-less, graceless, abandoned wagon and buggy which could be dragged from the back-lot waste patches of the community; there tottered sway-backed horses, lame mules, a blind and bloated pony.

Signs glared and waved: huge painted signs, black letters staring on white backgrounds, washed in flame.

"No Horse-and-Buggy Legislation Needed."

"Do You Want to Vote for a Horse—?"

"—Or a Ryder?"

"Shall We Turn the Legislature into a Livery Stable?"

Many more signs like these were displayed, and the old mules made their awful sounds in frightened discord. The largest, grayest, most scrofulous mule carried a sign of his own: "A Vote for Steele Is a Vote for Me."

Thin and limping nags were preceded by a pedestrian carrying a banner announcing, "We Are Steele's Promises," and they were followed by another pedestrian garbed as a street-sweeper, complete with wide-bristled brush and clean-ing cart: "Keep Our Kountry Klean." There were baby car-riages, buckboards, two-wheeled carts; and an overgrown lummox in a white nightshirt who sat doubled up on a child's coaster-wagon with a nursing bottle in his hand. The sign said: "I'm Going to Vote for Brother Benny."

All the way up Sixth Street, about-face at Maple, back to Hazel again, south on Hazel, far south past the Courthouse Park, patrolling through the residential section, the tatterdemalion tide went flowing. Ben stood laughing on the Wildwood porch; Dolly was furious, and finally hid her face. She realized the efficacy of this derision, and felt her strained hopes falling away.

Alfred Pittenger said, "Ben, they couldn't find any other way to attack you; they had to act like a gang of fools," and with this observation several others agreed. Ben himself was not at all disturbed.

The appeal was being directed openly and obviously against a witless bloc of voters: the little minds ready to respond to obvious suggestion, the inconsiderate louts hanging like deadweight around the margin of every political unit in a democracy. Ben Steele lost the election.

It may be believed that the one hundred and thirty-four votes by which he lost, were won to the Ryder faction solely by the spectacle presented on Monday night. Ben piled up a promising margin in every rural district except one; but he saw his lead diminish and finally vanish as the town's final votes were counted on Wednesday forenoon.

He was wounded by the blow. He had been confident that he would win.

Dolly's hatred against the unacknowledged enemies who had broken down her hope and her delusion was now a fever inside her. She went to bed with a sick headache before dinner Wednesday noon. She told Larry that she should not be called, though commiserating friends telephoned, and Agatha

Cook stopped at the house, trusting to console Dolly, and walked away disappointed.

Ben came home about three o'clock and went up to the front bedroom. Dolly lay with a folded handkerchief across her eyes.

"How are you, darling?"

"All right, I guess."

"Well, it's too bad."

She wanted to rise from the bed and throw her arms around him. She did not have the strength. She was wondering stupidly about another election . . . it would be two years before there could be another election.

"Would you run again?" she asked feebly.

"No. I gave it everything I had. The folks— Well, I guess a lot of them did want me, but not enough." He growled a tired homily: " 'Shoemaker, stick to your last.' "

Dolly asked, "Just what is your last, anyway?"

He stared at her in astonishment; she felt his gaze coming hard. She sat up, supporting herself by one elbow, and took off the cloth which was drying on her face, imprinted across the bridge of her nose and the hollows of her eyes.

"For God's sake!" Ben cried angrily. "What do you mean—what *is* my last? My business, by God! I'm going to stick to it."

Dolly whispered, "I hate your business. It's the very thing that defeated you."

"Defeated me? Why—"

"I mean that. I know it, and you know it."

"I don't know anything of the kind. Do you mean that parade Monday night? They were just trying to—"

"Whatever they were trying to do, they did it, Ben. Everybody knows how you hate automobiles and things. It just gave them an opportunity to talk about horse-and-buggy legislation. Oh," she screamed in a released frenzy of resentment against his stubbornness, against his trade, against the hateful appurtenances thereof, "that God damn livery barn! I wish it would burn down!"

Ben was standing by the front door, looking out through glass across the little balcony, gazing down at the sidewalk and street beyond, watching the tags of crumpled maple leaves, the fewer elm leaves still brown and wadded on their twigs. He did not turn in rage; he only said, "So you wish the livery barn would burn down?"

"Yes, I do! It's insured, isn't it? At least you wouldn't build a new livery barn and a new wagon shop and everything. You'd be rid of it. Oh, it's like the handwriting on the wall: automobiles and— You idiot, can't you see? You've simply got to understand! There's no reason why you've got to spend your life this way. Ten years from now, Ben, the automobiles are going to—"

He spoke a coarse and angry word. Dolly was affronted by the obscenity he uttered.

"Very well," she said coldly, "just go ahead and use words like that. It won't alter the circumstances, not in the slightest. All I can say is: there's no excuse for you to be so blind, so—so mule-headed, merely because your grandfather and your father—"

Ben roared at the top of his lungs, "You shut up about my father!" He gave her one glare and then stalked out of the room.

Dolly sat on the bed, wondering what he was going to do, wondering how soon he would come back and make up to her. He did not come. Distantly she heard him speaking to

Larry; she heard his footsteps for a time. It sounded as if he had gone out of the back door; she couldn't be sure.

She waited the best part of an hour without stirring from the room. She lay back and cried for a while, and the tears improved her condition of mind. At last she got up and went to the bathroom. She dressed herself carefully; she knew what she would do. She had not been the moving factor in a reconciliation after any of their recent minor quarrels; but this time she would take the initiative—she would go downstairs and telephone to Ben, she would tell him . . . Yes, she would . . . she would tell him that she wished he would take her for a *drive.*

Poor Ben . . . poor unhappy, politically-defeated— She thought of his laugh, she thought of his voice and his body, and an anguish of affection came to choke her throat.

Dolly hurried downstairs. Larry was stirring cake batter in the kitchen, and Dolly hesitated with her hand on the telephone receiver, there in the hallway outside the kitchen door.

"Larry, did Mr. Steele say whether he was going down to the shop or to the barn?"

"Yes, ma'am. He said he wouldn't be back for supper."

"Not back for supper?"

"No, Mrs. Steele. He said he was going out of town. Maybe he wouldn't be back tonight. He said to tell you."

Dolly's hand fell away from the telephone. She returned to the bedroom; and then she was too nervous to remain, greeted by a bland heaviness of mahogany and walnut. She looked at the bed; she thought of herself and Ben lying in bed; she thought again of their quarrel and of the harsh things said at other times . . . suddenly she believed she heard the echo of Ben's voice, crying out the imprecation he had shouted. . . .

She tried to consider a friend . . . but there was no one else whom she wanted to see. There was only Ben. Out of town? Where had he gone? Oh, was he going away? Was he leaving her with no more than that—not even another word?

Obsessed, she skipped down the stairs again.

"Valeria. Listen to me. Did he say where he was going, out of town?"

The gaunt young Negress turned a plaintive sympathy upon her. "No, Mrs. Steele," the soft, black voice said. "No, ma'am. He just said out of town on the train."

"On the train? But he said he was coming back, maybe, tonight?"

"Yes, ma'am, I think so. He said maybe he wouldn't be back tonight. I don't know."

Dolly went back upstairs. She had made one of the smaller side bedrooms next to Ben's into a sewing room. She had her machine in there, her work-baskets, a dress-form, and some forms for hats. Before the final energetic demand of the political campaign she had been trying to make herself a winter hat. It was to go with the marten fur and muff which Ben had given her as a belated wedding present.

(O little brooch of staring emerald and diamond flame . . . she saw it now; she saw her hands and those other nerveless hands fastening gems above the hospital nightgown, above that tired lace . . .)

She had been making a winter hat: brown velvet, with a cluster of gold fruit to adorn the crown. She had not had time to work on it much, lately.

Dolly sat at the table clipping velvet, draping and stitching, toiling until supper time. She ate almost no supper. A friend or two called; she did not want to take their calls. She told the maid to say that she was asleep. Larry said there was a show at the opera house: a traveling company—*The Virginian* they were giving this night, and Larry wanted to go. Dolly told her to go ahead, and she went back upstairs to the bad electric light. Her eyes were strained.

She was there with the hat, her fingers behaving badly, worry and terrors claiming her, when she heard distant shouts and soon the running of a stableman's feet, and pounding and yelling at the back door.

Thirty-Two

Emory Buckland had begun drinking about eleven o'clock that morning, when ominous reports of the election returns were first conveyed to the livery stable office. Uncle Em drank seldom—never to celebrate a happy event, never to brighten the spark of comradeship. He had found that the crutch of alcohol supported him in stress. He did not have a good head for liquor. He had been an active enlistee in the Cold Water Army of post-Civil War times; with a white ribbon affixed to his chest, he had marched in Temperance processions through the streets of Lexington, and had prayed loudly for the saloons to be closed and boarded up.

But in those days his wife and his two daughters were alive to see him march. They were no longer about, and his bereavement plagued him more odiously the older he grew. Instead of the square house with its pink-painted weatherboards, its nasturtium bed and solid well-cover—the house where he had lived his best years, even though the C. & N.W. trains scattered hot cinders on the roof and smoke in the muslin curtains—instead of this house, he had only a den above the resounding stables: a kind of box-stall adjoining the hayloft, a cot bedroom, built as tight as the grain-storage chamber which it had originally been.

Uncle Em did not dwell persistently on his lost youth and

the vanished people who had directed it, but he was sentimentally vociferous concerning that internecine struggle dignified by some as The War for Southern Independence but dubbed eternally by Uncle Em as The Rebellion. He did not talk much about Callie or the girls . . . years before, he had learned some poems by Will Carleton: these he recited to suitable boy listeners, to other veterans at monthly campfires of the Grand Army Post, to Ben Steele, to anyone who would listen.

Like many men of little accomplishment, men of hard-working futility and dogged, doleful lives, his wartime experience was the one sublime splint which held him erect. His domestic remembrance continued only in yellowed and dirty photographs in an old tin-strapped trunk, alone in the barn where mice scooted at night.

Uncle Em transferred the affection he held for his departed kin, and larded it over the Steeles. There was no one but Ben left now to give this love to. Emory Buckland knew remotely (spared the needle-prick of honest recognition)—he knew vaguely, without being told, without identifying the knowledge whole-heartedly—that he might not own the affinity with Ben which he had enjoyed with an elder clan.

But he had framed a gilt-edged marvel in his mind, during the campaign, and this panorama hung among his dusty dreams like the illuminated rosters of 1862 with their draped flags, their tinted cannon and ornate eagles. In the great fulfilment he had thought would assuredly come to Ben, Buckland saw a future joy, and he saw himself sharing it.

He imagined the State House in Des Moines . . . he could well imagine it; he had been there actually in presence; years before with Callie he had made a tortuous ascent to the Capitol dome. He imagined the State House, and Ben strolling through great corridors, past the cases of battle flags—proud but faded testimonials of Iowa's might.

Maybe the man at the door would tell Uncle Em that he couldn't come inside—no visitors admitted, maybe—something like that. "Oh, is that so?" Emory Buckland would say. "Let me tell you this, young fellow: you just go in there to the Legislature, and you tell Ben Steele that Uncle Em is out here!" The fancy gatekeeper would retreat, sneering and doubting still; but he would sing a different tune when Ben rushed out with hand extended and face split wide in a welcoming smile.

Ben would take him inside; Uncle Em would have a seat next to Ben; he would hear Ben make speeches; there might be a banquet later with the Governor in attendance. At the proper moment Ben would rise and say, "Ladies and gentlemen, I am proud to introduce to you tonight an old and valued friend, a veteran of that great conflict which made this nation one and indivisible: a soldier of the Third Iowa Volunteer Infantry. 'May the wreaths they have won never wither, nor the star of their glory grow dim.' "

From eleven o'clock on the morning of Wednesday, November 6th, 1912, Emory Buckland knew beyond a doubt that this happy legend of the future was not to be a fact shared and savored by him.

At first he was doubting; he scorned the reports; he bet fifty cents on the eventual outcome, swearing by all that was high and holy that this travesty of justice could not have been visited upon Dodge County by its electorate. When the horrid fact was proved beyond a doubt, Emory Buckland retired to his private quarters and was not seen for a while. Then he took some dollar bills from the little wad he kept in an old tobacco can, and by devious means, an hour or two later, he became the possessor of a quart of whiskey. This sustenance he absorbed throughout the afternoon. He had no head for liquor—that had been proved on other occasions—and when he tried to harness a horse about four o'clock, and announced at last that the horse was harnessed, although tug-straps were still trailing, the new manager of the livery stable cried in disgust, "Oh, the hell with this business, Uncle Em! You go sleep it off," and this Uncle Em tried to do.

He awoke after dark, chilly and uncomfortable, on the back seat of an old carryall in one of the sheds. He got out stiffly. He couldn't remember where his whiskey was; he guessed he had left it under the blanket on his bed, and so his steps took him in that direction. There was one clear thought active in Buckland's intelligence at this time, and it recurred again and again, spoken with a hollow voice like a chaplain's voice at a funeral . . . *he shouldn't have tried it. He was too young. He shouldn't have tried it now. He should have waited until he got older.*

Uncle Em knew in conscience that Ben Steele would not have essayed public office except at Dolly's instigation. At Friday night suppers he had heard proof sufficient to make him believe that. He had heard Dolly "nagging away at Ben" as Uncle Em expressed it to himself.

It was her fault. He shouldn't have tried it.

He staggered up the rough-timbered stairway to his room, and after much fumbling he lit the lantern that hung solidly on a wire hoop suspended from a rafter. Fire was the grave danger in all such places: they even had the common movable trolley by which lanterns were slid from stall to stall, hung tightly on their little track to avoid the danger of heat, of careless handling. There was the big tin cornplaster sign in the office, too, where bags or cans of tobacco hung safely, checked there by an ancient edict of the owners, to guard against stray whiffs and puffs in dangerous regions. The only flame ever burning within those quarters, aside from the necessary lanterns on their track, burned to illuminate the hard gray cot, the old washstand and slop-jar, the musty hay-smelling region where the veteran slept.

And he was careful, now, about bringing a flame to this lantern. He held a match with all the caution he could muster, though his hand was shaking. He heard the roar of a crowd applauding Representative Benjamin Steele; he heard the roar diminish and draw away and vanish, leaving only a smoky emptiness in which the gilded dome of the Capitol trembled.

"Shouldn't have tried it . . . she shouldn't have made him," he said again, and there was a balloon within his head. The whiskey bottle . . . he wondered where it was. He fumbled around the bed and found the big glass cylinder beneath an old comforter. He held it up to the light. Several inches of dark liquid still sloshed, tempting him on. "Too young," he gulped, half-aloud, and choking as he muttered the words. "Shouldn't have tried it. She made him." He drank heavily; he started to retch. He dropped the bottle and went staggering forward, feeling for the wall.

Emory Buckland wanted a place to hold onto: something solid to grip . . . his hand met glass and tin; the glass and tin were hot to the point of burning him, and painfully he struck this monstrous object aside. In another instant the place was alive with fumes and a great wide *whoof* of sound. Uncle Em fell into the middle of it.

There was a fantasy contrived many years afterward by a child who had every reason to build a sentimental and ghostly whimsy. By virtue of inheritance and sentimental regard, this child was empowered in a day-dream to construct a study which comforted him when he heard recounted (and told once more, and told again and again) the story of this disaster.

Thus, in an illusion remaining forever in the heart and mind of that child, Uncle Emory Buckland arose at last and walked aloof from the flames, and presently he found another man standing beside him. The other man made himself known. It was Long Dan Steele. He stood serene and contemplative, and when Long Dan walked away, when he progressed here and there through confusion of doomed sheds and other buildings and the yard itself, Uncle Em went with him.

"Well, Em," said Daniel Steele, "it's too bad. There isn't anything you can do about it now."

"No, I suppose not. I didn't figure on seeing you. I don't understand it."

"People never do."

"But it's awful to hear those horses!"

"So much that we listen to on earth, Em, is distressful for us to hear."

"Maybe so. I'm feeling a little weak."

"Take my hand. . . . Is it better now? Are you feeling better, Em?"

"Yes, I'm better. I didn't think it would be like this."

"They never do. I didn't myself."

"I want to see Callie and the girls."

"You will, pretty soon. Want to see Mad?" and Daniel Steele's call shrilled compellingly through the soaring flames, amid horse-screams and the running of men.

Madison Steele appeared to stand with them. "Why did you break that lantern, Uncle Em? That was a fool thing to do."

"I guess I got kind of drunk. What about Ben?"

"Wait and see."

"Is that what we do?"

"Yes. Hold our hands if you feel weak. Yes, that's what we do. We wait a long time—a long, long time, and we see everything."

Uncle Em jammed down the Grand Army hat which had appeared miraculously upon his head, though he had lost it in his last futile struggle when the lantern burst upon the floor and the flames leaped wide.

"Look, that's her—the girl! Yes, there she is. Somebody called her—"

Dolly was running down Fourth Street; she was bare-headed, she had a coat around her shoulders (everyone else who ran was bare-headed too).

"Where on earth is Ben?" Uncle Em wanted to know.

"On earth."

"But he ought to be *here*. . . . Look at her: she's broke loose from that boy who's trying to hold her. She's run hog-wild into the barn. She hadn't ought to have done that."

Long Dan Steele put his hand on the shoulder of his son. "Remember, Mad, that time last spring when we heard them talking? Ben was telling her about the time Libby's boarding stable burned, when you were little—the story you always told him—and how we got those horses out. He was telling her about putting something over their heads. Maybe she remembers."

"She's scared to death of horses," said Madison Steele scornfully.

"I guess she's worse scared of something else."

"What else?" asked Uncle Em.

"The Wrath to come."

"Is there any Wrath a-coming?"

"We don't know. We haven't met it yet. We just wait and see."

"Look!" cried Emory Buckland, and his voice was so skinny and alert—it seemed it must penetrate the howling of the fire, that it must slice amid yells and orders and countermanded orders of the people who toiled and ran, of the volunteer firemen who tumbled across their own hose-lines. It seemed that his call should carve among all mortals, and cause these people to stop and turn and look and fall silent before the miracle of Buckland and the Steeles, watching near.

"Doesn't do any good to shout," said Madison Steele in discernment. He put his hand on Uncle Em again to strengthen him. "They can't hear you. They never hear us. Maybe they'd behave differently if they did— I don't know."

"Look at that!" screeched Uncle Em, deaf to advice. "She got Barnum! She had her coat wrapped around his head—"

"Fellow's trying to hold her," said Long Dan. "She's quite a girl. There she goes again."

"Maybe she'll get Nagger," Uncle Em surmised.

"No, here's Nagger, right over here," and the horse whinnied behind them. "He's with us now. His stall was right under your room, Em. . . . There she comes. What's that horse she's hauling now?"

"He's going to step on her," said Uncle Em. "Look out there, lady! No, by golly, he didn't . . . I can't see exactly: she's got those grain sacks over him. Yes, it's Babe."

He said after a moment, "You know, those other horses—Oh, great God Almighty, I've seen a couple of other fires like this, and I just couldn't stand to hear those horses. But here—the way we are—I don't know how to say it. It's different."

"You'll find a lot of things are different," said Madison Steele. "How about it, Pa? Time for us to go, isn't it?"

Long Dan grinned slyly, and nodded.

"Come on, Em," they said, "we're going to show you things."

Emory Buckland fought against their persuasion. "But I better not leave, folks," he said. "We ought to stay here. It ain't over yet. Look at that: the blacksmith shop's on fire . . . they got their water going on the harness store; I don't think that'll catch. . . . I tell you, it ain't over!"

"It was over before it began," said Daniel Steele.

"How's that? I don't understand."

Madison Steele said, "You will."

"Yes," said Long Dan. "We were sent for you, Em—sent to take you—"

"Take me where?"

"Somewhere. You'll see. How would you like to see Callie and the girls?"

Emory Buckland laughed and cried in his eagerness. "Oh, yes, yes, I'd like that. Where? Oh, where? For God's sake—"

"How'd you like to hear some martial music—real old-time stuff? . . . What was yours?"

"Third Ioway!" Emory Buckland shouted proudly.

"That's it. How'd you like to hear martial music in the real old-fashioned way, like they used to play?"

"Oh, great God Almighty, let me hear it."

"Come on," they said, and they led him into space, with Nagger and two other horses following. This was the fantasy built long afterward by a child of Dolly and of Ben.

Thirty-Three

There was no way for anyone to notify Ben Steele. So he was not told until he climbed solemnly from the 10.23 eastbound train (forty minutes late because of a broken switch in the Fort Dodge yards). A man spoke to him at the edge of the platform, and he broke into a run. He ran across the Northwestern railroad tracks, past the Sixth Street intersection, past the Wildwood Hotel, and came finally to the glowing, smelly desecration of his material world.

The harness store still stood, and one building of the wagon works. Everything else was gone except a charred rim of corner sheds at Hazel Street. Amid those spiteful embers where the larger barn had been, men toiled near the fat carcasses of horses. They were digging around, trying to find what was left of Uncle Em.

Ben Steele waited a while. People came up and spoke to him; two or three gripped his hand. The grasp he gave was perfunctory . . . Believably he was not seeing them with his eyes. At last he went through the crowd . . . other people who observed his face: some of them had the inclination to speak, and then they looked at his face again, and the words were stopped before they uttered them.

He went up Fourth Street and cut across behind the Pryor

place toward his own back porch. There were lights burning in the house, and Larry was making coffee in the kitchen.

"Mr. Steele," Larry wailed, "I'm just as sorry as I can be!" She burst into tears, although she had been crying before. "That poor little funny old grandpa!" she sobbed.

"Where's Mrs. Steele?"

"Upstairs. She was crying and— She's just about beside herself, Mr. Steele! I was making her some coffee, hoping to tempt her. She wouldn't eat hardly no supper."

Ben went upstairs. He found Dolly in the bathroom; she wore her pink negligee, and she was trying to put cold cream on her face, but her hands were shaking.

She looked at him as if he were a hundred ghosts instead of one.

"Darling."

"Don't darling me," he said.

"Ben, I—"

"Well, you did it, didn't you?"

"Did what?"

"You burned it."

The face was a sheet of snowy flatness on which her large eyes swam. "For pity's sake, darling. You can't—"

He said, "I guess you got what you wanted. Do you know where I was? I was in Fort Dodge. I went over there on the train. I called up Mr. Harrick, and went out to his house, and made a deal. I didn't tell you: he wanted to buy me out last spring. He wanted that corner location to put up a big garage. So I had a proposition with him—a partnership, I guess you'd call it. I was going to sell everything: auction off the livestock, auction off the carriage stock, sell out the harness business. I was going to keep pace with the times, the way you wanted. You oughtn't to have been in such a hurry. And for Christ's sake"—this was the only time his voice broke in two—"why did you have to burn up Uncle Em?"

Dolly fainted. Ben did not catch her, he let her fall. He started forward as her knees sagged and her eyes rolled up. It was an automatic gesture; probably he was standing too far away to catch her, even had he wished.

At last he picked up the sprawled figure; he carried Dolly into the front room and put her on the bed. There was no light burning in that room. He stood briefly and looked down at the woman's figure, and he made a sound. Then he went to the stair and called, "Larry."

She answered him.

"Please come up here and take care of Mrs. Steele. She's fainted."

Larry clattered up the stairway, and Ben went back and turned on the light in the front room. He got a small bag out of his closet and packed a few things. He didn't know exactly what to take. All the time he packed, the servant was bathing Dolly's face and rubbing her wrists and muttering in alarm.

"Mr. Steele, what happened?"

"She just fainted."

"Where are you going?" blurted Larry. "You going away again? Mr. Steele, this is your wife; she's in a faint. . . ."

He looked at the two women: the one unrevived upon the bed, the other frightened and expostulating, revolving her eyes at him.

"Yes," he said. "You can tell her, when she wakes up, that I've gone," and he took his bag and walked out of the house.

He went west to Maple Street. He didn't want to walk past

the corner of Fourth and Hazel any more. Remotely, with voices still rowdy in his ears, he realized that any necessary arrangements about his life and his business could be made by letter when he was far away. What was the next train? Westbound . . . no, wait a minute . . . there was a southbound passenger about twelve-thirty, on the branch line to Des Moines. He could go there; he could call up Mr. Harrick and Mr. Pittenger the next day.

He strode through darkness of the railroad yards and walked down a side-track, thus avoiding the business district in its entirety, and keeping on across Hazel Street until he reached the Northwestern station. The office wasn't open yet: a yawning agent would appear before train time and unlock the door, and then Ben could buy his ticket.

He found a baggage truck in the sheds and climbed upon it. The punishment he had received would not allow him to feel an active hatred. He could experience no murderous resentment now—only a vast emptiness and silence. He shut his eyes and heard the cold wind in wires up above . . . there was the sad *baa*ing of sheep in a cattle car near the coal sheds.

After a while the baggage man came and unfastened a padlock, and moved the heavy door aside. Soon he was joined by the sauntering figure of a night watchman. They talked about the fire, and Ben tried to close his ears against their talk. He sat motionless, half doubled-up on the baggage truck, his arms around his knees, head fallen forward.

Suddenly the words, to which he had listened without understanding, soaked their way through his consciousness. He was alive and gaping now, and bright little bulbs were flashing inside the bones of his head.

". . . Damnedest thing I ever saw. She went into that barn

twice . . . got two of the horses out, pretty near single-handed."

"You wouldn't think a little woman like that would have it in her."

"Well, it was the damnedest thing I ever saw. Of course, she was crying and everything, and then a couple of men from the barn hung onto her, and they wouldn't let her go in again. It was real pitiful. She kept crying and saying, 'Oh, let me go.' She said, 'It's my husband's barn. I guess I got a right to go in!' "

They were both chuckling dryly, still shocked by the excitement and tragedy, still absorbed with their appreciation of a primitive courage which they could appreciate.

"How did it start?"

"Hard to tell. Old Uncle Em—I saw him about four o'clock —I was just on my way down to the city hall, coming to work —and he was there by the stable curb, and he was pretty drunk. Hard to say what started it; but most folks figure it started where he lived, up in the barn."

By this time Ben Steele was gone far away, stumbling across cinders behind the stores, and swinging south into the emptiness of Plum Street with its solitary yellow bulbs, one on every street corner. Ben wanted to run; he dared not run, he might fall down.

He went at a mechanical stride; he permitted himself one hasty glance toward the west as he crossed Fourth Street, opposite the Baptist church. There were still embers to be seen at Fourth and Hazel, and distantly the voices of men came to him, and there was steam going high: the fire department still poured water on the coals, and he could hear a remote hissing above the thunders in his head.

Ben hurried west on Third Street and tramped at last up the steps of his own house. He left the front door standing open—he could not take time to close it. He broke into a run and clambered, slipping and stumbling, up the shiny oak of the stairs. There was a light in the hall above; no light in any other room. Larry had gone to sleep, apparently.

Dolly was on the wide bed where Ben had seen her last. She had been lying there, crying . . . he did not know. She was a rumpled shape, rising through the gloom as he came.

"Dolly," he cried to her, "I heard! Why didn't you tell me? Why didn't you say something? I heard— About you and the horses and— Oh, Dolly, Dolly! Can you ever forgive me?"

Before long he was lying on the bed with her, bawling for the first time in ten or twelve years, pleading in grief, wondering at the great charity which ruled her and made her at last put her hands in his hair. On a near-by shelf waited the lace turban which had lured him earlier, and would be indicative of his desire for her again.

DATE DUE

MR 21 '67			
MY 2 '69			
NO 2 '70			
MY 15 '72			
OC 14 '75			

GAYLORD PRINTED IN U.S.A.